"No man came to my door to sweep me off my feet."

"I did." His thumb brushed her chin, forcing her gaze to him. The sadness in her eyes shamed him. He'd disliked her, he'd forgotten her, he'd tried to avoid her in town for years and married her for convenience's sake, but the truth was, his heart felt as new as dawn's first light whenever he looked at her.

"You didn't sweep me off my feet, Nick. You offered me an arrangement."

"Sure, I was trying to get my laundry done free, so I proposed."

"And I was trying to get a man to feed and shelter me."

"And don't forget clothe you. I did include new dresses in the marriage deal."

Tenderly. That's how he spoke to her. Gently, that's how he held her hand. She couldn't begin to say how much that meant to her....

* * *

High Plains Wife
Harlequin Historical #670—August 2003

Acclaim for Jillian Hart's recent books

Bluebonnet Bride
"Ms. Hart expertly weaves a fine tale of the heart's
ability to find love after tragedy. Pure reading pleasure!"
—*Romantic Times*

Montana Man
"…a great read!"
—*Rendezvous*

Cooper's Wife
"…a wonderfully written romance
full of love and laughter."
—*Rendezvous*

JILLIAN HART

High Plains
WIFE

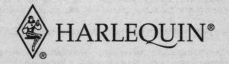

HARLEQUIN®

TORONTO • NEW YORK • LONDON
AMSTERDAM • PARIS • SYDNEY • HAMBURG
STOCKHOLM • ATHENS • TOKYO • MILAN • MADRID
PRAGUE • WARSAW • BUDAPEST • AUCKLAND

ISBN 0-373-29270-8

HIGH PLAINS WIFE

This edition published by arrangement with Harlequin Books S.A.

® and TM are trademarks of the publisher. Trademarks indicated with ® are registered in the United States Patent and Trademark Office, the Canadian Trade Marks Office and in other countries.

Visit us at www.eHarlequin.com

Printed in U.S.A.

Please address questions and book requests to:
Harlequin Reader Service
U.S.: 3010 Walden Ave., P.O. Box 1325, Buffalo, NY 14269
Canadian: P.O. Box 609, Fort Erie, Ont. L2A 5X3

Chapter One

Montana Territory, 1881

The high Montana prairie spread out like forever in all directions, broken only by small knolls and glens and the miles of fences. The land was bright green and new, for spring had come to the plains, and the sun was brilliant and warm. Mariah Scott swiped the afternoon's grit from her face with her sleeve and gave her slow-moving ox a snap of the reins.

"Git up," she ordered, but the animal didn't move one bit faster. Maybe there was no getting around the fact that she'd been swindled at the auction last week when she'd purchased the ox. Clearly a mistake she was sorely regretting.

And to add insult to injury, the beast *had* to slow down on the road right in the middle of Nick Gray's fields. Of all the places on the earth to linger, this wasn't the one she would choose.

She'd been in love with him once, a foolish young girl embroidering pillowcases for her hope chest. Some things were not to be, and it had been a hard lesson. It had been long ago now, but thinking of Nick Gray could still make her heart ache for what could never be.

"Nick is sure to be looking for a wife now that he's widowed," Rayna Ludgrin had predicted at Sunday dinner. "What with two little ones without a mother to care for them."

It's not likely to be me. Mariah smoothed her gloved hand over her second best dress—thin from years of wearing—and knew how much she'd changed. She was no longer young and faintly pretty, and now, whenever a man looked at her, he saw a practical hardworking woman.

No doubt that's what Nick Gray saw, too.

Enough dallying, Mariah. She had no time to waste on thoughts of that man. She had clean laundry to deliver and wouldn't get paid until she did. Mariah touched the thick leather reins on the ox's rump and bit back a curse when the animal locked his legs and the wagon groaned to a stop in the middle of the rutted road.

"Git up," she repeated.

The stubborn beast planted his hooves more firmly.

Exasperated, Mariah smacked him again, this time firmly enough to make a sound, but it wasn't hard enough to do any good. "If I could afford to sell you, then I would. You are a bad boy."

The gentle giant lifted his head, apparently unconcerned, and took advantage of the scant wind cooling his warm coat.

"I bought you because you were cheap, and that was my biggest mistake." Frustrated, she climbed down from the high seat. Her shoes hit the ground and dust clouded the air. Coughing, she tugged an apple out of her pocket. "Here's your bribe. Now will you pull my wagon?"

The big ox glanced at her through narrowed eyes, as if he were considering her offer.

"Even though I can't afford it, I *could* sell you to the stockyards," she bluffed.

As if he understood perfectly, he took the apple.

That was one problem solved. While the bovine crunched on the treat, Mariah patted him on the neck. He was a pretty creature, gleaming reddish-brown in the sun.

Turning to the wagon, she heard the smallest sound, sweet in tone like a lark but as heartbreaking as the wind. So quiet, had she imagined it? No, there it was again. A tiny sniffling sound like a child crying.

A child? Was one lost out here on the endless plains? She might be a spinster and never a mother, but she knew the dangers to a child alone on the prairie.

This time the sound was a muffled sob. Definitely someone small and in need of help. It had to be coming from the empty field next to the road. Unbroken new grass waved tall and proud and so thick, Mariah couldn't see anything but an ocean of green. There was no sign that a child—or anything else—was nearby.

The ox bellowed and swiveled his ears, lifting his huge head to gaze far out into the fields.

Maybe that was why the ox had stopped, Mariah realized. He could have known there was trouble. She patted him again, deciding maybe he wasn't beyond redeeming, and hiked her skirts up to her ankles. Dust whirled around her as she climbed carefully through the tricky barbs of the wire fence.

The crying sounded nearer. Tiny gulps of sobs that lured Mariah through the thick grasses until she spotted a flash of pink between the green stalks. The last thing she wanted to do was to frighten the child. "Hello? Are you lost?"

The stems parted and the flash of pink became a girl dressed in calico. Her pixie's face was streaked with tears. "You ain't my mama."

Poor child, lost and alone. Mariah's heart melted, just like that. She dug in her pocket for a bright shiny apple. "Are you hungry?"

The girl's blond curls brushed her shoulders as she shook her head.

"You don't like apples?"

"I got cookies." The child lifted her heavy satchel, tears trailing through the dust on her cheeks. "But I'm savin' 'em."

"Looks like you're packed for a trip."

"I'm goin' to heaven. That's where Pa said my mama went. I'm gonna go get her."

Mariah's heart cinched tight. Sympathy welled up in her so fast, she couldn't speak at first. She didn't know what to say to a child who'd lost a mother to suicide. While she tried to figure that out, she knelt until she was eye level with the little girl, who looked so miserable and alone. So helplessly small and precious. "Your pa has to be awful worried about you. He wouldn't want you to go look for your mama."

"He don't want me." The child leaned close to whisper, hiccuping on a sob. "He don't love me no more."

Sympathy ached like a nail driven deep in her chest, and Mariah couldn't resist sweeping a tangled lock of damp curls from the girl's cheek. Mariah knew what it was like not to be loved, and by all accounts this child of Nick Gray's was well treasured. The dress she wore was finely made without a wrinkle in it, her shoes dusty but without a single scuff.

Still, she understood how it felt to have a broken heart.

"That's my wagon right down there. Do you see my ox?"

The girl tilted her head, considering, and nodded once.

"His name is Bad Boy, but he's really very nice. If you bribe him with apples." Mariah held out her hand. "Would you like to feed him one?"

"I gotta find my ma."

"That's a long, long way. You'd better come with me, instead."

The girl's brow wrinkled as she considered. "I'm awful tired of walkin'."

"Good. Your satchel looks heavy. Want me to take it?"

"Nope. I can do it." She wrapped both hands around the thick handle and tugged the satchel along on the ground, over every bump and grass hump.

"I'm Mariah. I bet your name is Georgie."

"How do you know?" She wiped the last of her tears on her sleeve.

"I told you. I know your pa."

While Georgie apparently thought about that, she gave her bag another tug. "I'm awful thirsty. Do you got cider in that wagon?"

"I have water. Will that do?"

"Yep."

Mariah slowed her pace, waiting for Georgie. A chill snaked down her spine. It was suddenly so quiet.

No birds were singing. The prairie lay deathly still. Not even the wind blew. Bad Boy was fidgeting in his traces, a sure sign of trouble. With the height of the grass, a wild animal, even a wolf, could be stalking them and Mariah might not see the danger in time.

She stepped closer to the child. It would be best to get Georgie into the wagon as soon as possible. There was a loaded Winchester beneath the seat, and she knew how to use it if she had to.

"Let me carry that, Georgie. The faster we get to the wagon, the sooner we can get you a drink of—"

There was a streak of brown in the field ahead. In an instant it was gone and the green grass stood tall and motionless, as if it had never been disturbed.

Mariah knew better. It wasn't a wolf, but a coyote, and they always hunted in packs. She shivered, aware of the cold prickle in her bones. They didn't want her. It was the small child they'd scented.

She pulled Georgie to her skirts. Contented coyotes were one thing, but hungry packs roamed these prairies that were settling up fast.

She *had* to get Georgie out of this field. She swung the girl onto her hip and held her tight, walking as fast as she dared. Her skirts snapped with her stride and the sound of her breathing rang loud.

The coyotes emerged soundlessly in a perfect circle, cutting off her escape. There were a dozen of them, crouched, teeth bared, ready to attack in unison.

She skidded to a stop. What was she to do? Hunger gleamed in their eyes and she recognized an eerie determination. They didn't intend to back down.

Well, neither did she.

"Shoo!" She snapped the hem of her apron at the

coyote directly in front of her. You could never tell, maybe that would frighten him off.

Maybe not.

The leader of the pack didn't flinch or lower his gaze. He was hungry, she could see that in the ridge of bones showing through his matted coat. He crept closer, and the pack followed his lead, closing the circle. *Trouble*. Fear spilled like ice water into Mariah's blood.

She had to act fast.

''You leave us alone!'' She snatched an apple from her pocket and threw.

The apple hit the leader between the eyes. He dropped to the ground and shook his head.

Good thing she had more apples. She grabbed another and lobbed it at a second coyote. It struck him in the shoulder and knocked him to the ground.

Out of the corner of her eye, she saw a streak of brown. Georgie screamed the same moment Mariah felt teeth clamp at her nape. A heavy weight settled on her back and threatened to drag her down. How dare that coyote! Mariah whirled around, beating him in the nose with her fist until he slid from her back, taking her chignon with him. Her hair tumbled into her face. There were so many of them. How could she fight them all?

Georgie screamed again. The leader was on his feet and leaping, lunging for the little girl's throat.

Mariah tossed her last apple. The coyote howled at the impact. In pain, he slunk into the grass. Already the rest of the pack was backing away.

A gunshot echoed across the field, and Mariah swung around to see mounted men emerging over the grassy knoll, their guns raised.

She'd never seen a more welcome sight. Relief left her weak as the coyotes dispersed into the grasses, disappearing as if they had never been.

"Pa!" Georgie screamed as she slid from Mariah's arms and waded through the grass toward one of the approaching riders. "Pa!"

With his dark Stetson hiding his face, Nick Gray bent to scoop the little girl into his arms. She held him fiercely, clinging to his wide shoulders. He looked stronger than ever, holding his child.

Mariah couldn't hear his words, only the mumble of his voice, distant and low and soothing. She tore her gaze from him, fighting to ignore the hitch of longing deep inside. The sharp twinge of emotion shamed her.

She was too old to pine after some man she didn't even like. Tucking her hair into some order, she gathered her skirts and turned her back on Nick before he recognized her. The last thing on this earth she wanted to do was to have to talk to him.

Riders galloped past her, searching out the fleeing coyotes.

"Are you all right, ma'am?" one of them asked.

"Fine." She didn't look at him as she trudged through the thick grasses.

Georgie was safe and in her father's strong arms. There was no reason for her to stay, or for Nicholas Gray to say a single word to her. She was running late, and she had deliveries to make. She had no time for small talk.

"Ma'am! Wait up." A deep, captivating male voice rumbled across the prairie.

Nick's voice.

She cringed. So, he still hadn't recognized her, had he? She walked faster.

"Ma'am, you're bleeding."

"I'm fine."

Hooves clipped behind her, vibrating the earth. "You don't look fine. I saw that coyote jump you, and I feared the worst. He scratched you up pretty bad. Your dress is torn."

So, he still hadn't recognized her, had he? She kept her back to him and refused to comment. Maybe if she ignored him, he would go away.

But no, Nick reined his gelding to a stop in front of her. The big brute was blocking her path, and she wasn't referring to the horse. The years had drawn lines in his face and wariness into his eyes as blue as a Montana sky, but no amount of time had changed his attitude.

The brim of his hat shaded his face, but she could see the strong square of his jaw quirk as if he were surprised. "Mariah Scott. I might have known it was you. Not many women in this county can take on a pack of hungry coyotes and win."

Not many women, huh? She ought to be used to that attitude. As if, because she'd never married and her youth had begun to fade, her feelings had gone, too. It hurt.

Good thing she had a thick skin. She lifted her chin and circled around his horse so she could continue on her way.

"Aw, c'mon, now." Hooves clomped on the hard earth behind her. "I only meant you have the fortitude to scare off any rascal. Can't you accept a man's thanks?"

"Sure, when a man thanks me."

"Mariah, I didn't mean it that way. I'm grateful to you."

"Fine. You're welcome." *Don't look at him.* Looking at him would make her forgive him—just a little bit. There was no way she wanted to own up to the smallest feeling for Nick…unless it was a comfortable dislike.

She grabbed hold of the fence, careful of the barbed metal hooks.

He halted his horse beside her. "You're angry with me."

She wasn't angry, but she could never explain it. She'd do best to ignore him, and that's exactly what she intended to do. Let Nick Gray think she was angry, what would it matter? He may be looking for a wife, but she was smart enough to know he'd never consider her.

"'Bye, apple lady!" Georgie called across the field.

"Goodbye." Mariah waved at the little girl clinging to her uncle's arms. Somewhere along the way Nick must have handed off his daughter to his brother.

Georgie's fingers waved in response over her uncle's shoulder, so sweet Mariah felt her cold heart warm. At least the child was safe.

As for Georgie's father, Mariah refused to acknowledge him as she slipped through the fence as fast as she could. Her hem caught in a wire, and she stumbled, but at least she was on the other side.

A safe distance from the man on his horse, sitting so tall and proud he touched the sky.

"I was glad it was you, Mariah. That you were the one riding along at the right time."

"Me, too."

She stumbled onto the rutted road, dust kicking up at her quick step. With every step she took, she could feel Nick's gaze on her, bold as a touch. Why was he even speaking to her? She blinked fast to keep her eyes from blurring. Walked faster to get away from him.

She reached the wagon and pulled herself up. Was he still watching her? She turned her head just enough to see him at the edge of her vision, astride that black horse of his, one arm crossed jauntily on the saddle horn, the other at his hip.

He looked invincible. As if nothing could ever scare him. Or diminish the confidence he radiated like a midsummer's sun.

She would give anything to possess his courage. Maybe then she'd be able to look him straight in the eye, but she tumbled onto the wagon seat. She heard the gate hinges creak. It would be better to leave and leave fast before the shaking deep in her stomach radiated through the rest of her.

There was no way she was going to let Nick Gray see how frightened she was. Why were her hands shaking like that? She took a deep breath. The worse part was over, wasn't it? The coyotes were gone. The child was safe.

Except Mariah could still feel the hot breath on her neck and the weight of the coyote on her back. One rein slipped through her fingers. She scrambled after it, dropping onto her knees.

"Mariah?" Nick's horse halted at the side of her wagon. His shadow fell across her. "Are you okay?"

"I told you, I'm fine." She had to be. What choice did she have? She wasn't Georgie—she couldn't lean into Nick's arms and find comfort. She had no comfort anywhere in her life. The last thing she intended to do was to admit it. "Where did that blasted rein go?"

"Here. It's on the ground." Nick leaned forward in his saddle, leather creaking with his movements, and reached for the thick strap.

His big, sun-browned fingers snatched it, the movement masculine and commanding, and she hated noticing it. Noticing him.

He straightened, looking her up and down with his steel-blue eyes. No emotion flickered in their depths. "You're in no shape to drive. Maybe you ought to rest a spell. Let me take you up to the house."

"Sitting here isn't going to get my laundry delivered." Pretending that his concern didn't matter, she snatched the leather strap from his gloved fingers. "You go back to Georgie and keep her safe this time."

"Still as prickly as ever, aren't you, Mariah?" His jaw tightened. "Fine. Have it your way. Sure you're all right?"

"Positive." She snapped the reins. "Goodbye, Mr. Gray."

To his credit, Bad Boy moved forward, leaving Nick in a wake of dust. She glanced over her shoulder and saw the outline of him through the chalky cloud—lean and wide, all man.

She couldn't help longing just a little. It mortified her to think that she still hid a yearning for him after ten long years. Time had changed her, drawn lines on her face and given her a shield around her heart. But inside she was still that young woman who wanted to believe in love. In possibilities. Who dared to wish that the handsome, dashing Nick Gray would fall in love with her.

But he would choose another.

It doesn't matter. It's all in the past. She tried to be sensible. She was no daydreaming child, so why did she feel the same as she had so long ago? Because when Nick looked at her, he probably saw what everyone else did. A cold, hard-hearted woman who'd never been courted.

Not once.

Bad Boy drifted to a halt in the middle of the road and she didn't have the strength to scold him. She reached under the seat and found the gunnysack by feel.

"Mariah." A broad warm hand lighted on her shoulder.

She jumped. An apple shot from her grip and rolled across the wagon floor. Why couldn't he just leave her be?

Nick's shadow fell across her, towering between her and the sun. "That was a real fight you put up. You have the right to be shaken up."

"Me? Those coyotes didn't want me. They wanted your daughter."

"I know, Mariah, and like I said, I'm obliged to you."

"You should have been watching her. You left her alone and she wasn't safe. Georgie could have been killed." She realized his hand was still on her shoulder, hot and comforting, and she shrugged away, breaking the connection. "What kind of father are you?"

"One who isn't going to let that happen again."

"See that you don't." She snapped the reins again, and this time Bad Boy moved, slow and stubborn.

"Your ox could use some training." Nick rode past her to take the animal by the yoke and speed up his gait. "I'd be happy to work with him. Don't know what else to offer you for rescuing Georgie like that."

"I don't want anything from you. That isn't why I helped your little girl. Anyone passing by would have done the same."

"Either way, you still need help with this ox."

"That's none of your concern."

"So, you don't want my help. That's nothing new." Bad Boy slowed down and Nick gave a hard tug on the yoke. "The trouble with you, Miss Scott, is that the rumors are true."

Rumors? What rumors? Fury rolled through her, hot and fierce. See what came from trying to have a civil conversation with the man? Nick was bold and overbearing and couldn't mind his own concern if she paid him to. "Let go of my ox."

"I'm trying to thank you for saving my daughter's life, and you won't accept it."

"I'm not uncharitable. I simply do not require any assistance." It hurt her that he still thought so little of her.

Her chin shot up and she sent Bad Boy into a lope. Dust rose up to sting her eyes and the bouncing wagon rattled her bones, but it felt good to leave Nick Gray behind in the dust where he belonged.

She refused to feel sorry for her harsh words. Or for losing her temper. Nick had a real life, and he had children of his own to love.

She had no life at all, just her laundry business and a house that echoed with loneliness.

When she looked over her shoulder, he was still in the middle of the road, watching her, the dust settling around him like mist.

The trouble with you, Miss Scott, is that the rumors are true. Nick believed that and so did nearly everyone in the entire county. Oh, she could probably figure out what people thought. She was strong and iron-willed and prickly…and far too independent for any man to show any interest in her. Well, that was true enough. She didn't need any man. She was getting along just fine. She had her own business, her own home and her own ox and wagon.

You should have let Nick help you, Mariah. She closed her eyes briefly against the glare of the sun and certainly not because of the stinging sensation behind her lids. Nothing good would have come from letting Nick Gray train the ox. Not one thing.

She had to be practical. Had to accept the kind of woman she was. She was meant to be alone. Not everyone had a heart that could love.

So it *couldn't* be her heart that was hurting as she turned the wagon toward the Dayton ranch, late for her next delivery.

Chapter Two

Holding his gelding steady, Nick watched Mariah disappear in a trail of dust. That woman could get his dander up like no other, that was for sure. Not even his late wife could get him het up so fast as the Spinster Scott could. Maybe he didn't like independent-minded women, but what other woman would have battled coyotes to protect his little girl without wanting so much as a thank-you?

Hell, it would have been civil of her to accept his gratitude. She could have taken him up on his offer to train her young ox. But, no, not Mariah.

He swept off his hat in exasperation and raked his fingers through his hot, sweaty hair. The air felt good, almost as good as the relief of knowing his little girl was safe and sound and in his brother's care.

The wind warmed him, but that wasn't enough to stop his shivering. The image of hungry coyotes circling Georgie and Mariah chilled him to the meat of his bones.

"Darn lucky she came along when she did," his brother Will commented as he handed Georgie over. "No other woman in the county could do what she did. Miss Mariah Scott is tougher than a bad-tempered grizzly. Even those danged coyotes know it.''

"So they say.'' Grim, Nick cuddled his little girl to his chest. What would have happened to her alone in this field? He was damn glad he'd come along when he did. Glad his son had run to him, telling of Georgie's escape.

Best thing to do would be to head home and give Georgie that serious talking-to she needed, but there was Mariah's wagon, tiny in the distance. He could still barely make it out, a small brown dot rolling along the expansive prairie. As he watched, her vehicle dipped down a rise and out of sight.

Mariah Scott. He hadn't cause to think of her in a long while. But he thought of her now.

"Pa, I want down. That lady said I could go with her and her ox.''

"I'm here now and so I'll give you a ride on my horse.''

"But you don't love me.'' Georgie's sob rattled through her. "My mama does.''

A well-honed blade could not cut his heart this deep. Nick grimaced. He held his daughter with more gentleness. Searched for words that would explain this fierce jumble of pain inside him. And failed.

He didn't have the words. He didn't need to ask Georgie where she'd been heading. This wasn't the first time she'd done this, running off in search of her mother gone and buried.

Poor Georgie. Lida's death had hurt her the most of all. He pressed a kiss against the crown of her sunbonnet, willing to do anything to take away her grief. "I love you, baby.''

She sighed deeply, feeling frail and ready to break.

Such a little girl, and not even his comfort seemed to help her. Georgie's arms wrapped tight around his neck. "Is heaven long gone and far away?"

"Very far away. Not even my horse can get us there. If I could, I'd take you to see your ma. It just can't be done."

Georgie's arms tightened, her face pressed hard against his throat. "Not even an ox can get there?"

"Nope."

Georgie wiped her tears on his collar and said nothing more.

He held her, all sweetness, until the big house came into view. The orchard's gnarled black branches shielded the porch from sight, but he knew his son was waiting there, too small to be seen from a distance but keeping careful watch.

Sure enough, there was Joey, darting into the path between the trees. Worry was stark on his pale face and his blond locks were waving on the wind.

Nick's chest punched. Joey had always been a serious boy, with a frown between his brows when he considered something mightily. But in the three weeks since Lida's death, he'd changed.

Their lives had changed.

Joey planted his boots and shook a finger at his sister. "You can't go runnin' off like that. You're in big trouble, Georgie."

"I am not!" Her mouth compressed into a tough line. "You are."

"The both of you, code of silence, right now." Nick knew he sounded too stern and too tired.

He was just wrung out, that was all. He was at the end of his rope dangling by a fraying thread, and he had to hang on. His children and this ranch needed him. Look at Joey, all twisted up with worry, shivering in the cool wind. His trousers were wrinkled, his boots scuffed, his jacket crumpled and hanging crooked on his shoulders. "Joey, button up that coat and go to the house."

"Yes, sir." There was a tired look to the boy, as if Lida's death had used him up, too.

Nick wanted to curse her for her choice to leave the children like this. Wanted to hate her. At least he'd been the one to find her, crumpled in the field near the small grave where they'd buried her baby last fall. A baby he knew wasn't his.

Bitterness filled his craw and he tamped down a blinding rage he refused to give in to. The woman was dead. She'd suffered enough in this life, and he'd torn himself inside out trying to make her happy.

Georgie whimpered against him, bringing him back to the present, cuddling close. Her hold on his neck was choking tight.

It hurt, seeing her like this. Hurt worse to hand her over to his father, who ambled out on the porch, looking frayed and exhausted.

"Glad you found her, son." Pop nodded once in approval, said nothing more as he settled Georgie in his arms.

She cried, begging for her mama.

Pain twisted in him like a knife. He felt torn and lost and defeated. So damn defeated. Georgie pushed at Pop, struggling to get down. Georgie didn't understand death, and by God, neither did he. He'd never understand Lida's actions, so how could he explain to a child?

Georgie was hurting, and he dismounted, leaving his horse standing in the cold. Took the porch steps in two long strides. Had Georgie clutched against him by the third, taking her from Pop's arms and into his own.

"Pa," Georgie wept against his flannel collar. "Mama left."

"I know, princess." He kissed her brow, and wisps of her silken hair caught on his whiskered chin. He'd forgotten to shave again.

Hell, he was forgetting everything. The world was crumbling into bits around his boots. None of it seemed to matter as he cradled his daughter to his chest, holding her as gingerly as when she'd been newborn.

There was nothing but the sound of her broken sobs and the echo of his heels on the parlor floor. The scrape of the rocker as he eased into the chair. The squeak of a spring. And the feel of heartbreak.

He held Georgie tight and rocked her until there was only silence.

Will emerged from the shadowed depths of the barn. "How's Georgie?"

"Asleep." Nick yanked on the stall door. It didn't give, the damn thing. The hinge was sprung, leaving the wood door jammed into the frame. He kicked it hard, and wood scraped against wood, freeing the door, but not his frustration.

He could still feel Georgie curled against his chest, sobbing so hard her little body shook.

He hurt for her. Would take every grief, every anguish, every bit of pain from her if he could. The door crashed against the wall. The loud crack startled the mare in the stall. She whinnied and sidestepped, her head lifting high in alarm.

That's it, Nick. Scare the horse while you're at it.
He pushed aside all thoughts of Georgie, but not his
troubles. The feel of her sobs stayed with him as he
reached for the mare's bridle, speaking low.

He was in trouble. Up a creek without a paddle at
the mouth of a waterfall. He was wise enough to
know the plunge would be swift and lethal. He wasn't
on the boat alone. His children were with him.

Will plopped a saddle on the nearby four-by-four.
"You look troubled, big brother."

"Real sharp of you to notice." Nick kept his voice
gruff, because it kept the young man in line. "Got
enough ammunition in that pack of yours?"

"I'm packed and waitin' for you." Cocky, Will
tipped his hat. "You know what you need?"

"A clean blanket. Fetch me one, will you?" Nick
slid the brush over the mare's withers in a few quick
swipes. Her tail swished side to side, calmer now, but
he couldn't say the same.

Something had to change. One thing was for sure,
he couldn't last another week like this. Neither could
the children.

"Know what you need, big brother?"

"A foreman that does more work than talking?"

"Funny. What you need to solve all your problems
is another wife." Will tossed the blanket.

"A wife, huh?" Nick caught it and smoothed the
length of wool into place. "Just goes to show what
you know. A wife doesn't solve troubles. She's the
source of 'em."

"A little bitter, huh?" Will hoisted the saddle easily onto the mare's back. "Matrimony isn't supposed
to be bliss, from what I hear. Torture or not, it *is*

something you're gonna have to do sooner or later, so why wait?''

Nick hated it when his brother was right. Jaw clenched tight, he unhooked the stirrup from the saddle horn, letting it swing into place. He'd be the first to admit life had been damn near impossible with Lida, but without her…

"Pa?" Joey ambled into sight with his Stetson crooked, jacket still open, shirt half untucked. He looked uncertain and small and…nine years old. Hell, he was a boy missing his mother.

Leaving Will to cinch the saddle, Nick came down on one knee. "What is it, cowboy?"

"Georgie's sleepin'. I'm gonna make sure she doesn't run off again." So serious, as if he had the weight of the world on his shoulders.

Nick put his hand there, on the slim curve of his son's shoulder. One day Joey would be a good man, strong and hardworking and upstanding. The man he would be was easy to see in the boy, his chin set fierce and determined.

Nick's chest ached. He wanted life to be better for his son. "You're a good brother, but your grandfather is responsible for watching Georgie. You want to come riding with us?"

"Grandpop falls asleep sometimes." Joey bit his bottom lip with indecision. He glanced over his shoulder at the house. "I'd best stay and watch over them both, I reckon."

There'd been a time when the boy never turned down the chance to ride his horse on the range. Another thing Lida had stolen from him.

What am I going to do about Joey? Nick had no answer as he watched the boy amble back to the house, his boots dragging in the dirt. Would a new wife make a difference? A woman to lift the burden from Joey's shoulders?

A housekeeper couldn't do it. It would merely be a job to her, and one day she'd leave for a better opportunity.

No, his children deserved more than that. Needed more than that. They deserved stability and commitment. A woman who would always be there for them.

Joey disappeared from sight. The door slammed behind him, the smack of wood on wood carrying on the wind, sounding lonely and final and accusing. The image of Mariah Scott, holding Georgie in her arms, flashed into Nick's thoughts.

Nope. Forget it. If he had his way, there would never be another woman in his life. Ever.

Will handed over the reins. "Children need a mother to grow up happy."

"*You're* an expert?"

"Not from personal experience, but I am a keen observer."

"Of pretty women, maybe." Nick gathered the reins and shot his foot into the stirrup.

"A pretty woman is one of life's necessities. Another is a wife who can cook. We can't keep eating our brother's cooking. Dakota is likely to kill us with that slop he calls food."

"Mount up. We've got cattle to check on. Save your great wisdom for someone who needs it."

"If anyone needs wisdom, it's you, big brother."

"I'm wise enough to know I shouldn't listen to you." Nick eased into the saddle. "Are you comin'?"

Leather creaked as Will mounted up. "Know what you ought to do? Go to the fund-raiser they've got tonight for the town school. There'll be plenty of women there. Maybe one of them wouldn't mind getting married to an ugly cuss like you.''

Nick decided to let that one pass without comment. He didn't feel like trading jests.

''Don't say no right off, not until you think it through.'' Will bent in his saddle to unlatch the gate. ''The dance tonight will give you the chance to see what your options are. You could even dance with the lady of your choice. *If* she lowers her standards.''

Nick nosed his mare through the gate and waited with the wind knifing through his jacket while Will hooked the latch.

Go to the dance? Look over the marriageable women like horses lined up at an auction? That didn't sit right. He had no interest in taking any woman to wife.

Except his children were what mattered, what counted.

The high plains rolled from horizon to horizon and gave no answers.

A wife? He had to consider it. Maybe he would go to the dance tonight. Look at his options. See what could be. Marrying this time would be different. He was older. No one expected a man his age and with children needing a mother to marry for love.

A marriage of convenience. Isn't that what he and Lida had anyway? They'd lived in the same house and each did their work. Then fell into separate beds at night.

Troubled, he rubbed his chest. The spot behind his breastbone kept growing tighter and tighter. He didn't want a wife, but Lord knew he needed one.

His children needed a mother.

* * *

"Your angel food cakes smells like heaven," Rayna Ludgrin praised as she set her big wicker basket on the kitchen table. "Why, it's as perfect as could be. You'll put us all to shame at the supper tonight."

Mariah blushed. She didn't like praise, but she could see her friend only meant to be kind. "My cooking can't beat yours, and you know it. Let me grab my apron and I'll be ready to go."

"You aren't wearing that, are you?"

Did she detect a note of criticism? Mariah lifted a laundered and folded apron from the shelf. "It's my Sunday best. I figured it would be good enough."

"Good enough, why, yes." Rayna didn't even have the grace to look guilty. "Surely black isn't the best color for tonight. This is a supper and a dance, Mariah. Men will be there."

"Good for them." Mariah slipped the glass cover over her best pedestal cake plate and lifted it into Rayna's basket. "I've volunteered to help in the kitchen tonight, so black is a sensible color. What are you up to, anyway?"

"Not one thing. You might want to wear your beige calico. Quite fetching on you."

"I see where this is going." Mariah's face heated. "You're wasting your breath. The bachelors in this town are too young for me."

"Not Nick Gray. In our day, I thought you two were going to be quite the couple."

"Nothing came of it then, and I'm not about to change my dress just to please the likes of Mr. Gray."

"What a shame." Rayna snapped the lid shut on her basket. "A lot of women in this town don't think the way you do. They'll be all gussied up in their finest, praying for the handsome widower to ask them to dance.''

"Then he'll not miss me." Mariah kept her chin high, refusing to let even the slightest regret into her voice. She didn't need Nick Gray. Not to dance with. Not to marry.

Maybe if she told herself that enough times, she would believe it. Then—*maybe*—it wouldn't hurt so much.

Rayna hummed as she stacked molasses cookies from the cooling racks onto a plate. Her gold wedding ring caught the late afternoon light. Rayna would never understand. She was happily married and a mother of three sons.

What did she know about rejection? About watching the man you secretly loved marry someone pretty and vivacious? About spending every night alone in the same house for years, wishing another man would come along. Wishing for just one man to love her, despite her faults.

Mariah grabbed the oven mitts and swung open the oven door. The aroma of chicken potpie made her mouth water. The crusts were golden, the gravy bubbling through the little flowers she'd cut into the dough. Dry heat blazed across her face as she knelt to rescue the pans.

"Nick will need a wife who can cook."

"Plenty of women can cook. One thing Mr. Gray won't be doing is asking me to cook for him." It didn't matter that he would find himself another young and pretty woman. Truly, it didn't bother her one bit.

"Nick *was* sweet on you years ago."

"He isn't now." Remembering Nick's look of disdain today on the road, her face flushed again.

All right, so maybe that *did* hurt—but just the tiniest bit. What she needed to be was practical. Earlier today she had seen it as plain as daylight on his face—she'd grown too hard and too sharp. Over time, her cold heart had grown colder. She hated that, and hated that it showed so much.

Laden with the heavy basket, Rayna lingered at the back door. "A man never forgets his first love."

"We were not in love."

Rayna frowned. "Maybe not, but only because your father wouldn't allow him to court you."

"Nick didn't try hard enough." Bitterness still ached in her breast, and she turned away. The years of loneliness settled in a hard lump in her throat, making it hard to breathe and harder to talk, so she opened the pantry door and pretended to be very busy.

It was a good thing she loved her volunteer work. Her cherished spot on the Ladies' Aid had given her great satisfaction. She didn't need a husband to be happy. Why, look at her kitchen. Not a speck of mud or a man's grimy boots in a messy pile on her hand-polished floor. See? Her life was in perfect order, just the way she wanted it.

And if her conscience bit at the lie she told herself, she ignored it.

"Oh, speak of the devil." Rayna's tone held delight. "Some man is driving up in his fine fringed-top surrey. A man by the name of Mr. Gray."

"Stop teasing me and grab the basket I have by the door, would you? I've packed extra dish towels." As the vice president of the Ladies' Aid, Mariah took pride in her experience serving and washing. "Surely, there will be a lot of dishes to wash—"

A rattle of a harness in the yard echoed through her kitchen. That couldn't be. Surely Nick Gray wasn't in her driveway…

He was. Her breath caught as a matching team of sleek bays pranced into sight. They stopped, looking as graceful as a waltz, their long black manes flickering in the wind. The sunlight gleamed on their bronze coats and the new surrey behind them, where Nick Gray held thick leather straps between leather-gloved fingers. He was real and not a daydream, right? Mariah blinked, and sure enough he was still sitting there.

Why *was* he here? Suddenly her black dress was too plain, her hair too sensible, her shoes too scuffed. But he was as fine-looking as ever. His black Stetson framed his dark eyes and matched his finely tailored black suit. He looked so masculine and dashing, he made every part of her tingle. She hated her reaction to him.

"Good evening, Mrs. Ludgrin. Mariah." He climbed handily from the high seat to the ground, every movement deliberate and predatory and somehow breathtaking. He moved with confidence, making it clear he'd come for a purpose.

To talk to her? She couldn't imagine why. She noticed Nick's brother Will in the second seat of the buggy, his arm slung over the back of the seat, dressed up as well. Were they going to the supper and dance tonight?

Rayna's smile was all-knowing as she hurried down the porch, lugging both baskets. Leaving Mariah alone to face Nick.

That wasn't fair.

Nick stepped aside on the walkway, all gentleman. "Can I get those for you, Rayna?"

"Don't you mind about me. Looks as though you two need time to talk." Rayna glanced over her shoulder at Mariah and winked. "Good luck."

Good luck? Mariah watched her friend hurry off to her parked buggy. Alone with Nick? Twice in one day? The longing within her ached. It took all her willpower not to march back into her house and lock the door. Was it too late to pretend she wasn't home?

He swept off his hat. "You're dressed up real nice. Suppose you're serving at the supper."

"I am."

"Seeing you today got me to thinking." He stared down at his hat. Dark shocks of his hair tumbled over his brow, hiding his eyes. He looked troubled. Contemplative. "I'm sorry for the way I treated you on the road today."

"I need to apologize, too. I *was* frightened from the coyotes."

"Yeah, well…" He looked flustered, picking at the stitching on his hat brim. "I'm awful grateful to you for protecting Georgie. 'Thank you' seems awfully small sentiment for what you've done."

"It's more than enough."

As their gazes locked, Mariah's breath caught. The longing in her chest crescendoed until it was all she could feel. Why was he here? He'd already thanked her at the time. Why make a trip out of his way to do it again?

He raked one hand unsteadily through his thick locks, leaving them deliciously tousled. Confident Nick Gray looked remarkably uneasy.

And why was that? He'd apologized. Why wasn't he leaving?

He rubbed his thumb across the Stetson's brim, brushing at an invisible spot. "Like I said, I kept thinking about seeing you today."

"You did?"

"Sure. Couldn't help it. You were on my mind all afternoon." He lifted one big shoulder in a shrug.

He thought of her all afternoon? Her? Mariah Scott? The notorious town spinster? Her heart started to race. He wasn't about to ask her to the dance, was he?

He can't be. Shock left her speechless. Maybe he was. Why else would he be standing here, hat in hand? As unbelievable as it was, Nicholas Gray had come to ask her to accompany him tonight to the supper and dance.

He rubbed the back of his neck with his free hand. "I got to thinking, with me widowed and you alone."

"Yes?"

"I know there's Mrs. Gunderson, but she's at the other end of town, and after what you did today, I'd like to give you the business."

"W-what?" She couldn't have heard him correctly. What did business have to do with the supper and dance?

"My laundry." He held out one steely arm to point toward the buggy.

Then she saw the baskets of clothes on the floorboards behind the front seat. Nick hadn't come to ask her to the dance. "You've come to hire me?"

"Sure, if you can handle it. I know you've got a booming business going."

Of course. He wanted her to do his laundry. What

did she think? That he would actually want her after all these years? Mariah leaned against the threshold, suddenly weak. She somehow managed to take one breath after another.

Nick went on, unaware of the blow he'd dealt. "You turned down my offer to train your ox, and so I thought you might appreciate more business."

"You *thought?*" It was amazing the thoughts—or lack of them—that went on in men's heads.

"I was just trying to be nice, Mariah. I should have known you wouldn't want my business. No hard feelings. Hope you have a real good evening."

"Wait, I—" A thousand different emotions warred for words, but she didn't give in to the anger or the hurt.

What was the point? Times were hard, and she could lower her pride. Making a living was important, and she would always be a spinster. No doubt about that. It looked as though nothing could change it.

She straightened her spine, stood on her own two feet and approached the porch rail. "I charge more than Mrs. Gunderson, but I iron and she doesn't. I'll put you on Monday afternoon delivery. Will that be all right?"

"No complaints." He appeared relieved. "That settles it, then. Good evening to you." His smile was as slow and smooth as pure maple sugar.

Desire swept over her as she watched him go. The polish on his surrey reflecting a soft purple hue in the light of the setting sun.

She'd always held a softness for Nick. She couldn't deny it. It would be hard watching him tonight as he danced with other women. Younger women. Prettier women. Harder still to do his laundry and deliver it punctually every week, while he courted and married a more suitable bride.

She tucked away her disappointment and hurried inside. The pies were cool enough to pack into her last basket. The Ladies' Aid was waiting. She had important work to do and didn't have the time for wasting on thoughts of Nick Gray. Or her regrets.

Chapter Three

"You blew it, brother," Will commented from the back seat. "I didn't think I'd live to see the day when the perfect son, Nicholas Gray, would make a mistake of this magnitude."

"You think I should have went with Mrs. Gunderson?" Try as he might, Nick would never understand his younger brother. He gave the reins a snap when the horses slowed on the busy main street.

"It isn't about the laundry, man. The woman thought you were going to ask her to the dance."

"Mariah? Don't be ridiculous." Mariah was a practical woman. Sensible. She wasn't given to romantic foolishness, and he knew that from firsthand experience. "Mariah wouldn't have me if I begged her."

"I wouldn't be so danged sure. You didn't see the big, bright moon eyes she was giving you?"

All he'd noticed was the way she'd been standoffish, leaning against the door, more beautiful than the day they'd met. "Moon eyes? Mariah?" The sky had a better chance of falling to earth.

"I'm telling the God's truth."

"Is that so? Then why hasn't a lightning bolt struck the back seat of my buggy?"

"It isn't gonna. I mean it. You were bumbling around saying things like 'I kept thinking about you' and 'You look pretty.' What was she bound to think?"

Maybe Will did have a point. But this was Mariah they were talking about. "She wants to be a spinster. She tells anyone who asks."

"When a man tells a woman that he's been thinking about her and shows up at her place right before the big town happenings, she expects an invitation to the dance. Heck, brother, you even had me thinking you were gonna ask her."

The reins slipped between Nick's fingers. *No.* How could it be? Mariah hadn't wanted him ten years ago, at least her father hadn't. In the years that passed, she hadn't so much as given him a polite greeting in public. She'd just march past him on the street as if he didn't exist. As if he were dead and buried to her.

No, Will couldn't be right.

The schoolhouse came into sight, so he reined in the horses and parked the surrey. Folks were everywhere. His neighbor called out a greeting across the busy crowd. Nick waved back, taking stock.

Looked like the ranchers were gathering in the shade, smoking and discussing wheat prices. They'd fallen again. Not good news for the local ranchers. He set the brake before climbing to the ground. Headed toward the grounds with his brother in tow.

A pretty young woman cut in front of them, carrying a wrapped platter balanced just so, and damned if Will didn't look his fill as she sauntered up to the schoolhouse steps.

Nick knew trouble when he saw it. "You behave yourself with the ladies. No kisses in the moonlight. I don't want some angry papa coming after you with a shotgun."

"Aw, it ain't my fault. I sometimes get carried away by a woman's beauty and lose all sense. You're a man. You've got to know how that is."

Only too well. "It's called willpower. Use it. That's my advice."

"With that outlook, you're never going to find a new wife."

Nick ignored the jesting. He was no fool. He wasn't going to get trapped into marriage a second time. He'd keep his male needs under steely control. If he chose to wed again he'd choose a woman using logic and not his...

Mariah Scott caught his eye. Could anyone explain to him why his gaze shot straight to her? There had to be fifty women milling around, carrying baskets and platters from their wagons to the schoolhouse. Why couldn't he notice one of them? Why didn't his gaze stray to their bosoms?

He kept on walking. The other ranchers had gathered near to a keg of homemade ale that smelled like heaven on the breeze.

"Been waitin' for you, Gray." Al Ludgrin thrust a foaming tankard in Nick's direction.

"Just what I need." No truer words had ever been spoken. Nodding in greeting to the other ranchers, young and old, he took a sip and noticed Mariah again.

She was climbing down from her wagon, dressed all in black. The high proud curve of her bosom sure did look fine. Desire stirred in him. No doubt about it—she was surely a finely made woman, hard and tough, true, but soft where it mattered.

Alone, she tethered her ox. Alone, she lifted two heavy-looking baskets from the floor of her small wagon. Had she always looked that sad?

He didn't know, but it was on her face plain enough for anyone to see. The straight line of her mouth, down-turned in the corners. The town's formidable spinster wove her way through the crowd of children playing, a tall and slim shadow touched by the last rays of the setting sun.

Nick took a long pull from the tankard. The ale was bracing, just shy of bitter, but not strong enough to make him forget the troubled feeling churning in his guts.

Mariah squeezed between the table rows in the crowded schoolhouse when she saw Rayna Ludgrin bringing a fresh pot of coffee. Finally! They were sending in the reinforcements. She was dead on her feet and could use a few minutes' break.

"Don't get too hopeful," Rayna told her, speaking loud to be heard over the merry din. "They need you to keep serving. Careful, the handle's hot."

It sure was. Mariah's fingers felt seared in spite of the thick pad as she took possession of the coffeepot. "We never expected such a good showing."

"There isn't an empty seat," Rayna agreed. "So, are you going to tell me?"

"Tell you what?"

"What Nick Gray had to say to you. I noticed he hasn't taken his eyes off you all evening. Does that mean he asked you to the dance?"

"Why would he? We're not even friends." Mariah

tucked that piece of disappointment away and filled an empty cup of coffee for old Mr. Dayton.

"Then what did he come for?" Rayna sounded bewildered.

They were far from being alone and Mariah wasn't about to let anyone overhear her conversation and make the mistaken assumption that she was mooning after Nick Gray. "I've taken on his laundry, that's what. I didn't want to do it, considering the man and how I feel about him, but business is business."

"Mariah, I didn't know you still disliked him so strongly." Rayna winced. "I never would have teased you about him. I'm sorry."

"No apology necessary." Hiding her feelings, Mariah hesitated, not sure what to do, until someone called her from a nearby table, holding out his empty cup.

She didn't blame Rayna. She blamed herself. Across the crowded room, a group of men were leaving. Probably heading over to the stable yard, where the dance was to be held, to help themselves to their stashes of beer and tobacco. Nick was one of those men, but to her, he always stood out in a crowd.

The last thing she ought to be doing was noticing that man. What she'd said to Rayna was true. They were not friends. She couldn't stand Nicholas Gray. He was arrogant and domineering and stubborn... She didn't want anything to do with him. Really.

And that was the story she intended to stick with. From this moment on she'd have no other feelings for Nick than those she had for her other customers. She would wash and rinse, starch and iron his shirts and collect her fees. That was it. That was all.

She'd never let one vulnerable feeling in. She refused to waste one more regret. Father was right, she did have a cold heart. She might as well use it to her advantage.

There Nick was, looking at her again. Jerking his gaze away to listen to his brother. Nick wasn't sweet on her. He was probably wondering how much she planned to charge him for his laundry.

"Thanks for the refill, Miss Mariah." Kol Ludgrin nodded coolly at the brim-full cup, and she stopped pouring.

Goodness, she'd almost forgotten what she'd been doing. And look how her gaze crossed the room right to Nick. Didn't she have any more willpower than that? No, because he *did* look handsome tonight. She couldn't deny that Nick was easy on the eyes. A woman wouldn't get tired of looking at his face across her kitchen table. Not in a lifetime.

Not your kitchen table, she reminded herself. She wasn't the only female looking in Nick's direction.

Folks were finishing their desserts and leaving the tables. Children clamored through the aisles, mothers scolding, with babes on their hips. Those women had their duties. And she had hers. She was vice president of the Ladies' Aid.

Her duties kept her occupied long after the second story of the schoolhouse emptied, and she'd spent two busy hours on the first floor, wiping down the last of the dishes. There was a dozen women who stayed to clean up, to take apart the board tables and wash the floor. Now, this was accomplishing something. Mariah treasured the rare sense of satisfaction as she packed the last dessert plate into the last basket.

"I'll help you to the wagon with these," she offered when Rayna bustled up to take the heavy baskets. "Let me take the bigger one."

"What do you plan to do after loading up my wagon?"

"Load my own and go home." What else? She had no obligations at the dance. The president of the club was in charge of that end of the fund-raiser.

"That's simply not acceptable." Rayna tsked, tossing the wadded towel into Mariah's nearby basket. Trouble glinted in her narrowed gaze. "You're coming with us. Betsy, are you ready?"

"Sure am. I've got rope to hog-tie her with, if that's what it takes for Mariah to have some fun." Longtime friend Betsy Hunter snared Mariah by one hand while Rayna took the other. "We're all going to the dance, whether you like it or not."

What was wrong with everyone? "I don't dance, and you both know it."

"You don't have to dance," Rayna pointed out, tugging on Mariah's arm as they approached the stairs. "We can listen to the music."

"That's right," Betsy concurred far too quickly. They'd planned this. "Old man Dayton brought his fiddle. It ought to be a real treat."

"This wouldn't be about Nick, would it? Please tell me you two haven't been scheming. I don't like the man."

"This is about your duty as the vice president." Betsy released her death grip and held open the wood door to the cool evening breeze. Faint strains of a fiddle rose and fell in merry delight.

"No, I'm not going." She had no desire to see Nick swirling other women around the dance floor.

"I know how you feel about dances, but if you want a chance to be president in the next elections…"

O-oh, Betsy knew exactly what bait to use. Mariah knew she ought to get angry about this blatant use of manipulation. The truth was she did like old man Dayton's music and she *did* want to be president one day.

The setting sun's lights streaked bold purple and magenta against the sky and made the schoolhouse windows glow like a dream. Dozens of lamps and lanterns marched on stakes through the clipped-grass field, guiding their way, and the music sounded sweet and merry.

Maybe attending the dance wouldn't be too bad. She'd treat herself to a sarsaparilla, listen to a few toe-tapping songs and then help out, if the refreshment committee needed her. She'd be too busy to notice a certain man.

The makeshift stage was lit like a Christmas tree. The call of the fiddle and the twang of a banjo made it hard to concentrate as she searched for a path through the crush of people to the refreshment tables.

"Excuse me, Mariah," a man spoke at her side.

Surprised, her feet felt as if they'd frozen to the ground. Heart racing, she gazed up at the town gunsmith.

He held out his hand, but not to her. "Sorry, but could you step aside? I was hoping Betsy might honor me with a dance."

Betsy blushed. "Why, no, Zeke, I couldn't—"

What was a little disappointment? Of course he hadn't been about to ask her to dance. What was wrong with her tonight? Mariah stepped aside. "Go on, Betsy. Have fun."

"But—" She hesitated. Zeke took command and whisked her away.

"He's a good dancer," Rayna commented as the music lifted in harmony and boots tapped on the hard-packed earth.

"Yes, he is," Mariah answered blindly. The flaring skirts on the dance floor all blurred together.

Ridiculous, watching folks dance like this. She ought to be doing something productive. Something useful. She turned her back on the merriment, heading straight for the refreshment table. Surely there was work for her to do.

There always was.

"You're not dancing, big brother." Will handed Nick a tin cup of lemonade.

"I didn't come here to dance. We both know it." The cup was cool in the heat from the crowd, and the liquid puckered his tongue. It wasn't as satisfying as beer, but he needed a clear head right now.

He was on the hunt for a bride. A bride?

He couldn't do it. He couldn't pick out a wife, because every female here in this area was a stranger. He'd been married for a long time, and he wasn't a man with a wandering eye. He'd been faithful to Lida every minute of their time together. Having another woman had never crossed his mind.

So, how did he start now? It felt wrong, even with Lida gone. But his children needed a mother. They all needed a woman to cook and keep house for them.

So, what did he do? Just pick one? He was at a loss.

"You look like you're having troubles, big brother." Will smirked, looking as though he was enjoying this. "There are lots of pretty women in this town. Lucky for me, I don't have to settle on one. I can shop around."

"That's what you think. You just wait." Nick wasn't going to take any ribbing from his more obnoxious brother, especially when he wasn't even wet behind the ears where love was concerned.

"I'm going to go pick a female right now, but only for one dance." Will polished off his lemonade. "What you need, Nick, is to get out there and start dancing. Maybe you'll find a pretty young thing you'll want to keep."

Nick swirled the lemonade around in the bottom of his cup. A pretty young thing? Hardly what he considered good wife material. He'd had one of those once, and look how it had turned out.

Bitterness made the lemonade on his tongue curdle. Nope, he wasn't going to go near one of those young marriage-minded women lined up on the other side of the dance floor, looking at him with hope in their eyes. Females like that were nothing but trouble. He wasn't attracted to them. He didn't want a real marriage. Those women were looking for love. Every single one of them.

Just because a woman had a pretty face didn't mean she'd be good to his children.

The song ended, the crowd parted, and he caught sight of a blond-haired woman behind the refreshment tables, soft wisps escaped from her tight bun to curl gently around her face. A heart-shaped face that would be beautiful if it hadn't been for the dark smudges beneath her eyes.

Mariah. She was standing behind the lemonade pail beside two elderly ladies. All three wore black. Did she have to dress like a widow? Sadness pierced him sharp as a well-honed blade. Mariah had no husband and no children, unlike the other women her age. The women dashing after children, or sitting around the tables off to the side, or holding babies and talking about whatever it was women spent hours talking about.

Mariah was dressed in black, serving lemonade.

He couldn't help remembering the smiling young girl she'd been, once, when he'd been smitten with her. When it had hurt like a punch to the jaw to look at her.

He couldn't say why he slammed his cup onto the corral rail and left it there, or why his feet carried him through the crowd and past the dance area to the tables beyond. He only knew he was doing the right thing. He felt it down deep.

As he approached the refreshment table, he overheard Widow Collins. ''I hear he's hunting for a wife. That's why that man's here tonight.''

''What man?'' Widow White adjusted her spectacles.

''That oldest Gray brother.'' Widow Collins tsked. ''Those Grays have always been trouble on two legs.''

Trouble, huh? Maybe that was a sign. *Maybe I should turn around right now. Before Mariah sees me.*

It was too late. Mariah plunked the tin dipper into the pail, staring up at him, her gaze surprised beneath thick lashes. Then amusement curved the soft corners of her mouth.

Amazing. He'd forgotten her smile. How it could light her up from the inside and make her as soft as an angel. Funny how he'd forgotten that after all this time.

"Nicholas Gray." Mariah sounded as cold as stone. "Parched from hunting for a wife? Have some lemonade."

He held up both hands. "Not looking for lemonade. But I would like a dance with you."

"With me?" The dipper tumbled from her fingers and clanged against the tin pail. "Oh, I see. This is about Georgie, isn't it? You're asking me out of a sense of obligation. The same reason you hired me to do your laundry."

He blinked. What was she saying? What obligation? "I saw you standing here. Noticed you've been working all evening. Thought you might like a spin on the dance floor. Listen, they're just starting up a waltz."

Mariah stared at him as if she found him less than worthy of a single, obligatory waltz. Was asking a woman to dance always this nerve-racking?

"I don't approve of this close dancing." Widow Collins shook her head as she rescued the dipper from the depths of the lemonade bowl. "It gives young people all sorts of ideas. And at their age, they have enough of them. Mr. Dayton promised me there would be no more than two waltzes the whole night."

"Scandalous," Widow White agreed. "Mariah, I highly suggest you wait for a nice schottische. Something more decent than a waltz."

Nick could see Mariah wavering. He had to convince her now, before the widows said another word. "After all these years, you're still the prettiest girl here. Dance with me."

"Me? Dance with you?" she repeated.

''I dare you to.'' He flashed her that grin, the one that made the dimples stand out in his cheeks and his eyes twinkle.

Mariah felt its effect all the way to her toes. She was a sensible, practical spinster well past the fancies of youth. She was helpless to say no.

Out of the corner of her eye, Mariah could see the widows close together, stunned into silence. Beyond them the colorful women's dresses swirled in time to the music. What did she do? She could stay here where she belonged and not make a fool of herself. Then she'd watch another woman dance in Nick's arms.

This time, she wouldn't be left out.

He was waiting for her answer, one brow crooked in question, one hand held out, palm up. His fingers were broad and strong and warm when she touched him.

She wasn't aware of weaving through the tables or walking toward the stage, where the banjo and fiddle made music beneath the open sky. She knew only the weight of his hand in hers and the shivery feeling drifting through her. As if something wonderful was about to happen.

As if in a dream, Nick Gray pulled her to him. Not touching, exactly, but so close she could see the smooth skin of his shaven jaw and smell the night air on his shirt.

''Just close your eyes,'' he whispered, his breath warm against her ear, ''and follow me.''

She placed her hand on his shoulder, as strong as steel, and let him whirl her to the sway of the music beneath the light of the rising moon.

Chapter Four

If only this dance would never end.

Mariah closed her eyes, savoring the wonder of it. With Nick's hand at her waist, they moved together as harmoniously as the music. In a sweeping, gentle rhythm that felt like the heart of a dream. Slow and steady, and as light as air.

So *this* is what dancing feels like. Dancing in the arms of Nicholas Gray. Breathless. Exhilarating. She was intoxicated with it. The stars overhead were more brilliant than diamonds. The music from Mr. Dayton's fiddle sweeter than any she'd ever heard. And the man who held her was more captivating than she wanted to admit.

"You're as light as the music, Mariah. You're a good dancer."

"You sound surprised. I may be off the shelf, but I can waltz. I *am* surprised that you're not tripping over your feet. Or my toes."

"Go ahead and tease me. I'm man enough to take it."

You are all man. She bit her tongue so the words wouldn't accidentally slip out. His shoulder was pure iron beneath her fingertips, and just the feel of him was…*masculine.* There was no other word to describe him, staring at his chest, so muscled and solid and…

Down low, her stomach fluttered.

It wasn't because she was attracted to him, to this man she hated. Because she did hate him. She really did. And he disliked her with equal force. *He's simply doing me a favor, dancing like this, for saving his child's life. Remember that.*

When this brief dance was over, his duty done, he would escort her back to the punch table where she belonged. She couldn't fault him for that. Then he'd choose a prettier, younger woman to dance. One he would court and marry.

That won't be you, Mariah. Disappointment dug into her heart, but she refused to think about it. She stared hard at the button at Nick's collar. A thread holding it had frayed, and it could come loose. She'd have to remember that when she found this shirt in the next batch of laundry, and sew it on snug and tight. She always prided herself on doing a thorough job, the best in town, and never charged extra for the small touches. Yes, she'd do well to remember that button.

"That was a mighty fine chicken potpie you made. Rayna Ludgrin made a point of telling me you'd cooked it."

"I'm glad you thought so." It figured that he'd talk about food. See? He wasn't out to charm her. She knew that. Then why did it hurt so much?

"I enjoyed your angel food cake, too. Rayna took it upon herself to make sure I got a slice. I can't figure out why." He sounded amused, not on defense.

"She's a busybody who can't mind her own business, that's why." And a dear friend, Mariah didn't add, touched at her friend's thoughtfulness. Rayna didn't understand that Nick Gray wouldn't want her. "I'm glad you enjoyed the cake. It's my mother's family recipe. Maybe that would make a fine wedding gift for your new bride. The one everyone says you're here to find."

"Oh, yeah. That's why I'm here."

He sounded so sad. Mariah's heart punched with regret. She should have treated him better, even if she didn't like him. He'd lost a wife he loved. "I'm sorry for your loss. I never had the chance to tell you."

The strong shoulder muscles beneath her fingertips stiffened. He paused, letting the music move between them for a few short beats, his breath harsh, ruffling the tendrils at her temple, as if he were in terrible pain.

She ached for him. Maybe she'd been wrong to bring it up.

When he spoke, his voice was strained. "I never sent a note around for the food you prepared for the wake. I should have thanked you."

"You didn't need to. I understand. It's a sad time."

He simply nodded in response, his jaw brushing against her forehead. The fiddle sang sweetly, without a care in the world, but she could feel his heart, heavy and hurting. She laid her hand there, in the center of his chest, on the warm, hard, heat of him and felt the steady beat of his pulse. So much pain.

How was it that she could feel what was inside him? She didn't want to. She didn't want to watch as he chose another woman to marry, another woman to take his name, to live with him, to lie with him warm in his bed at night, to be loved by him, body and soul.

Anytime now Nick was going to release her, his duty done. She was prepared for it. She stared hard at the button on his collar, the one she intended to fix. Hardening her heart against the inevitable. She could see the younger women in the crowd watching him with hopeful eyes. Which pretty one would he pick to marry next?

For a second time Nick would pass her by to marry someone else. Her chest ached something fierce, and the button began to blur. She wouldn't think about that. She'd concentrate on that button. Remember to look for this shirt in the next batch of his laundry—

He pulled her to his chest, tucking her beneath his chin, against his heart. She settled against him as if she were made to fit right there, her forehead nestling perfectly against the column of his throat. *Oh, my.* Everything within her stilled—her pulse, her blood, her thoughts. All she knew was the scent of Nick's warm skin and the heat of his solid male body against hers. The music, the night, her anger at him, faded into nothing.

Being held by him was sheer heaven. Made her lighter than any soap bubble drifting on a summer's breeze. Made her heart feel bigger than the wide spread of the night sky overhead. She closed her eyes, breathing in the solidness of him, the incredible feel of his arms banded around her, of his body's heat, of the masculine way he was made....

"Is this all right?" His voice was a warm puff against her ear, making her tingle, shudder all the way to the soles of her feet.

All right? It was heaven. She nodded, closing her eyes, snuggling against him. Oh, to relax against the hard, wonderful plane of his chest. She breathed in the warm manly scent of his skin, letting him move her to the music, shuffling more than sweeping. His hand at her waist pressed her harder against him, as if he felt this, too, this yearning, this need to be closer. His free hand curled around the back of her neck, cradling her head against him. So tender…

He's not going to choose you, Mariah. So don't even begin to start hoping.

But holding him this close, feeling him so thrillingly male and comfortingly solid, made her ache. Ache for something she'd wanted since she was a schoolgirl. She wanted love. She wanted passion. She wanted to look into a man's eyes and see the depths of his love for her, tender and endless and true. To know that she, Mariah Scott—afraid, lonely, and so deeply flawed—could be loved. Accepted.

Cherished.

You're too cold-hearted for love, and you know it. Pa had told her this all her life. And it was true. She was too much like her mother for a man to ever find something to love in her. She was useful, a hard worker, good at cooking and cleaning, and she ran a fine laundry business. The best in town, in her opinion. She prided herself in that. In her accomplishments. She didn't need a man to make her feel good about herself.

But being held like this was so wonderful. Nick shifted, bringing his cheek to rest against the side of her head. It was tender and snug, and heat gathered low in her stomach. A strong liquid want, heavy and demanding, made her lean into him. Her softness to his hardness. She wished she could be held like this forever. By this man, the one she'd loved all her life.

She would never be good enough to be loved by him.

"You've been on your own a long time." He spoke low, so only she could hear him. "How long since your father's passing?"

"Five, almost six years."

"You've been alone all that time."

Alone. That's what she was, and she ached with it. She closed her eyes, sinking against Nick's chest. He wouldn't understand. He wasn't lonely, he had a lot of family, and his own children.

"I know now that life with your father was hard. Maybe painful. I should have seen that. I should have understood." His hand at the base of her skull moved in slow easy caresses.

Mariah shivered from the pleasure all the way to the soles of her feet. "It wasn't your fault. I wanted to blame you, but I couldn't. Lida was pretty and warm and loving."

"She was my children's mother and I won't say a bad word about her, but I regretted what I did. Telling you I wanted to court you and then marrying someone else."

"You fell in love."

His hand stilled. "Your father told me that you changed your mind that day."

"I didn't change my mind." She could clearly remember sitting at her bedroom window, ready for him to come calling, wearing the new dress she'd worked so hard to afford and had sewn during the late hours when her daily work was finally done. Fidgeting with anticipation, nervous, checking the mirror at least a dozen times to make sure her hair was all right because of the wind through the window.

Her first beau. Her young heart had sung with happiness. Other girls in school had boyfriends to take them driving on Sunday afternoons. She'd listened to their tales with such yearning. Now it was happening to her! Trembling, she leaned far out the open window, straining to see as far as she could around the bend in the road.

Was he late? Had he forgotten? He'd asked her in school that Friday; a whole day had passed and he could have forgotten.... No, wait. That was a small dust cloud rising on the rolling prairie, then suddenly a horse-drawn surrey appeared around the corner, the matched pintos trotting handsomely.

He'd come! The most handsome boy in school had come for her. She'd flown from the window, checked the mirror one last time to tuck an unruly gold curl beneath her poke bonnet and torn down the stairs.

Just in time to watch her father send Nick away. Dust flew in his wake, a big brown cloud obscuring him. When it faded, the dust settling back to the ground, he was gone.

He hadn't wanted her then. Nor had any man wanted to court her since. She refused to be sad about it. She was a grown woman, she didn't need anyone. Really.

"I have regrets," she admitted quietly. Wishing with all her heart that she could go back in time and change the parts of her that had brought her so much unhappiness. Wishing she could have been different. More loving. More…something. She didn't even know what it was. She just wanted to be loved. Was that too much to ask?

"I regret how I treated you. I was young. I made

mistakes. I still wind up making a few now and then.''

"Just a few?''

His chuckle rolled through her, starting in him and lashing through her like a wave against the shore, moving her when she didn't want to be moved.

This hurt too much, being in his arms. To think of the past. The one that had brought her here, alone, dancing not because she was wanted but because Nick Gray felt obligated to. It hurt that she wasn't like those other women, so soft and pretty and young. The best part of her life felt over, and she hadn't lived it.

Despair made her feet heavy, as heavy as her broken dreams. There would be no family for her, no children running to clutch her skirts calling "Ma, look!'' Because there was nothing about her that anyone—especially a man as fine as Nick Gray—could love.

She broke away from his embrace. She had her pride left, and she refused to lose that, too. It took all her courage to meet his gaze, so he wouldn't know how she felt. "Thank you for the dance. Consider your debt paid in full. I've got to go—''

"No.'' Nick's hand caught her wrist, stopping her. So tall he stood, his face set. "The dance isn't over.''

"It is for me.''

"You're not in charge here, Mariah.''

"There you go, thinking because you're a man that you're in charge and I—''

"But you gave your word.'' He took her other hand and settled it on his wide shoulder, his touch firm. "I don't think you want half the town to witness that the formidable Spinster Scott breaks promises right and left.''

"Oh, I'm sure everyone will understand my reluctance to dance with a man like you."

"Hmm? That so?" His hand settled into place at her waist. "I'm disreputable?"

"Of the worst kind. You overheard the widows talking about you."

"Seems to me that your reputation could stand some tarnishing, so come here."

She gasped, startled when he hauled her tight against him, into the snug shelter of his arms, where she could press her forehead to the hollow of his throat. She couldn't stop herself. Not one thing in her life had ever felt this good. This safe. This…right.

His hand curled around her nape, cradling her to him. A steady rhythm began to beat quietly in her blood, then picked up speed. *I'm in big trouble. Any more of this and he will know how I really feel about him.* Everyone in this room would know. Because they would see it on her face. See the love she hid deep in her heart for this strong man she'd never stopped wanting. Even if he'd broken her heart by marrying another.

The fiddle sang the last tender note of the waltz and the dancers fell away from one another, applause rising in the night. The stars twinkled, laughter and chatter rose, and Nick Gray's hand at her waist remained, a steady pressure that did not fade.

His heart raced beneath her hand, beating faster and faster. She gazed up into his eyes, so dark, so full of stormy emotions she couldn't begin to name, but still she felt the loneliness inside him that went all the way to his soul. Amazing, that she could feel that in him. Maybe because loneliness beat so strong within her.

She didn't know, but it hurt like a broken bone, healed and mended and throbbing in the winter.

Why did she have to feel this for him? Hands trembling, she broke away from him as the next song started, a lively schottische that had partners scurrying. Dancers were bumping against her skirts, because she was standing stock-still in the center of the dance area.

She wasn't doing anything but stepping out of the arms of the man she'd always yearned for. Away from the man who could still turn her inside out with only a look.

More than anything she wanted Nick's love. His real love. The kind her friends whispered about in those chaotic moments before the club meeting was called to order, with secret smiles of understanding about what went on between a wife and her man.

But the crowd of young women, all of marriageable ages and as pretty as could be, were waiting patiently for Nick to finish his obligatory dance with the town spinster. She couldn't compete, she knew it. So she tucked away her hopes right along with her disappointment and walked away.

"Hey, wait. Mariah—" His voice rang low, easily drowned out by the music and stomping feet of the dancers, so it was easy to pretend she couldn't hear him.

She walked past the pretty young women with hope sparkling in their eyes, pushed past the refreshment table where the widows stared at her in tight-lipped disapproval and out into the quiet of the schoolyard, dark and silent and empty.

Only then did she let the tears burn her eyes. Despair settled around her. She was alone. She had to face it. Just like her father had told her. No man was going to come courting her. Not now. Not ever.

She hated that the mean old cuss was still right, after all these years. Instead of heading back to the dance, to see which of the young women Nick had chosen to dance with, she headed toward the schoolhouse. Surely there was still some work there needing to be done.

Glad to be alone, Nick shook out the match, dropped it into the dirt at the side of the road and covered it with his boot.

The sweet, rich cigar smoke calmed him, and he dragged deep. He couldn't get Mariah out of his mind. The independent-minded, aggravating spinster who looked as prickly as a roll of barbed wire had melted against him like warm butter, fitting against him the way a woman was meant to. All curves and softness and heat.

This is a marriage of convenience, you want. Remember that, man. How Mariah felt in his arms didn't matter. That wasn't the issue.

His children were.

He dragged deep, blew out a long ribbon of smoke. The air was thick with the fresh, earthy scent of new grass growing and heavy with the sound of night insects and the birds that hunted them. He was looking true north, toward his property a few miles out.

Home. He warmed from head to toe, his worries melting away, thinking of his little ones tucked in for the night. His father would have put Georgie down first, after an hour of protests, requests for a drink of water and a lullaby. He pictured her snuggled beneath the thick comforter, covers pulled to her chin, her hair curled all around her face like an angel. So sweet. His heart hurt just thinking of her.

And fear hit him in the chest like the business end of a sledgehammer. He could have lost her today. Could have been at her wake, instead of a dance tonight.... Damn it. He couldn't stand it if something happened to her, or to his son...all it took was remembering the responsibility heavy on the boy's narrow shoulders to make Nick get off his butt and face what he had to do.

A wife might mean a lifetime of misery for him, but it meant security and happiness for his children. *Don't let those women scare you, Gray. You're the man. You're the boss. Pick one and be done with it.*

Aw, jeez. Not one of those young women—fresh-faced and immature—was what he was looking for. What he needed was a sensible, practical wife who understood that marriage was a legal agreement with separation of labours and knew that the job was tough. He needed a woman who would work hard and take good care of his kids. Someone who would leave his heart in his chest where it belonged and not shredded on the ground at her feet. Who on earth could fill those shoes?

A shadowed movement from the back door of the schoolhouse caught his attention. Mariah Scott, her basket slung industriously over one arm, was leaving. Backlit by the flaming torches set up to light the dance area, she was easy to pick out against the crowd, even in silhouette. Her purposeful stride was unlike any other woman's—not swaying and seductive, not dainty and airy, but no-nonsense. With every snap of her skirt, with every step she took, Mariah Scott meant business.

She marched past a gaggle of younger women, who huddled together talking near the bonfire. The moment she turned her back to the women as she swiftly marched down the worn path to the road, one of the young women mimicked her. They all burst out laughing.

Nick's chest tightened. Good thing he wasn't interested in one of those women. They were cruel, no matter how soft and feminine they looked. It was too dark to see Mariah's face, but he knew she'd been hurt. Her shoulders stiffened. He could see it. Just as he could feel the pride holding her up as she kept walking, without missing a beat. As if laughter was not lifting on the wind behind her, drowning out the first sweet strains of a new waltz.

She breezed past where he huddled on the shadowed bank, the row of parked buggies and wagons hiding him from her sight. He couldn't help noticing that while her shoes were patched, they were polished and serviceable. Just like the woman. Practical Mariah. She was hardworking and wore black like a widow, already given up on life.

He wanted to keep hating her, but how could he? She'd been as tied to her father's cruel demands as he'd been to the mistake he'd made with young Lida Brown. They'd both been trapped in unhappy lives. He knew the pain and the sting of the regrets that came with it.

He could make her life better. And his children's. With one simple question.

He climbed to his feet, dragging deep on his cigar. Maybe the rich smoke would give him the courage he needed as he made his way down the rode. "Hey, Mariah."

"Nick." Startled, she dropped her basket in her wagon bed, stiffening like a porcupine ready to strike. "What are you doing out here? Or have you found your bride all ready?"

"I found her. Least ways, I hope so."

"Oh, why that was certainly quick." Her voice came as sharp as the crack of the tailgate as she slammed it shut. "Let me be the first to offer my congratulations."

Her voice sounded strained. Hurt? That didn't sound at all like Mariah. "Don't go congratulating me yet. I haven't gotten around to ask her."

"Why not?"

"Because she's one of those do-gooder, busybody types. Always doing for some event or another. Like this fund-raiser tonight."

"Oh, then I must know her." She turned her back on him and hiked her skirts up to march into the tall grassy field. "You must mean Betsy. She's a good friend of mine. Truly, she'll make a good mother to your children. She's kind and I—"

Was her voice wobbling a little? Nick snatched the picket rope before she could grab it and yanked hard on the lead to bring the young ox to heel. "It's not Betsy I intend to marry. It's you."

"Me?" She froze in midstride, her skirts tumbling from her hands, and the air from her lungs.

He kept walking, leaving her behind. As he hitched the animal to her wagon, he stole a couple glances at her standing there, frozen as a statue, washed in patches of silvered moonlight. She was a beautiful woman with a gently sloping nose, the high delicate cut of cheekbone, the soft full mouth, and he knew, blue eyes so bright they could make the sky look pale by comparison.

His heart thumped in his chest, simply from looking at her. Still some of the boy in the man, he supposed. The boy in love for the first time—after all the bitterness of marriage, the heart didn't forget. But it was not his heart that saw the woman now.

No, it was the man appreciating her soft, full bosom. He'd never quite noticed how pleasantly she was proportioned. A narrow waist, not too tiny, but just right. How well his hand had fit there when they'd danced. Her skin as soft as warmed silk. Her hair fragrant with lilacs and soft against his shaven jaw. How small she'd felt against his chest.

"I told you, your obligation is over and done. Got that?" She marched right up to him, skirts flaring, and yanked the reins out of his hands.

"Yep, I heard you loud and clear, ma'am." He took her elbow, since he knew she'd refuse a hand up, and helped her into the wagon.

"I don't need your help or your pity, Mr. Gray."

"Pity? Mariah, I was being sincere."

"Sincerely charitable, I suppose. Good evening." Her chin shot up, all fight, all pride. The fierce spinster to the core as she snapped the reins hard enough to startle the ox into forward motion, jerking the wagon swiftly away from him.

But not before he caught the sparkle of tears in her eyes.

Aw, jeez. He'd hurt her. He stood there a long while, watching her wagon disappear into the darkness. What did he do now?

Mariah felt her way up the porch in the dark. The night felt so quiet as she stood there in the shadows, hesitating to turn the key in the lock because she didn't want to go inside. There was no one waiting for her. No husband to welcome her, no children running in their nightshirts who'd missed her all evening long.

Regrets. Why did she feel things so keenly tonight? She wished she could push them aside, but they remained, a heavy sharp blade in her breastbone. Did it have to be so darn quiet here? The door hinges squeaked like chalk on a board and her shoes tapped as loud as a war drum on the wood floor she'd polished only yesterday. The emptiness echoed around her and did not fade when she hurried to light a nearby lamp. The faint glow of the flame on the wick only illuminated the truth of her life—rooms in perfect order, not a speck of dust in sight, but without anyone to fill them.

Just her. It didn't seem enough. Not tonight. Not after dancing in Nick's arms. Not after what he'd said to her.

Marry him? She couldn't marry him. He didn't like her. She didn't like him. He'd proposed to her out of pity, for heaven's sake. *Pity.* As if she were a sad, lonely old spinster in need of charity.

Angry, she dumped her reticule on the hallway table. There was her reflection staring right back at her, the face of a woman no man could love. Or so Pa had told her, and told her often. And as time passed and she went from schoolgirl to spinster, she'd come to believe it.

Nick *couldn't* have meant his proposal. She was old, and getting older by the minute. The dim light accentuated every wrinkle and imperfection on her no-longer-youthful face. Not that she was ancient, it was just that life had a way of marking a person, like rings in a tree. Sadness had marked hers, and she hated seeing it there. Had to wonder if Nick had seen it, too.

Oh, stop thinking about that man! She shrugged out of her shawl, hung it with a curse on the wall peg and made it all the way to the kitchen before she realized she'd forgotten her basket in the back of the wagon. What was wrong with her tonight? Even standing in the dark of her kitchen, surrounded by the sounds of emptiness and the wind scraping the lilac branches against the siding, she couldn't seem to make her mind stop reeling her back in time to the sensation of waltzing in Nick's strong arms.

It's not Betsy I intend to marry. It's you, he'd said in that deep dark voice of his, as intriguing as a rogue's, making her shiver from the roots of her hair to the tips of her toes. He couldn't mean it. She didn't know why he'd even asked, and maybe he didn't, either. He had to have proposed knowing she would reject him. Right?

Breathing in, she could remember Nick's scent and feel the warmth of his shirt against her cheek, the security of his strong arms holding her. A part of her would always yearn after him, as she had when she was young, watching him marry another woman. And, as the years crept by, offering congratulations on the birth of his children. Watching from her father's kitchen window as his family surrey swept by on the way to town, with Lida at his side.

Pain filled her, at the loneliness of her own life. It wasn't better being alone. She didn't care how right her father was. If she could pray for any one thing and have it granted, no holds barred, then it would be to have a heart that could love. A heart that wasn't cold and used up, like a hunk of winter's ice. One that bloomed like the wild prairie roses, and no harsh winter or dry summer could stop their stubborn blooms.

But she was her mother's daughter. Ice to the core. Good for only one thing—hard work. At least she did that well.

Taking solace where she could, Mariah crossed the dark kitchen, petticoats swishing in the silence. She felt proud of how hard she'd worked tonight. Her contribution made a difference. They'd raised more than half the money they needed for the school addition. See? Her life had meaning enough. The children of this town would have new desks and plenty of room so they could become better educated, and a new heater to keep them warm through the winter.

She found the match tin by feel and snapped open the lid. The curtains were open, giving a view of her backyard and orchard, and a glimpse at her neighbor's house. Lights blinked on in their windows like beacons in the night, drawing Mariah's gaze. Their curtains were open, too, and she caught sight of the Bryants, returning from the dance, no doubt. Mrs. Bryant balanced her year-old son on her hip, while herding her other two small children through the front room toward the bedrooms in back.

It was just a slice of their lives Mariah could see through that window, but how warm it looked. How cozy. Mr. Bryant came into view and laid a gentle hand on his wife's shoulder. She gazed up at him with a smile. How happy they looked, man and wife. There was love there, a kind Mariah knew nothing about. She closed her eyes and turned away.

No, she belonged here. In the house she grew up in. In the house where she'd cared for her father until his death. It was hers now. And she would live out her days here, not troubled by the demands of children and a husband and by her own inadequacies.

No, she was happy here—*alone*—and she was content with that. Mariah snapped the curtains shut against the night and other people's bliss.

She vowed not to think of Nick again. And she didn't. Not when she fetched the basket from the wagon and unloaded her dishes. Not when she prepared for bed. Not even once, in her dreams that night, or any of the nights that followed.

Chapter Five

"Mariah!" Rayna Ludgrin's knock echoed through the warm house the next Monday morning and was followed by the squeak of the hinges. "Mariah! Are you in here? I'm a little early, I know. Some of your dishcloths got mixed up with mine. I'd best return them while I'm here, or I'll forget all about it."

"Good thing, because I have some of yours." Mariah sprinkled water on the collar of Nick's blue muslin work shirt. "How much did the dance bring in?"

"We topped last year's in donations." Rayna bustled through the door like a whirl of gaiety and dropped a neat pile of a dozen dishcloths on the crowded table. "Oh, you look busy. Your business is growing."

"It's improving." Mariah had told no one, not even her closest friend, how hard it had been making ends meet. "Have you heard from Betsy? She was dancing with the gunsmith when I left."

"Betsy ought to be here in a few minutes. She'd never miss our weekly tea time. Speaking of Friday night's event, what about you? I saw you waltzing in

Nick Gray's arms.'' Rayna helped herself to the tea water simmering on the stove. ''It was the talk of the dance.''

''Hardly. It was one waltz.''

''Yes, but did you see the way he looked at you?''

''I *did* happen to notice. That's why I've vowed never to speak to him again.''

''Mariah! If you keep this up, you'll never marry.''

''Marry? What does that have to do with Nick Gray? Oh, sure, you mean his act of pity. He danced with me out of his conceited, self-centered sense of obligation.'' She blinked hard and stabbed the point of the iron into the seam of the muslin's narrow collar. ''So, he must have chosen a wife by now. Those children of his need a woman's care. Who's the lucky bride?''

''I have no idea— Wait, I hear Betsy. Why, Betsy, good morning.''

Mariah's hands stilled for a shocked moment. What was wrong with Rayna? Why was she avoiding the subject of Nick Gray?

''Good morning, or, well, a few minutes to noon.'' She waltzed in, looking happy as a lark in a pretty blue calico dress with a matching bonnet, balancing a pink bakery box in her gloved hands. ''Guess what? Zeke asked me to go driving with him on Sunday.''

''He's a good man, Betsy. I'm glad for you.'' Mariah set the iron in its stand. Maybe this romance would work out for Betsy, but what about Nick Gray?

He'd proposed to someone else.

Pain pierced like an arrow into Mariah's chest, making it hard to breathe. She couldn't let her feelings show. Keeping her chin high, she turned the shirt on the edge of the board, smoothing the fabric until it was perfect.

There. Another shirt done. She folded it precisely and laid it on the stack of others.

It's all right. You didn't expect he really wanted to marry you. But that didn't stop her heart from breaking or the disappointment from welling up like a geyser. She hadn't realized how much she wished Nick's proposal had been a real one.

Blinking hard, she set the iron aside, her work done for now. She had a few hours to spend with her friends. This afternoon she had more garments to iron and deliveries to make.

Nick Gray's choice of bride was not her concern.

It was just as well. She was content with her life. Look at all she'd accomplished. Rayna was right— her laundry business was beginning to flourish. The fund-raiser had been a success. She had friends, her own house, and her independence. What more did a women need?

"A good man." Rayna waggled her brows as she gathered china from the corner hutch. "Betsy, did you hear what Mariah said? He's a good man, she said of the gunsmith. What did you mean by that?"

Mariah blushed as she snatched the stack of plates from Rayna. "Just what I said. Zeke is a good prospect for a husband. He's an honest businessman. He's kind. He makes a good wage. I think you ought to let him court you, Betsy."

"That's what I'm going to do." Betsy smiled. "Rayna, did you hear what Mariah said? She said a man who's a good prospect for a husband is honest and kind."

"Huh! Mariah, just goes to show what you know."

Rayna winked, sharing a private grin with Betsy as she gathered small plates from the high shelf. "Mariah has never been married, so we'll have to forgive her ignorance."

"Hey! I'm not ignorant!" Mariah protested, used to the ribbing of her friends. "I can't imagine why you two think marriage is such a joy—"

"Not a joy," Betsy corrected. "A pleasure."

"Oh, yes, it's that." Rayna nodded, blushing. "Oh, the pleasure."

"You two, I'm shocked at you. To think I call such lusty, indecent women my friends." Laughing, too, Mariah grabbed the bread plates from Rayna, stacked them on top of the china she already had and marched toward the dining room, pushing through the glass door.

Really. They were talking about intimacy, and as embarrassed as Mariah was, she was more curious.

"Me? Indecent?" Rayna blushed harder. "Why, I should hope so."

"That is what I miss most about being married." Betsy sighed with longing, the fondness in her voice unmistakable. "Charlie was a thoughtful man. Oh, and so tender. As much as I miss him, I miss that tenderness with a man. That intimacy."

Mariah set the plates on the lace-covered table, alone, listening to her friends in the other room, voices low, talking of marriage with such fondness. Remembering how thrilling it had felt to be held in Nick's arms, snug against his chest, made her wish for the first time that she knew what her friends were talking about. What true intimacy with a man felt like. Was it that wonderful? Was it special to be so loved?

Yes, it was. Why wouldn't it be? Longing filled

her so sharp and sweet, tugged at the cold edge of her heart like spring's first sunshine on frozen tundra. What she would give to know that wonder. To be treasured and held like that. To have Nick hold her in that special way.

He doesn't want you, Mariah. Nick would marry someone else, just as he had last time, and the man she'd loved forever would be out of her reach. The same man that her father had sent away when she was young and halfway pretty, when she'd had a chance of being loved.

Now that chance was gone for good. Mariah could see her reflection in the mirror over the fireplace. She didn't like what she saw. Hers was the stark, unhappy face of a woman who looked older than her years.

That's not me, she thought. It couldn't possibly be.

But it was. Time had changed her on the outside. There was no doubt about it. She couldn't go backward. She really didn't want to. It's just that... She sighed. The longing within her was the sixteen-year-old schoolgirl she used to be, who had never stopped loving Nick Gray.

I hope his new bride, whoever she may be, makes him happy. He deserves that. And his beautiful little girl, with those wonderful gold curls tangled and falling everywhere, she deserved a kind mother. Mariah ached, remembering the child. Remembering how hard Georgie's small fingers had held tight with a mountain of determination. So fragile and dear and amazing.

She'd give anything to have a child like that. A child of her very own. If only...

Some things were not to be.

The room echoed with the joyous chatter of her

friends as they rescued the meal out of the oven—
chicken and dumplings. This would not be a day of
sadness, but one of joy because she wasn't alone. She
had friends she treasured.

Truly happy for Betsy and Zeke, she finished setting the table before she hurried to the kitchen to join
in the merry talk. But today, for some reason, visiting
with her friends could not chase away the sorrow inside her.

The sorrow of what could never be.

The Gray's ranch house loomed ahead of her, and
it may as well have been a tornado heading her way.
Facing a twister head-on would be less fear-inspiring
than pulling the wagon to a stop in the shade of
Nick's front porch.

Remember, you're glad for him. Glad he found
someone who could make him happy. Mariah set the
brake, taking time to gather her courage. She could
do this. She'd handled more painful situations than
this, and she could walk into that house, deliver the
laundry, look Nick in the eye and find it in her heart
to be happy for him.

Yep, that's exactly what she would do. She gathered the rucksacks and pillowcases stuffed with fresh-
smelling, perfectly ironed garments, and began leaning them in a tidy row up against the side of the
house.

The screen door snapped open and bare feet
slapped against the wood porch. ''It's the apple lady!
Hi, apple lady!''

''Why, hello, Georgie.'' Mariah hefted the last of
the five bundles. ''That's a pretty dress you're wearing.''

"My mama gave it to me." Georgie's eyes filled as she smoothed the pretty yellow gingham with the flat of her hand. "Did you come to take me?"

"I came to deliver your laundry." Some of the garments she'd washed and ironed had been Georgie's sweet little dresses. "Where's your pa?"

"Don't know." Georgie bit her bottom lip, as if considering something of grand importance. "My Grandpop's in the chair."

"Want to go fetch him for me?"

"No." Georgie headed straight for the wagon.

Where was the child going? Mariah leaned the last full sack against the others in a flash, intending to go after the little girl, but the screen door sprung open. A slender woman wearing a sky-blue calico dress flew across the porch. The screen door slammed shut.

"Mariah!" Theresa Dayton skidded to a halt, breathless, her hand flying to her chest. "Goodness, I didn't see you there. Where's Georgie? Oh, there you are, you rascal. Didn't I tell you to stay in the kitchen?"

So, that's who Nick decided to marry. The neighbor's pretty granddaughter, who had grown up on a ranch. She'd make a busy rancher like Nick a fine wife.

"I want to offer my congratulations," Mariah managed, surprised at how much it hurt.

"Congratulations? Oh, thanks, I guess." Theresa took off after Georgie. The little girl was a few steps away from the wagon and began crying when Theresa caught up with her.

"Gonna go to heaven," Georgie insisted. "I miss my mama."

Poor little girl. Poor Theresa. The woman knelt,

trying to pull the distressed child into her arms, but Georgie fought her. Mariah ached watching. She didn't know what to do, how to comfort the child. She'd tried the other day, with little success.

She knew nothing about being a mother or a wife. It's just as well Nick was marrying someone like Theresa. Even if it hurt. Mariah took an unsteady breath, staring hard at her red, cracked hands made rough from long exposure to lye soap. She would have disappointed him.

"Hey, what's all this fuss?"

Speak of the devil. There he was in all his male glory, gray cotton shirt stretched over his capable frame, looking like something out of every woman's most secret dreams. The sight of his wind-tousled hair made her fingers itch to run through those untamed locks.

She turned, taking a step away from the man who strode across the porch and into the yard. He gathered Georgie up into his arms.

"What's the matter, princess?"

"I'm goin' with the apple lady. Long gone and far away. To heaven."

"Is that right?"

"Yep. I wanna go real bad."

"So I see." Nick leaned his broad forehead against his daughter's little one, gazing right into her eyes.

Mariah didn't know much about children, but she knew what it felt like to be a little girl, unsure of the world around her. What a wonderful father Nick seemed to be—and that was hard to admit.

"Heaven is far away, and I'm going to miss you if you go." Warmth deepened Nick's booming voice and it rumbled like a caress on the afternoon breeze. "I think you'd better stay with me."

"But I miss Mama."

"And I'll miss you. I'd be lost without my little girl to love." He gave her a smacking kiss on her brow. "Let's get you back inside, okay?"

Georgie shook her head, then threw her arms around his neck, holding on for dear life. So lost and alone and hurting.

"Thanks, Theresa." With one last kiss to his daughter's face, Nick handed over the child into his fiancée's gentle arms.

"I'll make sure to keep a better eye on her, I promise." Theresa cradled the girl and carried her into the house.

Yes, Theresa would make Nick a good wife. A loving wife. A kind stepmother.

Something that Mariah didn't know how to be. Now, a good businesswoman, that's where she had some experience. That was the only reason she was here. Not to regret the path of her life. Not to remember the sweet thrill of being held against Nick's broad chest.

She averted her gaze as he faced her, so she wouldn't have to remember. Wouldn't have to feel vulnerable and feminine and have to acknowledge the terrible longing inside her. The longing to be in his arms.

"Mariah." Nick's voice sounded strained, as if he wasn't at all pleased to be alone with her. "Glad you could fit us into your deliveries today. This was my last clean work shirt."

Business. Yes, that's all they would ever have between them. The last fraying thread of hope snapped.

How deep did her love for Nick go? So many years of quietly loving him, and hating that she did, only to be his laundry woman.

There would be no second chances for her. For them.

She didn't dare lift her gaze to his. Her despair felt as enormous as the Montana sky and as easy to see. If she didn't have a warm heart, she did have her pride. And by God, she would not lose anything else to Nick Gray.

Fine. This is the way it's meant to be. She was woman enough to accept it. He was *not* the love of her life, but a customer. Nothing more. Not ever. "I'm glad I could fit you in today's schedule, then. I found several buttons that needed tightening and patched quite a few garments. All included in the price, of course."

"Sure do appreciate that."

"I'll send a bill at month's end. I'd appreciate payment upon receipt. Good day." She pushed past him, staring hard at her feet as she breezed by. *That's right, keep going. Don't look at him. Don't look back.*

"Wait. You forgot something."

"I didn't forget a single shirt. I delivered the same five bundles you brought to me."

"Not the laundry. What about me?"

"You? That's right. You and Theresa. I must offer my congratulations." Mariah forced the grief from her voice because she *wasn't* sad. Really. She *refused* to be sad. "I'm nearly finished crocheting a lace tablecloth that should do fine for a wedding gift. I'll include it with the recipe I promised—"

She choked, turning away before he could see the pool of tears in her eyes. Shame on her, breaking down like this. She was a grown woman who ought to have more sense than to keep hoping she'd be good enough for a man like Nick.

"Wait. Mariah. Come back here." His boots pounded in the dirt behind her. "I'm not marrying Theresa."

She stopped, grabbed the wagon's sideboard, and let her head fall forward. She was breathing hard, and the world was nothing but a blur. She blinked hard, fast, as Nick skidded to a stop behind her. She couldn't have heard him right.

"I hired her. For a few days. Until you give me an answer."

"An answer?" She didn't understand. He wasn't marrying Theresa? He certainly wasn't interested in *her*—an old maid who didn't know the first thing about being a wife or a mother.

"I believe I tried to propose marriage a few evenings ago. To you. Do you remember?"

She shook her head, willing the wetness from her eyes. "I would have declined your offer of marriage, serious or not."

"It was damn serious, Mariah. Why else would I ask? So I'll say it again. Will you marry me?"

His hand settled on the dip of her shoulder and the imprint of his hand burned like a stove-hot iron. Be Nick's wife? She could see the ranch house clearly, the windows open to the temperate breezes. There was Theresa in the kitchen, clanking open the oven and lifting out a cookie sheet held in a thick, cumbersome mitt. Georgie's voice rose in excitement along with a little boy's whoop of delight.

A home. A husband. Children to call her own. Her chest constricted until it hurt to breathe. Was this a second chance for her? The opportunity to change her life? Was this fate giving back the one thing she regretted most losing?

She could see that day in her memory as clear and precise as if it was that very day more than a decade ago. When she'd raced down the stairs, skirts flying, hopes as high as the fluffy clouds in the pristine Montana sky. There was Pa, closing the door behind him, stepping out to speak with Nick.

"Mariah don't want you to come courtin'," Pa's rough baritone had been faintly slurred with drink and rang with a mean note. The one that said he meant business.

She froze, not believing her father had turned Nick down. Not believing as Nick climbed back into his buggy and drove away. He never looked back.

The heavens above were giving her another chance to love the one man she'd secretly wanted through all the lonely days and nights since. Did Nick feel this way, too?

When she turned to face him, it wasn't the past she saw, but the present. She was no longer young, but neither was Nick. Lines of character and strength marked his face. And he may still be too confident and cocky, yet he was more handsome to her than any man in the world. Did they have a chance to find happiness? Or was love, once gone, always gone, never to be renewed, never breathed back to life like the last embers of a banked fire?

She didn't know. She didn't know how to answer. Or what to say. The woman she'd become was hard as stone, as cold as a dark January night, as unfeeling as a razor's keen edge. She was nothing like Theresa, cheerful and caring, or like those young women in town, soft and coy.

She could only be herself, the practical woman she'd become. Was that enough? But then Nick smiled, as if he could see the answer in her eyes. She felt the young woman she'd once been. Just a hint of her. The young woman full of hope, who still believed she was worth loving.

Her chest tightened as she made her decision. Took the biggest risk of her life. "What are you doing tomorrow, say, around two o'clock?"

"Will I be marrying you?"

"Yes." Her knees started to tremble and her petticoats rustled. Nick had to hear her quivering. He had to guess how afraid she felt, afraid and vulnerable.

Then he smiled. A small ghost of a smile that reminded her of the young man he used to be, kind and gallant, the man who had once captured her heart. Who lived inside the steely, remote man and his confident manner.

The tightness in her chest eased. Hope beat there, steady and strong. *Hope.* For the first time since she was young, she felt new, expectant, as if the future held more than the sounds of an empty house echoing around her. Tomorrow she would be a wife with children to care for and a real home to call her own.

And Nick. She would have Nick as her husband to hold through the night, no longer alone.

"I'll swing by in the surrey to drive you to church. Will that do?"

"Just fine."

"Just so you always know." He leaned close, his breath a hot caress against the shell of her ear. "I proposed to you and no one else. I can't think of any woman who'd make me a better wife.''

''I can.'' It was only the truth. She was practical enough to be honest. ''Just about any woman around knows more than I do about being a wife and mother. I've been a spinster for too long.''

''I know deep down you're a kind woman. That's all I ask. That you be kind to my children. Raise them up right. Love and protect them the way a mother should.''

''I'll do my best.''

''That will be more than enough. You're a hard worker, Mariah, and your best effort is a far sight better than anyone's.''

A hard worker? Her father's words had a strange echo in the empty places in her heart. *What man would want you, Mariah? You're as cold-hearted as your mother, and there's only one thing a woman like you's any good for and that's hard work.*

No, Nick didn't mean that. He only meant he admired her work ethic. Right? That he trusted her to care for his children. Right?

''Marriage is hard, I won't lie to you.'' He caught her left hand and cradled it between both of his, a deliberate act, and his touch was as firm as his words. ''I promise you this. I won't make you sorry you married me. I'll do my best by you. I'll give you my all. I'll do every damn thing I can to make you content. As long as you take good care of my children. That's all I ask. This isn't a marriage for love. You know that.''

Not for love? Mariah squeezed her eyes shut as pain exploded like a bullet through her chest. Of course, she was being foolish. Nick was mourning his beloved Lida. He wasn't ready to love again, not until he'd finished grieving. She shouldn't be foolish hoping for the impossible. Right now Nick needed her to care for his children and for him. In time, he would need more from her.

And she would find a way to give it to him. Her father couldn't be right. She refused to believe it, not now, with Nick towering over her, blocking her view of the world. He was all she could see as he leaned close and brushed a kiss to the side of her face. A warm, brief caress of heat that left her ears buzzing and her skin tingling.

"I promise you won't be sorry that you chose me. You could have asked anyone, and I—" she paused, swallowing hard "—thank you."

Nick felt as if she'd gut punched him. She was thanking him? No, he was the one who ought to be grateful to her. She was saving him from marrying one of those young, idealistic women who were no different than Lida had been. Always grasping for something to make them happy—love, romance or pretty bobbles from the town mercantile. Believing that marriage was some blissful state of happily-ever-after where they got every damn thing they wanted.

Mariah. She confused him as nothing else on this earth. But he knew her down to her hard, steel core. Mariah was capable and hardworking and good, down deep. This proposal meant a lot to her. More than he realized. Odd how her lower lip trembled like that, how she closed up as if she'd said too much by thanking him, shown him how much it meant.

She wanted a family. He felt it in the way her fingers clung to his, holding on so tight with a need she wouldn't admit to. Pride. He knew something about that. Yet she was fragile, too. Her hand was small against his, delicate, her nails short, her skin rough from the lye soap she worked in. Hardworking, trustworthy. A woman who wasn't after his heart. No, not Mariah. She wanted a place to belong. He ran his fingertip over the crescent of her thumbnail. Yes, she was so fine-boned, so female, and it cut him to the core.

"No, I am the one who's grateful." He cupped her hand gently between his, this woman he could trust. "Do you think we can manage a peaceful union? We don't much get along."

"We don't get along at all."

"Yeah. Well, I figure we've got something to build on, don't you? We've got respect. I hope we have friendship. That's more than most marriages I can name."

"True," Mariah agreed. It wasn't a promise of love, but it would come in its own time. Right? She studied the back of his hand, his sun-browned knuckles were scarred and battered from hard work, but there was no answer there. No reassurance. "It will take a lot of hard work to get along with you. You're too sure of yourself. I may have to take you down a peg or two."

"Yeah? I could say the same about you." The tiniest smile touched the corners of his mouth. "You're bossy and independent. Set in your ways. Good thing I like a challenge."

"Bossy? I'll make you pay for that one. Don't be surprised if you find too much starch in your drawers."

His eyes twinkled, as they once used to. "Is it too darn late to take back that proposal?"

"Absolutely. I haven't yet begun to make you suffer."

She loved the way he tipped back his head and laughed. The wind tousled his dark hair, making him look untamed and rugged and handsome enough to tug to life a strange, sweet yearning.

One that made her chest hurt as if an ax had sank deep into her rib cage. There was magic between them. Some strange, powerful force that could not be seen, only felt.

Maybe—just maybe—they could find happiness together. One day. After Nick was through grieving Lida.

"I'll see you tomorrow, then." He cupped her elbow, helping her into the wagon seat. "I'll send Will by in the morning to help you pack. He'll move whatever you want. How's that?"

"I'd appreciate it." She waited while he untethered the ox, smoothing her dull gray skirts with small, nervous movements.

Mariah, nervous? Nick had to think about that. He wasn't used to seeing a vulnerable side to her. "Guess this is goodbye, until tomorrow. Until I make you my wife."

"I'll be waiting." She snapped the reins. The ox groaned, not at all certain he wanted to move.

Nick slapped his behind and the animal took off, hauling the old rattling wagon down the driveway. Mariah sat so tall and straight on that bench seat, her slim shoulders set like a soldier's.

"I heard what you said to her." His father was there, wearing a look of disapproval that made a full force twister look friendly in comparison. "You're out of your mind. You can't marry that woman. She'll tear you apart by the end of the first week.''

"I know what I'm doing, Pop.'' If Mariah made his kids happy, then Nick figured he would do anything for her. And it started now, with his respect.

He would respect this woman and take care of her. Provide for her and protect her. "I'm marrying the spinster. If you have a problem with that, you keep it to yourself.''

"That's no way to talk to your father. I'm still tough enough to whip you, boy.''

"When did you ever whip me, old man?'' A lifetime of affection for his father warmed him, and he clasped Pop on the shoulder. "Just be good to her, okay? I've got a lot riding on this.''

"She can cook, I grant you that. But, son, are you sure? A woman like that will bring a man nothing but heartache.''

"A woman like what?'' Nick thought of Lida, so beautiful and everything a young wife should have been. But she'd had no heart, not really, no loyalty, no strength, no character. When put to the fire, she melted like wax.

But Mariah, she was steel. She wouldn't melt. She wouldn't break. She wasn't the kind of woman who would take a lover or her own life. No, Mariah was loyal and steadfast. Mariah was getting older and didn't want to be alone anymore. That's why she was marrying him.

Marriage was a serious commitment and it could tear a man to pieces if he let it. But he could handle Mariah, and he knew, gut-deep, that this marriage would be different. This time he'd keep the upper hand. He'd be good to her, but love her? He had no heart left for that.

Good thing she didn't want that anyway. The look on her face when she'd thanked him for proposing... He couldn't believe it. How sincere she'd looked. Not all prickly and self-righteous, like the Mariah he knew. But the soft, open young woman who could make him grin from just looking at her.

A few days ago he never would have predicted he'd be standing here, watching her drive away, glad he'd proposed. He had no idea how hard her life had been with her father. How little kindness she must have received in that house over the years.

Yes, he was glad he'd chosen her. More grateful that she'd said yes. By marrying him, she was solving a great many of his difficulties. But maybe by his proposing to her, he was helping her, too.

It was something to consider as he watched her wagon journey down the road, nothing but a small dark spot against the prairie. Sadness filled him, heavy and deep, and he didn't know why.

Chapter Six

"Are you ready?" Nick's warm voice brushed the shell of her ear as he held the door for her.

"As ready as I'll ever be." Mariah took a deep breath and stepped into the empty church. If only her pulse would slow down to a mere gallop. She wanted to marry Nick, so why was she so frightened?

Because you can fail him. She went cold all the way down to her toes. If she turned around right now and walked straight down the aisle and out those doors, she would be safe. She'd remain the crusty old reliable Spinster Scott with a business and a house and an officer in several of the town's most prominent social clubs. But if she did, then Nick would marry another woman. And she'd be alone, watching him drive by on the way into town with another woman at his side.

Pain hit her like a falling brick and the impact left her trembling. She was afraid. It was that simple. Afraid of her own inadequacy.

You can do this, Mariah. She took a deep breath against the tight stays of her corset. Women get married every day.

Nick's hand caught hers and held tight. "I've done this before and survived it."

"That's not comforting."

"Maybe this will be." His fingers laced through hers, joining them together in front of the pulpit. He looked fine in his tailored black suit. "When this is done, you aren't going to be alone anymore. You'll have me."

"And you will have me," she vowed.

His smile was all the reassurance she needed. He understood. This was a life-changing moment. Joy made her feel as light as the sweet afternoon sunlight drifting through the stained-glass windows.

"Shall we begin?" the minister asked, storming into the sanctuary with an air of purpose.

Betsy clamored in the back door, lifted a hand in a silent wave and slid onto the front pew. "Congratulations," she mouthed.

Congratulations. Yes, this felt like something to celebrate as the minister's "dearly beloved" boomed into the stillness.

Mariah knew every word of the service by heart because she'd been to so many weddings. This one was hers. Hers and Nick's. She squeezed his hand as he held on to her so tight. He towered above her, a perfect pillar of calm masculinity, but his palm was damp against hers.

He was nervous, too. His gaze latched onto hers and she could see the flicker of caring there. He didn't need to say the words, but his concern for her was clear as he captured her other hand in his. And so he held her, hand to hand.

"I take thee, Mariah Elizabeth Scott, as my wedded wife." Nick never wavered as he recited the sacred vows in his booming baritone. Promising to cherish her for the rest of her life. From his unflinching gaze locked on hers to the unyielding grip of his hands over hers, to the strong immobile stance, Nick Gray meant every word. "Until death do us part."

She shivered clear to her soul. Emotion welled up in her heart, a thousand powerful feelings too difficult to name. Her eyes burned, her throat ached. Her past, her sorrows, her regrets lifted from her shoulders, leaving her changed. New. She had to clear her throat and find her voice, for it was her turn to speak. "I, Mariah Elizabeth Scott take thee, Nicholas Adam Gray to be my husband."

Husband. She stumbled over the word. She was really here. She was marrying him, and he squeezed her hands, encouraging her, his kind, steady touch a silent reassurance. He wanted her. Her, and no one else. Tears blurred her vision as she spoke her vows, the words slipping past her lips, promising to love, honor and obey him, to cherish him for the rest of her life.

Oh, she would. With all her heart. With all her soul. She wasn't going to be alone anymore.

Nick lifted their joined hands and brushed at her cheek with his thumb. The pad of his thumb came away wet with her tears.

"You okay?" he whispered as the minister spoke.

"Fine." More than fine. Her heart, so cold and frozen, felt like a pond cracking at the season's first thaw. Tiny little cracks radiating from the outside in. Hurting with the pressure of the coming spring.

Suddenly the ceremony was over, the minister pronouncing them man and wife. "You may kiss the bride."

They were married. Mariah watched Nick smile as he wiped away the last of her tears. Never wavering, never uncertain, he leaned forward. She caught her breath. She didn't know what to do. She'd never been kissed. What if she disappointed him?

Then his mouth slanted over hers, his top lip fitting gently against the seam of hers. He felt like heated velvet and tasted like passion. The caress of his mouth thrilled through her like lightning crackling across a midnight sky. He pulled away, leaving her mouth abandoned and tingling.

I want him to do that again. But he was turning away to give the minister a tip for his services. Betsy hopped up from the pew, dark curls bobbing around her smiling face.

"I can't believe it. You're married now." Betsy wrapped her in a warm hug. "And to the most eligible bachelor in five counties. You did well, my friend."

"I'm shaking like a leaf caught in a twister." It was over, and she and Nick were wed, so why was she trembling like this?

"Don't worry, you're going to be fine. Rayna didn't come because she was busy with a surprise. Gather up your new husband and make him take you home. To your new *home.*"

Betsy understood. What else were good friends for? Mariah blinked hard, unable to say the words. Her own home. Her own family. Her own husband.

Look at him, standing there so wonderful, looking no different than he ever did. But he *was* different. He was hers. The man she would take care of for the rest of her life. It would be his bed she slept in. He would be the man she reached out to at night when the lamps were blown out and silence filled the house.

He would teach her the pleasure made between a man and a woman. He would father the baby she would carry one day.

A bright warmth sparked to life inside her, right behind her breastbone. A strange warmth that made her chest ache and her throat fill. It hurt and made her glad all at once when Nick turned from the minister, smiled at her, and held out his hand.

She placed her left hand against his calloused palm, her wedding band glinting new and flawless in the muted light.

"Let's go home," he said.

Home. Nothing had ever held such importance. Unless it was the tenderness in Nick's touch as his fingers threaded through hers and held tight.

His kiss. It was all she thought about sitting beside him in the front seat of the surrey, while her wedding ring sparkled in the warm sunshine. Nick's kiss. The heat of his lips, the caress of his mouth. The thrill that arced through her from head to toe. Her first kiss ever. It had been wonderful. Fantastic. She'd never dreamed the simple brush of a man's lips could be so…fascinating.

No wonder the women in her social circle whispered in delight. And to think that was only a kiss! What would it be like to lie in his arms at night, against his strong chest, skin to skin? What would it be like to be loved completely? Tonight she was going to find out. She shivered, afraid and curious all at once.

"Are you cold?" Nick's baritone slashed through her thoughts like a well-honed blade. "That shawl you're wearing looks pretty thin. I'll give you my coat.''

"No, I'm fine—" She wasn't cold in the slightest, but how could she tell him that? The weight of his wool jacket settled over her shoulders, smelling of wind and leather and Nick. A pleasant combination that took her breath away.

"That better? There's a nip in that wind. Can't have my wife getting cold.''

"You didn't need to do that." She ran her fingertips over the soft wool, thumbing the fine stitching at the hem. "I can take care of myself.''

"I see. It's going to be like that, is it?" He glanced at her sideways, beneath the brim of his hat. "You're going to fight me every step of the way?"

"Fight you? I'm not fighting you. You simply didn't need to give me your coat. I—''

"Mariah." His hand covered hers and even through the leather warm from his skin, she could feel the jolt of awareness that passed between them like the crackle of static in the air before a storm. "Let's get this straight. I know you can take care of yourself. That's why I married you.''

"It is?" She bit her lip to hold back her thoughts so she wouldn't do something foolish such as speak without thinking. He'd married her because of their past together, right? For that one brief moment in time when they were both different people, younger and naive and hopeful. He'd married her because he wanted her, right?

Her chest pounded as she waited for his answer. Waited for him to reassure her. To tell her that she meant something to him.

"You are the strongest woman I know." He took

his hand from hers, breaking their touch, turning his attention to the road ahead. "You can take care of yourself, so I know you can take good care of my children."

He doesn't mean that the way it sounds. But she wasn't sure at all. Nick sat beside her, as stoic as stone. Her pulse throbbed in her temples as seconds passed, stretching endlessly. Had she made a mistake? Had she misunderstood?

Then he smiled at her, his eyes warming as his gaze found hers with a jolt of awareness. Her every nerve ending tingled, as if he had touched her. And she knew what he wasn't saying. That he needed her.

She felt as bright as the sun above in a perfect blue sky.

"Let's get another thing straight." He guided the horses off the main road and onto the well-tended driveway that cut between the fields and neat, split-rail fencing. "I know you're an independent sort and as strong as can be. But I'm your husband, so you ought to let me care for you. Got that?"

"You care for me?"

"Sure. It's my job. I just pledged my allegiance to you before God."

"Allegiance? That's to the flag."

"Well, then I promised my entire life to you. Just to you, Mariah. I've been here before, and I know what this means. Marriage will only work if we do things together. You take care of me. I take care of you. It'll be a far sight better than the lives we've been living alone. What do you say?"

"I could be coerced."

"Good. Then we've got a deal."

It felt like a weakness, and she should be ashamed

of it, the way she yearned for his affection. She didn't need anyone. Not even Nick Gray. She could stand on her own two feet. Get a coat or anything else she required.

The edge of Nick's jacket caught the wind and fluttered. She smoothed it back into place with her fingertips. How warm it felt. How good to have something she didn't need. She scooted closer to him on the seat, just a few inches.

The prairie winds felt sweet ruffling across her face and lifting her bangs as the surrey rolled up the road on Nick's land. On her land. This was hers now, too. The rolling meadows, the grazing Herefords, the house up ahead, hidden by the draw and roll of the plains. But she knew it was there. Her new home. Her new life. And her stepchildren. Thinking of Georgie and Nick's somber son made her bones ache with longing. She was a mother. Her chest felt too full to breathe. Nick had done this, made her so happy, and she wasn't married but twenty-seven minutes.

"Just think I ought to warn you." Nick leaned close, his words a soft, warm buzz against the outer shell of her ear. "Your friend Rayna came by this morning and took over the kitchen. Something about throwing a big dinner to celebrate. Right in the workweek, too, but I figured you've waited a long time for this. If we're going to celebrate, then we should do it right."

"Rayna's at the house?"

"Yep. Kicked me out and told me not to come back until I had my bride with me."

"She's fixing dinner for us?"

"Not just a dinner. A celebration. You know. With

lots of people. Food. Old man Dayton's bringing his fiddle.''

''But we just had a dance in town, and it's planting season and the calves—''

''Look at that.'' They'd turned the last bend in the road and the ranch house came into sight, the honeyed logs gleaming warm in the sunlight as if to welcome them home. A dozen vehicles lined the last ten yards of the driveway. It was a damn good sight to see that his neighbors had come to welcome his new wife.

Wife. That was going to take some getting used to. Still, being married to Mariah would be an improvement. At least she wouldn't be running off on him all times of the night to be with her lover.

He cringed. He couldn't help it. Lida's betrayal cut him deep. Still. Even after her death. He was angry and hurt, sad and bitter, and worse, he was a man who hadn't been able to keep his wife.

Mariah wasn't Lida. He had to remember that.

Mariah wasn't the kind of woman to cheat on a man. And he would be grateful to her every day of their lives to come. She was like a sparrow in her plain blue dress and her straw hat. When folks came around the back of the house to greet her, she didn't put on feigned delight like an actress, as Lida would have done. When Will was the first to extend his hand to help his sister-in-law from the surrey, Mariah didn't bat her lashes at him. Or smile coyly at Dayton's grandsons, all strapping young bachelors in their prime. No, instead of basking in the attention, Mariah blushed, studied the ground, and finally turned to him.

To him. Yep, there was no chance she'd be unfaithful. Not one. Pride made him strong as he handed his youngest brother Dakota the reins, circled around the surrey and tucked Mariah's hand in his. He'd chosen well. Damn well. He settled his free hand on her nape, sneaking beneath the soft fall of her golden hair. Her neck felt small, the round knobs of her vertebrae frail against his palm. She was not so formidable of a woman, after all. But as delicate and as fragile as any human being.

Tenderness ached in the cold shadows of his heart. Tenderness he didn't want to feel.

"Congratulations!" Rayna met her at the kitchen door and wrapped her in a warm hug. "To think you are now Mrs. Gray. How does it feel?"

"Different." Mariah stepped through the entryway, where coats hug on a neat row of pegs, and into the big room. A large white cake, iced and decorated with red spun sugar, sat in the center of the round oak table.

"I can't believe all this. That you'd come here in the middle of the week with so much work to do." Mariah swallowed hard. There was a baked ham cooling on the counter and a big pan of baked beans steaming on top of the stove. "Thank you, Rayna."

"It isn't every day a woman marries. I'm happy for you. You found a good man. He's worth the wait."

"Nick married me out of necessity."

"Yes, but he married *you*."

She still tingled from Nick's kiss, from his touch, from the regard he showed her as he'd walked her to the back porch. She could see Nick through the large window behind the table, speaking with several of the neighboring ranchers. He was shaking their hands, no doubt, and accepting their many congratulations. Except they didn't look too happy for him. Several of the ranchers looked very grim.

"Out of here. You're the guest of honor. You're not allowed to work." Rayna escorted her to the door. "Scoot. Go to your husband. This is your wedding day."

Mariah found herself back on the porch, squinting in the sun. Tables had been set up on the back lawn in the warmth of the sun, and a group of boys raced back and forth, shouting loudly as they played tag. The widows Collins and White were behind the re-freshment table, ladling punch into glass cups. Maybe she ought to go over there to see if they could use some help.

"...that spinster? What could he want with her?" a woman's voice rose above the din.

Mariah whirled toward the sound. Three of the lo-cal rancher's wives were huddled together, their backs to her, so they were unaware she was standing right behind them. But that didn't excuse their words. She turned away, determined not to listen. But the con-versation seemed to follow her with every step.

"...can't see why any man would marry her..."

"...maybe he got her pregnant and had to pro-pose..."

"...couldn't believe my ears when I heard the news..."

Mariah kept walking. She was thick-skinned. She could handle a little gossip. It wouldn't be the first unkind words she'd ever heard and probably not the last. Folks were bound to wonder why Nick had cho-sen her.

Nick. Her senses stirred at the sight of him standing a half head taller than the other men, his dark hair ruffling in the wind. Her fingers itched to smooth that thick hair into place. As if he could feel her, he turned, spotting her immediately, as if he was drawn to her and no one else.

He didn't smile or blink or nod in recognition, but she knew his intent even before he took the first step toward her, as steadfast and as invincible as a Greek myth, carved in stone and made immortal by legend. She knew before he cupped her jaw in the palm of his hand what he was going to say, as if he were a part of her.

"Hello, pretty lady. What do you say about going driving with me on Sunday?"

"The last time you asked me that question, you were a bit younger."

"Heck, I was still wet behind the ears. But you, Mariah. You still smell like lilacs."

"Are you protesting? Or approving?"

"Approving. It always was my favorite."

"Is that so? You're attempting to be charming, and it's not going to work."

"Then I'll have to try harder."

There was a part of her that could still dream, and she could feel it, the yearning to lean a little harder against Nick's chest, safe and snug in his arms, and never let him go. To let him kiss her the way he had in the church, with a caress that left her senseless and breathless and dazed. That made her blood heat like water on a hot stove.

He leaned close and breathed deep. "Yep. Lilacs."

She shuddered to the marrow of her bones. Tingles danced down her spine as she studied the curve of his mouth. His kiss. She wanted to feel it more than anything. *Just lean forward,* she wished. She didn't care if everyone was watching or how improper it would be in front of all these guests. All she wanted was the heat of his lips and the velvet caress of his mouth against hers.

Tonight, he'll do more to me than kiss me. Tonight was her wedding night. She would finally know what made her friends blush as they whispered of the marriage bed. Of the pleasures a man could give a woman. Of the love.

Nick's jaw brushed hers. Against her heated skin, she could feel his, even hotter, rough with a day's growth. His breath was hot as sin against the shell of her ear.

"Are you hungry, Mrs. Gray?"

She burned like a newly lit flame.

With everyone watching, Nick took her by the arm and led her past the rancher's wives to the head of the table.

Over the scrape of forks on dessert plates as twilight began to set, old man Dayton picked up his fiddle. The first tender notes of the waltz lifted into the air above the chatter and laughter at the board tables where her new neighbors pushed off the bench seats.

"Dance with me, Mariah." He said it just like that, his whisper a warm caress against her cheek.

His hand settled on her back in the space between her shoulder blades, a warm steady pressure that did not fade as she stood. His touch remained, guiding her to the center of the yard, where the neighbors stood in a wide circle as they waited for the newlyweds to begin the first dance.

The pleasant brush of his chin settled against her brow. "This seems familiar."

"Are you complaining?"

"Not a chance." He fit his hand around the back of her head, cradling her, gently pressing her face to the hollow of his throat. "From this day on, I will waltz only with you."

It was as if time stood still and the earth spun backward, taking time and a decade of heartache with it, making her new. Giving her the chance to try again. As if Nick felt this, too, his fingers at her nape tightened. It was a wonderful sensation, pulling her more tightly against him. As close as they could be, only clothing separated them.

I want to love him, her heart whispered, the most secret part of her heart. The hidden corner where not even her father's cruel words over the years had been able to touch. There was a part of her that could still dream, and she could feel it now, yearning to love Nick with all she was worth. Nick, her husband.

"How does it feel to be married to me?" he asked.

"I haven't found cause to complain yet."

"You just wait for tomorrow morning." His chuckle began in him and rumbled through her. "You'll be cooking for the whole lot of us, and we eat breakfast at four-thirty."

"Funny how you neglected to tell me this before the ceremony."

"Yep. I was afraid you'd change your mind, and then where would I be?"

"Frying your own bacon."

"No, I'd be starving because I can't cook."

"Then you'd better be real nice to me, or I just may oversleep now and then."

"Be nice to my wife? You can count on it." His breath shivered across her brow, warm and wonderful, as he guided them in a sweeping, slow three-step. They moved together, toe to toe, thigh to thigh, hip to hip.

His fingers began a slow, light caress on the back of her neck. Her nerve endings danced. Her skin tingled. Happiness filled her up, making it hard to breathe. *This is only the beginning.* Of being held by him, of being loved by him. The dependable thud of his heartbeat, the capable steel of his chest, the rhythm of his breathing and the caress of his fingertips against her bare skin overwhelmed her. Made her feel as if she were dancing on clouds. What would tonight be like?

She was going to find out. She was going to know the intimate touches a man gave his wife. The sweet caresses. The tender joining that would make them one, that would make her desirable and loved.

She longed to press her lips to his throat and to taste his skin. She couldn't stop her fingertips from caressing little circles against the curve of his neck and the dip of his shoulder. Tenderness, rare and new, took root in her heart.

"What did your father say when you told him we were to be married?" she asked, instead. "I notice he didn't come to stop the ceremony."

"He's going to love you, Mariah, because you're a fine woman." Respect boomed in his voice, both affectionate and irrefutable.

She glowed with it. No man had ever treated her this way. She felt valued and valuable. Just as with his vows today, he'd promised to honor her. To cherish her.

I will do the same for you. Strong with it, she lifted onto her tiptoes to whisper into his ear so no one else could hear. She chose her words carefully. "Your father doesn't look happy. He keeps frowning in my direction and shaking his head. Will our marriage cause problems between you two?"

"Not a chance. Pop and me, we get along."

"Your father doesn't like me. It's no secret. I haven't always been nice to him when I came across him in town."

"What's this? The fearsome Spinster Scott admits to being a curmudgeon?"

"You're teasing me."

"Because you deserve it." He gently forced her gaze to his. "You've been working pretty hard to keep everyone at a safe distance. I can understand that. Get too close to someone and they're just gonna hurt you."

"That's right."

She understood. Emotion punched in Nick's chest. Life taught everyone hard lessons, and the price and pain of them was sometimes hard to accept. He'd been busy with his own problems for so long, he hadn't given it much thought. But he did now, tucking Mariah to him, bringing her against him so sweet. "It's easier to be tough and scare folks away. Is that what you do?"

"Guilty." He couldn't see her face, but she sounded as if she were smiling.

Good. He wanted her to smile. Wanted her to be happy. "Are you going to do that here?"

"I wasn't planning on it. I might actually be agreeable to you. I know, don't be surprised. I *did* promise to be good to you before God and the minister. I'm a woman of my word."

"My kind of woman."

As if to prove to him she wasn't so prickly, she cuddled in his arms as the song faded away and the evening crickets picked up the melody. He waited, holding her close, his wife. This woman who felt small in his arms. Fragile.

If he closed his eyes, he could feel the real Mariah, soft and womanly against him, the pillows of her breasts, the slight curve of her stomach and the length of her thighs fitted against his. She clung to him, and he could feel what was inside her. Maybe because the same emotions lived within him. Loneliness. Heartache. Sadness that had burrowed down deep and lived there year after year until it began to weigh down your soul.

It will be different this time. Mariah's different. Marriage with her would not be bleak and painful.

He was grateful to her. She was tough and strong and independent. She didn't need anyone, not even him. She was going to make his children's lives better, and his, too. What a lucky man he was to have such a wife.

Old man Dayton's fiddle struck the note of a ballad. Nick shuffled his feet, taking her with him. Her hair against the backs of his knuckles felt like silk. The sweet lilac scent of her filled him up with a strange ease.

A single yearning tugged deep inside him. Maybe it was the young man still inside him, the one who'd been so taken by her beauty years ago, those soft blond curls rioting around her heart-shaped face, and those blue eyes so big and jewel-like, so sparkling with light. He'd done right by marrying her.

It was important that he treat her right. "You look mighty pretty in that dress."

"It was my mother's. I found it in her trunk. It was the most cheerful color I could find." She stiffened in his arms. "It's too bright, I know, but I didn't want to get married in my work dresses."

"Too bright? No, this is a beautiful color on you. The color matches your eyes."

"I feel like a peacock in it, instead of a sensible sparrow."

"Think of a humble blue finch, instead." Kindness warmed his voice.

And warmed her. Maybe the dress had been the right choice, taken from her mother's trunk at the last minute, a muted blue-gray spriggled lawn that was no longer in fashion, but pretty enough.

"You're not a spinster anymore. So make sure you take some time this week and stop by the dress shop. Get whatever you want, all right? I don't want to see you in black again."

Normally she would take umbrage at that kind of comment, but she could feel his caring like the brush of the twilight's breeze on her face. It felt good to be cared for. Strange and new and wonderful. She didn't deserve it, but she was going to do her very best to make this new life work.

To make Nick fall in love with her...

It was the middle of the workweek, and the ranchers all had early mornings ahead. Old man Dayton played one last song. The final sweet note signaled the end of the celebration. Folks offered their last round of well wishes as they headed for their wagons. It seemed to take forever, and Mariah caught herself glancing across the yard to find Nick. He'd be helping someone to hitch a team or chatting a few more minutes with Mr. Dayton, or giving his daughter a hug before Will carted her and Joey into the house and out of sight.

She buzzed with anticipation. Every inch of her felt aware. Alive. Tingling. Breathing in, she could almost remember Nick's scent, the warmth of his shirt against her cheek, the security of his strong arms holding her… And his kiss. The memory of it shivered through her and the tenderness of it beat within her.

Across the yard, over the top of old man Dayton's head, Nick smiled at her. Not a broad, happy grin, and not a casual acknowledgment. But a slow, heated curve of his lips that was a promise of things to come. This was their wedding night. When the guests were gone and the house silent and dark, he would lie down beside her in bed and kiss her. Hold her. Cherish her. She tingled, feeling wanted. Desired.

Nick turned away, and still she felt it. Like magic bubbling through her veins. She was no longer lonely and unwanted. She was Mariah Gray. Soon, she would be in her husband's arms, even closer than tonight when they'd waltzed together. And she would know what it was like to be loved and desired. To be held tenderly and sweetly. From this night on, she would not be like the Widow Collins, who had grabbed Mariah's hand to offer good wishes. Then left alone in her small buggy, heading home where no one waited, no one cared, where no one loved her. *That is never going to be me again.*

"How are you doing?" Nick strode out of the shadows, all man and might. "It's been a heck of a long day. You've got to be tired."

Tired? So, that's how he was going to get her into

his bed. She blushed, pleased he wanted her. "It *is* getting late."

"Yep. Time to head to bed."

Did he feel this, too? This glow of anticipation? Happiness felt like wine in her blood, and her senses filled when Nick's broad hand settled in the small of her back, escorting her to the porch and into the house. Yes, he must feel this, too. He wasn't looking at her, and his jaw was tensed. A muscle jumped along the strong length of his jawbone.

Every step she took brought her closer to the bedroom. Their bedroom. Through the kitchen. Up the stairs. Anticipation danced through her until she was breathless with it. More than anything she wanted to let him peel off her clothes and cherish her.

Nick hesitated halfway down the hall. Moonlight slanted through a small window in the end wall, enough to shadow the closed doors to the children's rooms. It looked as though his brother Will had taken care of everything, and that meant Nick was hers. And she was his.

He faced her. *This was it.* She was nervous and thrilled all at once. She was about to learn what it meant to be wanted. To be loved and desired...

"My brother put your things here." Nick opened one of the closed doors. "This will be your room."

"My room?"

"It used to be Lida's. I'm sorry about that. I had her personal things moved out, but there isn't an extra room in this house or I would have put you there."

"But—" She stared at the threshold, unable to see anything but unrelenting darkness. He didn't want her? "We're married, and I thought...well, that I'd be...with you."

"Mariah." His deep voice stroked her name with regret. "You know this is a necessary marriage for me."

"Of course I do." She edged against the wall, where the shadows were darker. She didn't want him to see on her face or in her eyes how she really felt. The tingle of excitement faded. "I didn't know we would be sleeping alone, that's all."

"Oh." He sounded relieved, a man still and dark as the shadows surrounding him. "Truth is, I sleep better alone."

"I see." Disappointment wrapped around her like a sheet of ice. Cold to the bone, she shivered. What had she been thinking? It had gone to her head, that Nick Gray had asked her to be his wife. She'd let her imagination run away with her, dreaming of impossible things that could never be. Nick Gray hadn't wanted her. Who would? She'd spent her adult life trying to drive everyone away, so they wouldn't see what she was really like inside. So they wouldn't know she was cold-hearted and inadequate and afraid to let anyone close. She'd done such a good job, she'd convinced everyone how unlovable she was. Even herself. Even Nick.

Who was she fooling? Only herself. He wasn't in love with her. He'd rather be alone than to so much as fall asleep beside her. She remembered what those women had said today, what she'd overheard. *…Can't see why any man would marry her.* And her father's words, said so often throughout the years they felt as if they were her own. *You're cold as ice clear through, just like your ma. Nothin' to love about either one of ya.*

The pretty dress she wore wasn't going to change

that. Or the fact that a circle of gold banded her fourth finger. Or that she had a new last name. She was still plain old Mariah, sensible, practical, useful. A necessary wife, a convenient wife. Not a real one.

Something broke inside her, like glass shattering into a thousand tiny slivers, embedding deep into her chest. She hurt from the inside out. *He doesn't want me. He's never going to want me.* She had to accept it. She could never let him know how she really felt. How she had hoped…

Gathering her strength, she took a shallow breath, ignored the cutting pain in her chest the best she could, and faced reality. Let go of her dreams. ''The truth is, I sleep better alone, too. This room will do just fine.''

''You sure?'' He looked deeply troubled, staring into the dark threshold as if there would be an answer for him there. Then he lifted one wide shoulder in a resigned shrug. He sounded relieved. ''Good night, Mariah.''

''Good night, Nick.'' She could hear the pain in her own words, they were so thin and wavering in the dark she couldn't believe they were hers. She was strong. She didn't need anyone. Least of all Nicholas Adam Gray.

He hesitated. He was so awesome, cloaked in the dark, solitary and strong, a man who didn't need her. Maybe not anyone. ''As long as you're sure, Mariah. I don't want to disappoint you.''

''You haven't.'' She lied. She had her pride. She had her dignity. Most of all, she didn't want him to change his mind. To take her to his bed out of a sense of duty.

Or pity.

"Sleep well," she said as lightly as she could. "Breakfast will be on the table at four-thirty sharp."

"You're a good woman, Mariah."

She wasn't. She opened her mouth to tell him that, but what was she going to say? Feeling her every flaw, her every failing, she said nothing at all. It took all her strength to march through that dark threshold. All her willpower to close the door and not be sad. To snuff out her disappointment like the flicker of a dying candle's flame.

The room felt empty. Vast. Alone. This was her life. Her future.

It wasn't different, after all.

Chapter Seven

The kitchen was peaceful in the dark hours before sunrise. Mariah's steps echoed on the wood floor as she put the bacon on to fry, but it wasn't a lonely feeling. Upstairs, the children were still asleep. If she peeked through the curtains at the window, she could see the glow of light from the distant barn. Nick and his brothers were there, already laboring hard.

The fire popped in the stove, calling her back to her work. She'd risen, washed and dressed and came down the dark stairs, expecting to find the kitchen cool and equally dark. But Nick had left a lamp burning to greet her. The fire in the stove was crackling merrily. He'd done that for her. Like a good husband.

Men built fires all the time. It was a courteous act. Nothing more. Nick had vowed to honor her, hadn't he? Despite his multitude of flaws, he was an honest man. So, honor her, he would. That explained his treatment of her yesterday, after they were married. The touches. The kind words. He was doing his best to take care of her, just as he vowed. But not to love her.

Her hands trembled as she turned the sizzling strips

of bacon. Fine, she could admit it. She was sad about
that. But she had to stop secretly wishing for the
moon.

The back door slammed open with a sharp *crack.*
Cool wind skidded across the back of her neck. Her
stomach tightened. Was it Nick?

Jeb Gray, Nick's father, banged the door closed.
The windowpanes rattled. The stove burners clattered.
He kicked off his boots with a thud.

Facing Nick would be easier than his father. Mariah's stomach tightened as she laid the spatula on the
worktable, taking her time. She could *feel* his dislike.
She didn't need to look up to see the scowl on his
face.

It's all right. She may be married, but she was still
the formidable Mariah Scott. She knew how to handle
difficult people. "Would you like some coffee, Jeb?
It ought to be done boiling by now."

His frown deepened and he hesitated. Did he think
she would try to poison him? She didn't have to wonder just how vehemently he'd disapproved of Nick
taking her as his wife.

"Sit down and I'll pour it for you." Annoyed, she
grabbed a mug from the shelf. "I've got biscuits in
the warmer if you'd like."

Jeb looked around cautiously, as if he were keeping
mindful of the exits so he could make a quick escape,
if necessary. He took a step forward, then another.
"Guess that'd be all right."

She'd serve him and get back to work. It would be
faster than having to try to make conversation while
he frowned at her. She filled the cup and set it and
the biscuits on the corner of the table. He watched
her every move, and it bothered her. Was he looking

for something to criticize? Her stomach squeezed, as if a belt was cinching up tight around her middle.

Don't expect the worst, she told herself. But it was hard not to as Jeb took a sip of coffee, scowled and set it back down.

"Too weak," he said. "Next time, better make it twice this strong."

No "please." No "thank you." Not even a soft tone in consideration of her feelings. Did he think she didn't have any? That belt around her stomach tightened another notch.

The bacon grease was snapping, hot and crackly, and the strips of bacon were toasty brown. Perfect. She forked them onto a plate. One glance at the clock told her she was a few minutes behind. If she put the eggs on now—

The door boomed open, slamming into the wall. Three sets of boots stomped against the floor. Mariah saw Dakota, the youngest of Nick's brothers, first. He was dark and lean, and he nodded a silent, intimidating hello. He took a chair at the table with his back to her. Will, Nick's middle brother, did the same.

"I'll have the eggs fried in just a minute." She hated the apology she heard in her voice. This was now her kitchen, darn it, and she was in charge of it.

"Smells good, Mariah." Nick strolled into sight in his stockinged feet. "We sure appreciate all your hard work."

He was trying, and she could, too. "When the eggs are done, I'll make a new pot of coffee. Let me set the pancakes out and you men can get started—"

"We'll wait for you." Nick wrapped a pot holder around the enamel pot and lifted it off the trivet.

"You aren't here to serve us, Mariah. You eat at the table with us, all right?"

"But the food will start to cool—"

"That's what the warmer is for. You're my wife. You have the place beside me at the table." He gestured to the two chairs in front of the window, where a gray light glowed on polished oak. "This coffee smells a far sight better than what we've been having lately. Go ahead and fix the eggs."

He strode away, shoulders squared, all confidence, at ease as he ribbed his brother Will for being too lazy to get his own cup of coffee and poured it for him.

Nick was helping her? The band tight around her stomach expanded to cinch in her chest, too, making it hard to breathe. She cracked an egg on the edge of the big black fry pan and broke it in two. Over the sizzle of the egg white hitting the hot bacon grease, she remembered what Nick had said to her. *We've got respect. That's more than most marriages I can name.*

Respect wasn't love. It wasn't being desired. It wasn't belonging.

But it was more than her mother ever had. Mariah pushed out the images from her childhood, of her mother exhausted and bowed from long hours of work, carrying a full plate to Pa at the table, serving him like a slave, back bowing lower with each bite of his criticism.

Respect was good. She would be grateful for it.

"I know it's a lot to manage before sunrise." Nick plunked the coffeepot onto the trivet with a clink, brushing the hard bulging muscles of his arm against her shoulder. "You're doing fine, and I sure appreciate it. Joey and Georgie will be up by six. If you set aside a few pancakes and sausages, that will be enough for them.''

''I'll see to it.'' Nick's children. Thinking about little Georgie made some of the tightness in Mariah's chest ease. Her stepchildren.

They would accept her, right? Why wouldn't they? Mariah broke the last egg into the pan. Yesterday neither of them had so much as spoken to her. Jeb had looked after Georgie all afternoon, while Joey had been playing with his friends. Both had eaten at the children's table during the celebration supper. Their uncle Will had taken them under his wing that evening and put them to bed.

Today they were all hers.

''You'll do fine with them,'' Nick assured her, as if he could read her mind. ''I've got the last of the heifers calving in the north field, and I've got to relieve Robert, the hired man. He's keeping watch over them. He'll be in for a meal shortly. What's left over will do for him.''

''Fine.'' Mariah concentrated hard on her work flipping the eggs. There wasn't one thing about Nick that offended her. Not his words, not his manner, not the efficient way he carried both the platter of bacon and sausage and the plate of toast to the table. Helping her with her work without a complaint, damn him. When she wanted to hate him. If she could find terrible fault with him, then maybe she could find release for the pain gathering in her chest.

But she couldn't. Even this early in the morning, with his work clothes wrinkled and his uncombed hair tousled, he made her heart stop beating for one brief moment.

"Looks like the eggs are done." He held out a clean platter. Something her father never would have done for her mother. Something Mariah couldn't believe he was doing for her.

Respect. It went both ways. And so she thanked him as she scooped the eggs from the pan as fast as she could. The band around her chest cinched tight again. Was he thinking about last night? How she had wanted him to take her to his bed?

Embarrassed, she slid the last egg on the platter and turned, intent on lifting the fry pan from the heat. She heard Nick's step all the way to the table. Heard the clink of flatware on enamel as the men at the table began dishing up.

"Wait for Mariah," Nick reminded them. "And don't you all have something to say to her?"

"The food looks real good, ma'am," Dakota boomed above the din. "Don't mind whatever Pop says. Both him and Will got their taste buds burned off drinking their own coffee."

"See? I'm not the only one glad you're here." Nick was at her side again, his eyes shadowed and his face somber. He held out his hand, palm up, waiting for hers. "Let me escort you to the table. It gets a little rough with all of us fighting over the food at once. We're like a pack of wild dogs, but I'll make sure you get enough to eat."

"You'll throw me the scraps?"

"Nope. I'll give you first choice."

When she laid her hand in his, her palm to his, his big fingers curled around hers and held her tight.

She didn't have his love. But she had the man and his respect. It was enough.

* * *

"Hey, big brother." Will ambled through the wet grass, ducking against the cool wind. "Got the feed unloaded. How's it goin' here?"

"Good. We've got the last heifer dropping and she's not having a bit of trouble." He gestured toward the cow on the ground, her side heavy and heaving.

The trouble was that the house was a fair distance away, nothing more than a thumbnail-size box on the far hill, but it was in his line of sight. A tiny gray thread rose in the air above it, smoke from the fire, and made him wonder how Mariah was getting along. He knocked rain off the brim of his hat.

"What's the matter?" Will stood shoulder to shoulder and followed Nick's gaze to the distant house on the hill. "You had big problems before you got remarried, brother. Looks to me like you've got even bigger ones now."

"I want you to be good to Mariah, Will."

"Be good to her? Hell, I'm scared of her. Can't see why you couldn't have picked one of those sweet things in town. Soft and pretty and pleasant to look at." Will sighed, too wet around the ears to know what was valuable in a woman. "Sure, breakfast was damn good. That was a welcome change around here, but, hell, brother, you married Mariah Scott. That's a guaranteed lifetime of hell ahead of you."

"That's marriage, no matter who you pick." Nick couldn't help it. Images of Mariah kept creeping into his mind. Of her opening the door to find him standing on her porch, come to take her to the church. She'd looked so different in that dress, a quiet blue-gray, instead of the dark grays and blacks she usually wore. He'd seen the young girl she used to be in the woman too practical to be young.

No, that wasn't quite right. Last night, as she'd hesitated in the hallway in front of Lida's old room, he'd seen something else in her. A longing for the dream of what a marriage could be.

And he'd disappointed her. He felt like the biggest jackass on earth. Never occurred to him that Mariah would want to share his bed. And not just to sleep.

Damn it, he'd tried to explain it to her. And judging by the way she'd looked at him this morning, expecting his disregard, instead of his friendship, she understood what he wanted now.

But she was still hurting. The thought of that tore at him. What was he going to do about that?

"But did you have to go and pick *her?*" Will swept off his hat and shook it hard. Rainwater splashed everywhere.

Nick swiped a drop off his cheek. "She's a good woman and I don't want to hear another word against her. She's my wife, and damn it, Will, I don't care if you like it or not. You'll treat her with the respect she deserves."

"You're sweet on her, aren't you? That's why you—"

"No," Nick roared, so mad so fast, he burned with it. "But I won't have the hell I had with Lida, and you alone know what she did to me."

"She was a weak woman. I know you hated her—"

"I never hated her. That was the problem." He hurt something fierce, as if a dagger had pierced his lungs, and he struggled for breath. For control. "Mariah isn't soft and sweet, but she's nothing like Lida was. She is a strong, tough-minded woman with standards that would put both of us to shame. She isn't going to sneak off at night or bear another man's child. You, above anyone, ought to know how much I value that.''

Will's throat worked, and he stared at the ground. ''Sorry, Nick. I know you're right. I just thought... you know...''

''I know, you were thinking down south, instead of with your brain. That will get you into a world of trouble. I made that mistake with Lida, and I learned the hard way.'' The hard way? He'd been young and hurting from Mariah's father's rejection, and had sought the quickest form of solace. A lot of whiskey and, later, a Sunday afternoon driving date with pretty Lida Brown. A forced marriage was the result five weeks later.

Nick's gaze strayed back to the house. Mariah was there, and she was strong enough to put his domestic life in order. He was thankful for her. He was grateful. But sweet on her? No, he didn't have the heart for that.

''I hate these pancakes.'' Joey dropped his fork against the plate with a clatter loud enough to wake the dead in the next county. ''They taste bad.''

Now what did she do? Mariah took one look at the boy's face and read the hatred in it. The challenge that glinted in his eyes as dark as his father's. No doubt the boy was as willful, too.

Great. Just her luck. She set the iron on the stove, turned her back on her work, and plucked a jar of preserves from the pantry. ''This might help. Georgie, do you want some jam?''

''Only if it's the red kind.'' The little girl glanced up from her plate, her fork suspended in midair. The syrup smeared across her face made her look more adorable.

"You're in luck. It's red." Mariah uncapped the jar. "Joey, you first."

"I hate red jam." His gaze narrowed. His mouth pulled up into a tight, belligerent line.

This wasn't about the pancakes or the jam. This battle was about her presence in this house. Mariah grabbed a second jar from the pantry. She hadn't expected her first day to be without a single wrinkle. "How about some blueberry jam?"

"I hate that, too."

"I'm sorry about that." She set the jar in front of him and stole the red one. His animosity followed her as she circled the table and sat in the empty chair beside Georgie. "Do you want this on your pancakes or on your toast?"

"The toast. But squished in the middle," the little girl instructed around a mouthful of pancake.

"Like a sandwich?" When Georgie nodded, Mariah went to work, slathering the sweet strawberry jam on the slice of toast, then folding it in two. "Like this?"

"Yep." Georgie grabbed it, pleased. "Are you still gonna take me to my ma?"

The knife slipped from Mariah's fingers and struck the table with an ear-ringing clatter. The kitchen seemed too quiet and still, as if the entire world had quieted to await her answer. Her pulse thrummed in her ears, and she got up too quick. The chair legs scraped against the floor, setting her teeth on edge.

"We're going to stay here today, Georgie." Mariah headed straight for her ironing board, set up on the worktable by the cookstove. "I have to finish up my work."

"You could take me in your wagon. With your big ox." A high note of desperation lifted Georgie's voice and her eyes shone with grief.

Mariah left the ironing untouched to kneel down in front of the girl's chair. "My mother went to heaven, too."

"She did?"

"Yep, and I hurt really bad for a long time, because she had to leave."

"Y-yeah." Georgie breathed in, pain raw in her voice. "She just left. Didn't take me or her dresses or nothing."

Mariah's chest twisted with a fierce emotion, too complex to name, but it brought tears to her eyes and a pain to her heart. "I'm certain she misses you very much."

"Y-yeah." Georgie rubbed her eyes with her fists. "Can we go see her now? Pa ain't gonna take me. He don't love me."

"That's not true. Your father loves you very much. Who couldn't love such a good little girl?" Mariah dared to touch those fine golden curls and stroked the girl's soft brow. "Why don't you stay here with me today? When I'm done with my ironing, you can go in the wagon with me to deliver all these shirts."

"No." Huge tears brimmed those big blue eyes and trickled in fat droplets down her cheeks. "I just want my ma."

Mariah's heart broke. She didn't know what to do, she'd never in her life comforted a child of her own the way a mother should. She felt useless and lost, wondering if she should hold the child or think of the right magic words that would comfort so much pain. Georgie leaned forward, her head diving toward Mariah's chest, and tumbled out of the chair.

Mariah caught the girl and pulled her into her arms, holding her safe in her lap. Georgie buried her face in Mariah's shoulder and wept. Mariah could feel each tremble, each sob, each spear of sorrow. She leaned her cheek against the crown of the child's head, wishing she could absorb the hurt. Georgie felt fragile and tiny and infinitely precious.

How could Lida have chosen to leave this little girl? Grief could be consuming, Mariah knew this firsthand, but to take one's life? And leave children behind? Children who needed her? Mariah vowed not to hate the woman, but it was hard as she watched Joey scowl, overturn his plate with a spark of anger and push away from the table in disgust.

She patted Georgie on the back, gently. It was the only thing she could think of to do. What did she know about comforting children? Not one thing. She doubted she had a single motherly instinct. Nick shouldn't have married her. He should have chosen someone more suitable. Someone soft and loving and who naturally knew what to do with a crying child.

''I got a bad owie.'' Georgie put the heel of her hand against her heart. Her eyes watered with a silent plea.

Mariah could only kiss the girl's sweet brow and hold her close. She didn't know what else to do.

Nick took one look at the kitchen and fought a growing sense of doom. There was a stack of laundry on the worktable. The kids' breakfast dishes were still on the table. There was no sign that the noon meal was being prepared—no roast cooking, no bread baking, no soup simmering. Where was Mariah?

He rummaged in the lean-to for a tin of bag balm. This was only her first morning here. He couldn't expect the day to go smooth. Even as efficient as Mariah was, she would need time to get things in order. Figure out their daily needs. And in an hour she'd have six hungry men at her table, in no mood to wait for their hot meal.

Maybe it was the day's storm, the wind and rain as cold as a March downpour, that was making his temper short. Or maybe it was the pitying looks his brothers and the hired men had been giving him all morning. Not one of them had the courage to say it, but he could guess what they were thinking. It wasn't hard, with the confused looks on their faces, as if they were trying to figure out why he'd taken the prickly, sharp-tongued town spinster to wife. He'd had enough of it, and he wasn't going to explain his choice. He knew what he was doing, damn it.

So, why wasn't the woman of his choice making dinner?

He stomped down the back steps, swearing when rain dripping off the eaves decided to drip onto his head and down the back of his neck. Splashing through the puddles, he realized his head was wet, too. Where in blazes did his hat go? Why was he so damn forgetful this morning?

Mariah. She was on his mind. The need in her last night, as palpable as the shadows, as revealing as the moonlight, as vulnerable as her voice when she'd told him she slept better alone, too. Why did this keep bothering him? He'd been honest with her up front. His conscience shouldn't be troubling him.

But it was. She'd expected him to be cold to her this morning. And when he'd helped her serve the meal and then sat her beside him at the table, she had been grateful. It had been in her shy smiles when he passed her the platters of delicious food she'd cooked. If she was disappointed, then she'd recovered well enough. Things should be going better now. So, where in blazes was she?

Maybe something had gone awry. His work could wait a few minutes. He'd best figure out where she'd gone to.

He tore through the kitchen only to find the fire blazing in the parlor, but no one there. Something felt wrong. Georgie could have run off again. That wind was cold, the rain mean and inclement for this time for year. If she'd forgotten her coat, she could have pneumonia by now, not to mention the hundred other dangers to a small child alone on the prairie—

He bounded down the hall only to find Georgie's bedroom door open. The soft glow of lamplight spilled through the threshold, illuminating a path through the door and into the room where Mariah sat in the old cane rocker, which had been his mother's, with Georgie motionless in her arms.

"She cried herself to sleep," Mariah explained in the softest whisper. "Every time I tried to move her to the bed, she stirred, so I decided to stay here and let her rest. I didn't know what to do. She was sobbing so hard, poor baby."

The fear drained out of him like water from a barrel. Georgie was safe. He propped his forehead against the door frame and took a steadying breath. He shouldn't have worried. Mariah could handle anything and quite well, if the sight in front of him was any indication. Georgie slept like an angel, her face tucked in the hollow of Mariah's throat, her little hands clutching her rag doll. The dried tracks of tears stained the curve of her cheek.

"Trapped in the chair, are you?" He kept his voice low, not wanting to wake his little angel, and knelt at Mariah's side. "How long have you been here?"

"Most of the morning. I'm afraid I'm a little numb from sitting in one place for so long." Lights glinted in her eyes, as gray as the storm outside, made dark with emotion.

Or maybe exhaustion. The lamplight on her face cast her in a radiant light, making her skin look as smooth as a cameo and tracing the lush curve of her mouth. A full bottom lip that he'd spent many hours of his last year in public school daydreaming about.

He had no right to be daydreaming about her now. She was here for his children, and nothing more. Look how content Georgie was. It would be a long row to hoe for a small child grieving her mother, but Georgie had Mariah to watch over her. For the first time since he'd found Lida lifeless that sad rainy morning, he felt a seed of hope. Georgie was going to be all right. All she needed was time. And Mariah.

You chose right, Gray. You picked a good woman. He felt proud of it and as sure as the wind howling against the eaves. He owed Mariah. And he would spend the rest of this convenient marriage letting her know it. She treated his kids well, and he would treat her like a queen.

"Let's see if we can get her into bed." Nick leaned close, close enough to breathe in the lilac scent of Mariah's hair and the soft woman scent of her skin.

Georgie cried out in her sleep at his touch and buried her face harder against the hollow of Mariah's throat.

"See?" Mariah cradled Georgie's head, holding the girl to her. "She was in so much pain, I didn't want to wake her. She needs to sleep."

"How about you? You said you're getting numb in places."

"Just where my person is in contact with the chair, but I'll survive. The real trouble is that I can't cook the noon meal from here."

"That's not a problem." He'd make sandwiches and heat up some soup. Even bring Mariah up a tray. He had a hard day of work waiting for him, but it could probably wait another hour. His daughter was safe, and that's what mattered, cradled on Mariah's lap, snug in her arms.

Nick climbed to his feet, his chest strangely tight, Will's accusation mocking him now. He wasn't sweet on Mariah, but he *did* respect her. With everything in him. "Thanks for taking care of my little one."

"It's my pleasure." Mariah smiled, the real Mariah. Not the cold spinster grown hard with loneliness, but the woman with a soft heart and a gentle touch.

He couldn't stop the tug of tenderness in his heart as he turned his back and walked away. "Want me to get you anything from the kitchen?"

"Isn't that my job?"

He didn't answer, disappearing down the hall.

The flame on the wick flickered in tiny beats of the draft from the window. Rain cuffed the glass and hammered on the siding, and it felt cozy in the small room, warmed by the chimney bricks that made up one wall. The rocker squeaked slightly as Georgie slept, as limp as her rag doll, a welcome heat against Mariah's chest.

Her stepdaughter. She couldn't believe it. She felt as if a light had come on in the dark places of her heart, a warm glow that changed everything. She pressed a kiss into Georgie's angel-soft hair at the crown of her head, grateful. Completely, thoroughly, to the reaches of her soul grateful.

She heard the sounds of a home, instead of a house empty and echoing with loneliness. The bang of the oven door in the kitchen below. The slam of the outside door. Men's voices rumbled pleasantly downstairs, and the sound of Joey's light, quick step in the hallway. His door slammed shut. No, she wasn't alone anymore.

Nick reappeared in the door, carrying a steaming cup in one hand. "Thought you might like some tea."

"You did?"

"Sure." He was the most thoughtful man she'd ever seen. He set the cup on the windowsill within her easy reach, as if he fetched tea for women every day. "I don't know how you take it. I put in a little sugar and cream, just in case you like it sweet."

"I do. Thank you."

"It was no trouble. I told you, Mariah. We take care of each other." He leaned close, the heat of his skin like a whisper against the curve of her face. He dipped lower to press a chaste kiss on his daughter's brow.

Something inside Mariah's chest squeezed tight and hard. It was an emotion too complex to name and too frightening to think about, so she didn't. She held her breath, instead, willing it to go away as Nick hesitated, a hair's width away, his gaze dropping to her mouth, her lips. His eyes went completely black, as if he was thinking about kissing her. As if it was what he wanted more than anything.

A pulse of desire beat low in her abdomen. A curl of desire that made her mouth tingle. She remembered the warm commanding caress of his kiss.

Maybe there's a chance. She couldn't help the wish from rising up out of the shadows of her heart. It was a hope that didn't dim when Nick left the room. It was a hope that remained strong as the rain fell and the wind moaned and the lamplight flickered.

Chapter Eight

Mariah prided herself on being a hard worker, but she'd never been so bone-tired as she felt that evening after supper had been served and eaten. Nick had warned her to cook plenty of food, and even then, she'd run short. Nick and his brothers polished off the entire roast before the platter made it around the table once. Tomorrow, she'd know what to expect.

But for tonight, even though twilight had come and gone leaving the kitchen in shadows, the stacks of dishes and pots remained. She'd been on her feet since four that morning, and one glance at the clock told her it was a few minutes past seven. *Best get to work.* Morning would be here before she knew it, and she would do this all over again.

It wasn't bad for a first day, she decided as she drained steaming water from the stove reservoir. The work overwhelmed her, and Joey had glared at her over his plate during supper, as if he were hoping that if he stared hard enough she'd disappear. He wasn't the only one. Nick's father and both his brothers kept on their best behavior, tensed as if she were waiting to smite them at the least provocation.

The men were in the parlor now, the scent of tobacco and the rustling of newspapers telling her she wasn't alone in the house. Deep, male voices rumbled in conversation. Mariah filled the washbasin and grated slivers of soap off the bar of lye into the steaming water.

She felt Nick's presence before she heard the pad of his stockinged feet on the polished wood floor. Before she smelled the scent of tobacco from his evening smoke still clinging to his gray flannel work shirt. She shivered from the intimacy in his voice before he spoke.

"You're in here alone with the dishes. That's not fair."

"True, but the dishes aren't complaining about being alone with me. So I won't complain about them."

"Sure, go ahead and joke. Guess you don't need my help."

"You came in to help me?"

"Sure. I was sitting in my favorite chair with my feet up, reading the newspaper when I heard you drawing water in here. I felt guilty. It ruined my concentration, so I thought, What the hell? I'll come in here and help her out."

"Oh, you think I need help?" She plunked one cup after the other into the dishwater. "I'm not doing a good enough job?"

She loved the way trouble gleamed in his dark eyes. She loved that he took a dish towel from the stack on the worktable and sidled up to her.

"I think you're doing an excellent job." His elbow brushed the side of her arm. "That's why I was feeling so damn guilty."

"You? Guilty? I don't believe it. I think you're the

sort of man who doesn't have a decent bone in his body. Too confident, arrogant, bossy.''

''Humph.'' He shook out the towel with a snap. ''I'm tough, too. Be careful, or you'll know the sting of my whip.''

''Whip, huh? That's a dish towel.''

''Yes, but I know how to use it.''

She blushed all the way from her collar to the roots of her hair. ''You're speaking about the towel, right?''

''Of course.'' The devil twinkled in his eyes as he flicked the towel again, snapping it crisply in midair. ''Hurry up with those dishes, or you're next.''

''You don't scare me one bit. I am also quite skilled with a dish towel.''

''Sure, at drying dishes with it.''

''Yes, but also at putting overconfident men in their places with it.''

He cocked one brow in an unmistakable challenge. ''Oh, so you play rough, do you?''

''I play to win.''

''So do I.'' Nick tossed her a clean dishcloth, folded so neat and perfect—the way Mariah did everything. ''Now get to work or know the sting of my wrath.''

''Hmm, maybe you'll know the sting of mine.'' She eyed him mischievously.

In the sheen of golden light, she looked amazing.

Soft wisps of hair had escaped the tight, no-nonsense knot at the back of her head, framing her heart-shaped face like small gossamers of sunlight. On a face made more beautiful by time, he'd swear to it.

Water splashed as she washed the first cup, thoroughly and quickly, her hands a blur in the sudsy water. Before he could think of something to say, she plopped the cup into the rinse water in the basin in front of him.

"There. Make yourself useful." She sounded stern, but she was only feigning it. He saw the corner of her mouth curve.

"Aye, aye, ma'am. I don't want to get on your bad side. You could probably whip me in a towel fight."

"I'm glad you finally accept my superiority." The flicker became a beautiful smile as she washed another cup. "Seriously, Nick, you were up before I was this morning. You ought to be sitting in the parlor with your feet up, not helping me with my work."

"Nope. The newspaper had boring articles in it anyway. I was falling asleep. Helping you is at least keeping me awake."

Mariah heard what he didn't say. He wanted to ease her burdens, lighten her load, just as he'd said. Just as she wanted to do for him. "Really, go sit and talk with your brothers. I'm almost done here."

"Sure. Look at that pile of dishes. It's a good hour's work, Mariah. I don't mind one bit. I'd rather spend the time in here with you."

"With me? The bossy, independent-minded wife?" The *convenient* wife.

"The truth be told, Will took his boots off and his feet stink something fierce. I came in here to escape the odor. You're doing me a favor by letting me stay."

He was lying, and they both knew it, and he was trying to make her laugh, too. Her chest ached with the thoughtfulness of it. Distance stood between them, but something snapped between them, a closeness or a connection, and it felt out of her reach. He wasn't ready, and she didn't know how to bridge the gap between them. She didn't know how a woman loved a man, not just physically, but in all those mysterious ways, using the right touches and words. Because she'd never seen that kind of love up close. Her father had been cruel and her mother brokenhearted.

Stop thinking about the past. She stared hard at the coffee ring on the cup she held, then dunked it beneath the water and scrubbed hard. "Helping the wife like this isn't something my father would ever have done."

"Your father was a hard man."

She scrubbed harder. Damn that stubborn stain. "He was hard to live with."

"You stayed with him, Mariah, instead of marrying. I'm not the only man who wanted to come courting, you know."

She dropped the cup with a thunk. Startled eyes met his. "That's not true. You were the only one who ever came calling."

"Do you think that no one wanted you, is that it?" Forget the dishes. He reached into the hot water to take her hand. Her skin was wet and hot, her hand so small against his. There were tears in her eyes, shimmering like diamonds in the lamp's soft glow, and it killed him as surely as a bullet to his chest to see her in pain. Maybe he shouldn't have said anything, but it was too late now. "Do you think you stayed a maiden because no man in town wanted to call you his?"

She dropped her gaze, those golden wisps of hair tumbling forward to shield her face from his scrutiny. Her bottom lip trembled. "After Pa died, nothing changed. No man came to my door to sweep me off my feet.''

"I did.'' His thumb brushed her chin, forcing her gaze to his. The sadness in her eyes shamed him. He'd disliked her, he'd forgotten her, he'd tried to avoid her in town for years, and married her for convenience's sake. But the truth was, his heart felt as new as dawn's first light whenever he looked upon her.

"You didn't sweep me off my feet, Nick. You offered me an arrangement.''

"Sure, I was trying to get my laundry done for free, so I proposed.''

"And I was trying to get a man to feed and shelter me.''

"And don't forget clothe you. I did include new dresses in the marriage deal.''

Tenderly. That's how he spoke to her. Gently, that's how he held her hand. The power of it rooted her to the floor as if her shoes had been nailed into the boards. The magic of his kindness felt like a balm to old wounds too numerous to count.

Old wounds that would not be reopened here. She couldn't begin to say how much that meant to her. "I know it's only been one day, but how you treated me... Is this how it's going to be?''

"It will get better, I hope. There's a lot of work to do here, and I'm sorry for that.'' Nick's thumb fit against the cut of her chin, a warm, rough caress that made her eyes water.

"I don't mean the work. I don't mind that. I mean you. You were good to me, Nick. What man offers to dry dishes after a fourteen-hour day in the fields?''

"One who honors his wife.''

Tears burned in her eyes. Honor. She didn't deserve that. "I didn't do a very good job today. You had to fix the noon meal." Georgie had cried herself to sleep after supper, and Joey had disappeared to his room with a book. The kitchen was a mess and she'd been far from adequate. "I know I'm not Lida, I wish—"

She didn't know what she wished, but she wanted it with her entire being. With all she was. She wanted to be the wife he didn't have to help with the dishes. She wanted to be the woman he needed. He loved. And it was so far out of her grasp.

Nick's forehead touched hers and he met her eye-to-eye, nose to nose, so close his breath was hers. "I thank God that you're not Lida. Remember that."

"She was so perfect. So…everything." Neat and slim and petite and every hair in place. Mariah would see her in town, in the mercantile an aisle away or walking down the boardwalk to the dressmaker's. "I know you had to love her very much, and I'm afraid you look at me and see a woman who could never measure up."

Nick released her and spun away. "Believe me, you outshine Lida in every way. I love her still, it's true, but not the way you think. She was the mother of my children, and I will always be grateful to her for that. But between us…"

"I'm sorry." Shock sounded heavy in her voice and in her step as she came closer.

He winced. He couldn't stand for her to know the truth. He couldn't speak out against his children's mother. How else was he going to tell Mariah what her steadfastness meant to him? He didn't know. Maybe it was foolish to say anything. It was in the past. What was done was done. He ought to leave it behind him. Be glad he had a wife who was happy with a little thoughtfulness. Who believed that his drying the dishes for her was a great thing.

"I know you still need to grieve Lida. I understand." Mariah's fingers slid over the curve of his shoulder, holding on, holding firm.

She didn't understand, and he couldn't tell her. Couldn't bring up the pain again. "Suppose I ought to keep my word and help you with those dishes. I'd hate for you to beat me in a towel fight."

"I would win, too." She leaned against him, her cheek to his shoulder blade, her breasts to his back. Her comfort felt like a warm blanket on a cold winter's morn.

A seed of affection took root in his heart. He couldn't help it. Couldn't stop it. A tiny seed that hurt like a burr in his chest. "Let's get this straight. No woman is going to beat me."

"Is that so?"

"You doubt my abilities."

"You underestimate mine." She still clung to him so sweet, providing comfort in her touch, tender and caring and all woman.

Her breasts pressed against his back felt as hot as the center of a flame. He'd been a long time without a woman, that was all, a man had natural needs. Refusing to let that dominate him, he took a step away from her comfort, from her soft, pleasing woman's form. He was strong enough not to need any comfort or any woman's softness in his life.

"Where do you think you're going?" Mariah was all tenderness, as if she could feel the pain gnawing like a hungry dog at his breastbone. "I thought you were a man of your word."

"Now and then, if the mood strikes me."

"Are you drying the dishes, or will I have to make you?"

"Make me." He turned at the threshold, where the shadows were darkest and the light did not reach. He was nothing but a black form, as powerful as the darkness itself.

Mariah ached for him. She could feel his sorrow as if it were hers. Feel his loneliness. Feel his need. A need that said, "You're not alone."

She snatched the dish towel from the edge of the worktable. "Remember, you asked for it."

"Hey, wait. I'm unarmed." He held up both hands.

"Do you think I'll give a man like you mercy?" She snapped the towel, intentionally falling short of his big, broad chest, giving him fair warning of what was to come. "No mercy, Mr. Gray. You don't deserve it."

"Fine attitude when you're holding the weapon." He prowled toward her like a panther, ruthless, fearless.

She flicked the towel hard, sending it straight for the center of his chest. His hand snaked out and tore the towel from her fingers. "Hey! Give that back."

"Now who's the one with the weapon?" Sounding pleased with himself, he circled the table, stalking her, towel pulled back and ready to fire. "And following your example, I intend to show you no mercy."

"Not very chivalrous of you."

"Do you think I care?" His arm shot out, the towel snapping a foot in front of her.

She reared back, changing positions. "You're keeping me away from the other towels."

"Very perceptive. At least I married a smart woman."

"And I married a ruthless man."

"No, a superior one. Admit it." He flicked the towel again, stopping her in her tracks. "Say it. Nick Gray is a superior man. Say you will rub my tired feet every evening after supper."

"I will not!"

"Now that's a shame, because I might do the same for you."

"I have no wish for you to put your hands on any part of my person." She knew he was teasing her, darn it, with his words and that damnable towel he'd stolen from her. She made a run toward the worktable and took a playful snap on the upper arm. "Hey!"

"Oh, sorry. Did I get you?" He didn't sound sorry at all. Not one bit.

"You're going to pay for that," she vowed, grabbing two towels, one for each hand. "You got the first blow, but I'll get the rest of them."

"Pretty confident for a woman."

"It comes from being around you."

She hit him square in the jaw, and he retaliated with a snap to her forehead. She cracked him twice, once in the chest and the other in the belly.

"Ready to surrender?" she challenged, jumping to the side to avoid the smack of his towel. "I've got you backed into the corner with no way out."

"That's what you think, huh?" He tossed down his towel, a big bulky form huddled between the window and the hutch. "Let's see you run, pretty lady."

He ducked his head and charged like a bull straight

at her. She felt a wild flutter of panic because he was twice her size and he could knock her to the ground in a second flat. Then she saw his arms reach out to grab her, and she knew she was safe. And at the advantage.

She hit him twice, the ends of the towels cracking him in the dead center of his head. It didn't stop him and she squealed as his arms came around her. His head brushed the dip of her waist. In one rush, he scooped her onto his shoulder, bottom up, her face looking him in the back, and swirled in a big circle in the center of the kitchen.

"Who's the victor now, little woman?" His laughter vibrated through him and into her, a wonderful life-affirming feeling that chased away the darkness in the room and the shadows from her heart.

She laughed, deep and loud, wrapped her arms around his broad waist and held on to his solid, hot, male body as they went 'round and 'round together.

"Are you ready to surrender?" he demanded.

"No."

He spun faster. "Are you sure?"

"Yes, except I'm getting dizzy."

"Ha! I thought that would get to you." Laughing, holding her safe, he lifted her off his shoulder, into his arms, and lowered her to the floor. He held her steady as she swayed on her feet.

"You broke the rules," she told him as soon as the room stopped spinning.

"What rules? I didn't hear you list any." He pulled out a chair and helped her sit. "Are you all right?"

"Absolutely not. I have a cheater for a husband."

"Hmm, you didn't say I couldn't wrestle you." He pushed the tangled hair out of her eyes with a tender swipe of his big hand. "But let's get this straight. I'm as faithful as the day is long, and I'll never cheat on you. To prove it, I'll be a good sport and help you dry the dishes. But don't forget tomorrow night to find enough time to rub my feet."

She opened her mouth to protest, but then his promise to her sunk in. He was a man she could count on. Trust. A man faithful only to her.

Surely that meant he wanted her in his bed, to love her as his real wife. In time, when his grieving for Lida was through.

Hope flared to life within her, big and full and glowing.

Spying the narrow line of light shining beneath his son's bedroom door, Nick gave a knock before he walked in. Joey's room was dark except for the faint glow of the lamp by his bed, turned to the lowest notch. It cast a wavering orange glow onto the book propped on the comforter, concealing the boy behind it.

"Past your bedtime, son."

Joey lowered the book. "Can I read to the end of the chapter?"

"How many pages is that?" Nick had been tricked by this one before.

Joey bent his head, diligently counting. "Four whole pages and a part of one."

"Okay, then." Nick took a step back into the hall, but something kept him from closing the door. A father's instincts, he suspected. Joey had kept by either him or Pop for most of the day in the fields, but he'd been unusually quiet. And spent a good deal of time, like his father had, casting long silent looks toward the house.

Maybe there were some things needing to be said. Nick let the door click behind him and padded across the darkened room. "We're both caught in uncharted waters, aren't we, son? There's this woman in the house cooking for us, and we hardly know her."

"I heard you laughing. You know her real good." Joey's brow furrowed and he bowed his head, staring hard at the open page in front of him.

Nick sat on the bed. "Scoot over. Make room for your old man."

Joey sighed, put down the book, and schooched over a few inches. "I know you're gonna say I gotta like her."

"That's not what I'm here to say."

"She told you, didn't she?" Joey's face scrunched up, a show of belligerence, but it didn't take a wise man to see the pain shining in his eyes. "She shouldn't a done that. She shouldn't a told."

"All right, time to ante up. Tell me what you did."

"Nothin'." Joey bit his lip to keep it from trembling.

"Is it something that upset Mariah?"

"I don't know. Maybe." That bottom lip trembled some more, but he was tough, bucking up. He didn't so much as sniffle.

Poor kid. This wasn't easy for him. "I know you miss your ma."

He nodded, dark locks tumbling forward to hide his eyes. There was a little-boy sweetness to him, but a solid strength, too.

Proud of his son, Nick cupped him on the shoulder,

man to man. "Mariah isn't here to replace your mother. You know that, right?"

One narrow shoulder lifted in an uncertain shrug.

Ah, the real problem. "No one can ever do that."

"Ma wanted to leave us. I know she did." Joey fisted both hands. "Before she passed on to heaven, she wanted to leave. I know all about that." The betrayal still stung deep, and Joey didn't know the half of it. Never would, if Nick had any say to it. A boy needed a mother he could respect. It made a difference in the man he would become. No good would come of the boy knowing his mother's quest for happiness ended up in more than one man's bed—men she wasn't married to.

"This lady, is she gonna leave, too?"

"Not to my knowledge." How could he make promises to his son that it wasn't up to him to keep? Nick would gamble his heart that Mariah would keep her vows, but his son's? "I have faith in her. I think you can, too."

"I heard Pop say that you made a real mistake." Joey let out a pent-up sigh that sounded suspiciously close to a sob. "That you shouldn't a done it. That we'd all come to regret it."

"Pop don't know everything there is to know. And he doesn't know Mariah. Not like I do." He'd hold his anger back until he could have a talk with Pop. Let him know he wasn't helping matters. "I wouldn't have married her if I thought she wouldn't pull through for us. She took real good care of Georgie today. Did you see that?"

"I guess." Joey's knuckles turned white.

"I'm sure this is gonna work out. Do you know why?"

The boy shook his head.

"Because Mariah used to live all alone in her house in town. She didn't have any family. Not a mother or a father. No brothers or sisters. And no children of her own. Don't you think that's got to be pretty lonely?"

"No." Stubbornly he set his chin. His brows crinkled together in thought. "Maybe."

"I married her because I thought she wanted a family more than anything. So that's why I think she's going to stick with us. Because that's what families do, right? They stick together."

"Through thick and thin." Joey's fists relaxed. He tugged at a thread in the sheet hem, pulling it until it was a few inches longer than it had been. "I don't care, for me, you know. But Georgie needs a mother. She keeps runnin' off."

"She didn't try it today. Mariah made sure of it, just like she's going to do from now on."

Joey didn't say anything, as if he wasn't willing to put too much belief in a woman who could leave.

Nick couldn't blame him. He had problems with Mariah, too. "To the end of the chapter and then I want this light out, partner. Do I have your word on that?"

The boy nodded, head bent, already escaping into his book.

Nick wished he could take on his son's worries and hurts, but that wasn't the way life was. Troubled, he closed the door tight. Mariah wasn't going to let them down, he knew it. And in time, Joey would see it, too. He'd understand that some women could be counted on.

He *felt* Mariah an instant before he heard the pad

of her step on the hallway carpet. It was an awareness of her presence, like an awakening of his senses, from dark to light, from silence to singing. And there she was, wrapped in a brown housecoat, the white ruffle of her nightgown showing above her stockinged feet.

"Nick, I should have asked. Did you want a warm cup of milk?"

"Are you joking? Tough men like me don't drink hot milk. We chew on nails when we can't sleep."

"Foolish of me to even ask. Next time I offer to do something nice for you, I'll just spare myself the display of manly arrogance and kick my own shin. It would be less painful."

Ordinarily, Mariah would have said that insult with a sharp hook in her voice that was as mean and keen as barbed wire. But this Mariah—his wife—marched coyly past him to her bedroom, her hips swaying beneath the smooth fall of brown fabric. Her hair was down, tumbling everywhere in a wild disarray of golden curls that fell to the small of her back and swished with the rhythm of her gait.

She spun to face him and the snug bodice of her housecoat clung to her unbound breasts, snaring his gaze. Her breasts were full and round and made for a man to appreciate.

"I have a few errands tomorrow. I have the last of my laundry deliveries to make and then I'm meeting a few of my friends in town."

He snapped his gaze to hers and kept it there. What did she say? He had no idea, so he said the safest thing. "Yep."

"Just so you know, I'll have dinner on the table before I go, and you're to leave the dishes where they are when you're finished eating. Your father said he'd keep Joey with him, and I'll take Georgie with me.''

"Sounds like you thought of everything." He had no notion if that was true. As if she was trying to distract him, she lifted the cup to her lush lips and sipped. His pulse thundered in his ears and through every single inch of his body.

Damn. His trousers were tight, and what did he do? He had to go and remember how she'd felt like paradise in his arms, soft and too good to be true. How womanly she was, real woman and not simpering girl, and she made him feel…

Well, in a way he was never going to feel again. Would *never* feel again. *What's wrong with you, Gray? Use some discipline.*

"I do appreciate this." Mariah was all aglow, from the shimmers in her hair to her pearled complexion to the dazzle of her smile as she took a step backward into her room. "We've been getting together like this since we graduated public school. It won't interfere with my duties here and my responsibilities to you."

"I trust you, Mariah. I don't doubt you for a moment."

She glowed even more brightly, as if he'd given her the highest praise. "You don't know what this means to me. How you treat me. I couldn't have a better husband. Thank you."

He knew her life had been hard, but he hadn't realized how much as he watched her walk into her room and close her door. Close the door that used to lock Lida away from him every night. And now his new wife, carefully kept far out of his reach, away from his heart.

You're making a mistake getting close to her. She's

only going to hurt you. Nick thought of Lida, of how harmless she'd seemed at first. How frail and pretty and in need of him, a big, strong man to take care of her, to love her like no one else. She'd been grateful, too. She'd been appreciative and complimentary and laughed in the kitchen when they were alone.

Look where that got you. Closing his mind against images too painful to recall, Nick stumbled down the hall to his room, locked the door and sat awake in the darkness until exhaustion claimed him.

Chapter Nine

"Mariah, tell us all about how married life is treating you." Rayna set the coffeepot on the end table next to her sofa in the comfortable parlor of her house. "You avoided the topic all through the meal, and I won't let you get away with it for one minute longer."

"That's right," Betsy agreed from the divan. "You look happy. Does that mean Nick is a good husband?"

"He's a good husband." Mariah slid two cubes of sugar into the pretty china cup she held before handing the matching sugar dish to Rayna. "He's a good man."

"Oh, is he now?" Rayna lifted one brow as she slid sugar cubes into her coffee. "A *good* man, is he?"

"Stop that, Rayna," Betsy scolded. "That's private between a wife and her husband. Poor Mariah might not be comfortable—"

Realizing what her friend meant, Mariah's face burned. She was glad Georgie was at the baby-sitters and wasn't close by to overhear. "I didn't mean... I don't want you to think—"

"Don't worry about it." Rayna waggled her brows. "I'm glad Nick has made you a happy woman."

Mariah blushed harder. How did she tell her closest friends that her marriage wasn't what it appeared? She thought of their separate rooms and their separate beds and it made her sad. She wanted Nick to desire her, to want her. "Nick is still grieving Lida."

"Of course he is. What man wouldn't mourn the passing of his wife?" Betsy spoke, compassionate as always, and a good friend. "It must be hard for him to be forced to remarry so soon, but a busy rancher with two small children, he had to be practical."

Mariah winced. *Practical.* There was that word again. She didn't want to be practical. She wanted to be wanted and to belong. She wanted a real marriage and to know real passion. She wanted to fall in love, real love, the kind that swept a woman off her feet, that filled her up and made her complete.

She'd had a glimpse of that last night in the kitchen with Nick. *Please, let him fall in love with me.*

"Shall we, Rayna?" Betsy asked, sparkling as bright as the crystal glasses on the small table between them. At Rayna's nod, Betsy rose to her feet with a sweep of skirts and a crinkle of petticoats. "Mariah, you know gifts ought to come with a wedding, and since your wedding was so rushed, we didn't have time to celebrate."

Mariah set the delicate cup into its saucer before she spilled. Her hands were already shaking and her chest felt tight. She hadn't given it a thought because it wasn't a real wedding, not yet anyway—

"We thought we'd have a little party, instead of

our usual hour of sewing and talking.'' Rayna brought a box of colorfully wrapped gifts out from behind the divan. ''Betsy's fetching the cake. We, my friend, are going to celebrate your marriage. Who knew you were secretly in love with Nick this whole time? To think you finally married your true love.''

Is that what everyone thought? Thinking of Nick, she surely hoped it would be true. In time. Hope lifted her up as she stood to help Betsy with the cake.

Already, Nick was opening up to her, moving away from his grief, and one day he'd be ready to love her fully. To wrap his arms around her in the kitchen for a casual, good-morning kiss. To take her into his bed at night, wanting only her love.

Soon. She could feel it in her bones.

Nick leaned on his shovel and swiped the rainwater from his face. It was a cold, mean day. The precipitation was wind-driven, blowing at a high angle that kept his hat brim from doing any good. The rain hit him right in the face as he blinked, using his sleeve this time to wipe off some of the wet.

''Where did that wife of yours get off to?'' Pop asked from the business end of a shovel.

''Town.'' Nick figured he could say that with some surety. Mariah had said she wanted to go to town today.

He hadn't listened, he'd been too busy noticing the soft, inviting swell of her breasts to pay attention to what she was saying. He was a man who hadn't been with a woman in over five years, and it was only natural that his desire for a woman was building, like damned-up water in a creek. So it was to be expected he might drift toward sexual thoughts now and then.

Be honest, Gray. He'd thought about Mariah in that housecoat cinched tight at her narrow waist and hugging her lush breasts for more than half the morning. And with the way it was going, the afternoon was about to wander down the same path.

"Not keepin' much of a tight rein on her, are ya?" Pop commented as he jabbed the shovel into the muddy earth. "I guess you don't need to worry. She's a woman past the first blush, and she can be meanspirited. Not one folk in town will argue with you about that."

"Mariah isn't mean. I thought we talked about this." His jaw snapped shut into a hard clench. "Mariah works hard and she deserves respect."

"You can't fool me, son. I know why you married her. She ain't gonna cheat on you, that's why. And how could she? She's not the kind of woman a man's attracted to—"

"Pop." Nick boomed the warning, but at the same time the blood kicked in his veins. Who wouldn't be attracted to Mariah? The woman he'd seen last night in the hallway with her hair down and tangled, her blond curls tumbling everywhere, looking as if she'd just risen from a bed where she'd been thoroughly loved. She looked like temptation with her cheeks a rosy pink. With the sway of her full breasts against her robe.

His groin pulsed hard, remembering that little detail. He'd been able to see the outline of her nipples, which meant she wore no corset. Possibly no undergarments at all. The notion of Mariah naked beneath that nightgown...soft, creamy skin made for a man's touch—

"Speak of the she-devil. Here she comes now,"

Pop drawled. "Sorry, son. I'll do my damnedest not to call her that again."

"See that you don't," he growled, already turning toward the south where a black surrey rolled across the green prairie.

It's her. He couldn't say why he was so danged relieved to see Mariah sitting straight as a post, the way she always did, so prim and proper and self-controlled on the front seat of the surrey. Because of the distance and the clear plastic rain sheets pulled into place around the vehicle, he couldn't see more than her shape and that of little Georgie seated beside her, but it was enough.

"I'm going to go and check on my daughter." Nick left the spade where it was and whistled to his gelding. The animal's head shot up and he trotted on over. Nick caught the dangling reins. "She's got Mariah now, but I still worry about her."

"Sure, go on in. Take all the time you need." Pop wasn't fooled, or it looked that way, as the old man bowed his head, trying to hide the smirk on his face.

What did Pop think? That he was riding in to see Mariah? Nick toed up in the stirrup, swabbed off the seat and eased into the cold, damp saddle. Nick had a hard time not thinking about her, but that was natural. A man noticed these things about a woman. It didn't mean anything beyond simple male appreciation of a pretty female. That was all there was to it.

And appreciate her, he did, but nothing more. He reined the gelding to a stop in the yard just as Mariah climbed from the covered surrey. His pulse *didn't* surge. His blood *didn't* heat. He *didn't* so much as notice the new bonnet, the same blue-gray as her eyes, serviceable but complimentary. Just as he didn't notice the new cotton dress in a matching shade that hugged her curves to perfection and brought out the beauty in her, so powerful he forgot to breathe.

"Pa!" Georgie squealed from the front seat, arms out, waiting for him to reach her down. "Come looky and see. I got feathers!"

Mariah, as if self-conscious, dipped her chin as she swept the rain curtain back on its rod. "You said I could go shopping, and Georgie and I took good advantage of that, didn't we?"

"I got pink feathers and purple ones!" Georgie stood up on the floorboards, waving the ends of the magenta colored boa wrapped around her neck and the other one flowing out behind her on the seat.

"Awful nice feathers you got there. Looks like you two females set me back a few gold eagles." Nick swept his little girl off the surrey and into his arms, boas and all. "Guess it's the cost for the privilege of having such beautiful girls in my life."

"I got diamonds, too!" George tugged a long strand of paste jewels from beneath her cloak, shining like the genuine article, so pure and flawless, it made his heart cinch up tight.

Mariah had found a way to make his daughter forget her grief. Momentarily, no doubt, but it was a step. He owed that woman. He hoped she'd cleaned out the dress shop; he wouldn't mind it a bit when the bill came, no sir. His throat felt tight, making it hard to find the words, so he carried Georgie through the rain and mud to the covered back porch and placed her gently on the top step.

Gratitude. That's what he felt for Mariah. A powerful, soul-deep gratitude. That's why it swept him away so. Why, when he turned to her now, he didn't notice the rain or the wind or the cold. He saw only her on tiptoe, leaning into the back seat of the surrey, gathering up fallen packages. He could hear the rustle of paper and her muttered frustration.

"That's the trouble with shopping," he began, setting a hand on the small of her back to gently move her aside. "Too many packages to keep track of. That's where a man comes in handy."

"That's certainly why I married you, since I'm a weak woman, unable to lift so much as a hatbox." She straightened so the palm of his hand that had been merely skimming her spine now held the dip of her waist and hip.

"I married you so I could carry your hatboxes and look powerful and masculine."

"That is one of your more positive attributes."

"Being powerful and masculine?"

"No. Carrying things for me." She reached up, as casual as could be, and rubbed a drop of rain off his chin with her gloved fingertip. "You make a pretty good pack mule. Better than my ox, that's for sure."

"Pack mule, huh? Know what I think? I think you like me for more than my hauling abilities."

"Truly? And what would those other abilities be? Hitching up the surrey?"

"I am darn good at that."

"Putting sticks of wood in the stove and setting fire to them?"

He pressed closer, so they were eye-to-eye, nose to nose. "Darn right. I am man. I make fire. I am powerful."

"I am woman. I can make fire, too."

"Then you're not impressed by me?"

"Not one bit." *Liar. He* impressed her, every bit

of the man he was, strong and protective and tender. His touch at her waist was possessive, a man claiming his woman, and her blood sang with exhilaration.

His gaze slid to her mouth. ''There's something else I can do well.''

''Put up the horses?''

''Huh! You're about to learn I have many talents.'' His hand at her waist dug in, pulling her across the scant inch that separated his body from hers.

She bumped into him, off balance, but he held her steady, full against the breadth of his chest and the span of his abdomen and the iron-hardness of his thighs. He was hot and hard and male and, when his mouth slanted over hers, possessive.

Like fire to iron, she molded her lips to his. His kiss was like a brand burning into her flesh, unyielding and overwhelming, and she wanted to push away from him in fear and pull him close in delight. The stroke of his lips against hers was a demand and a plea, a question and an answer and the single most pleasurable sensation she'd ever experienced. It was as if his kiss made her alive, as if she were sleeping beauty and he was breathing life right into her.

The tip of his tongue swept the seam of her lips, pushing his way into her mouth with a hot, wanton sweep, and she opened to him, melted to him, the way flame altered steel, changing her, transforming her, making her new. She clung to him, breathless and vulnerable and aching for more.

For the first time she could see what it was between a man and wife. It was a glimpse, a promise of what was to come. More than a kiss, breathless and consuming, it was being entirely alive and wanted.

He broke away, breathing as hard as she was, his

chest rising and falling beneath her fists. She realized she had a tight hold of his shirt and let go. Amazing. She was a little disoriented as she stepped back and fought for balance. Nick's hands slid to her elbows to help her.

"Guess I'd best bring in these boxes," he drawled in that deep baritone that rasped across her nerve endings until she shivered deep. Until desire curled hot and ardent, low in her abdomen.

"I would appreciate it. After all, I must find as many uses for you as I can." Feeling new, gathering her courage, she pressed her lips to the side of Nick's jaw, damp from the rain, before she grabbed her reticule and headed toward the back steps.

She had every right to kiss him. He was her husband, and look how he'd kissed her. They were married, and he was making steps away from his sorrow over Lida, if that kiss was any indication. Feeling warm and wanted and wonderful, she practically skipped up the back steps and into the warm kitchen, where Georgie twirled in a circle wearing only her chemise. Her dress was crumpled beside her on the floor. The purple boa was wrapped around the top of her head and the other snaked around her waist. "I'm a dancer!"

"And a good one, too." Contentment warmed her like soup on a cold day. Look how her life had changed.

Mariah untied her new bonnet and set her reticule on the table. For the first time in her twenty-eight years she felt as if she'd come home. *Home.* She had a real home.

"I'm all dressed up for the ball," Georgie announced, swirling to a stop and laughing as the feathers swung in an arc around her, still caught in motion.

"It's almost time to serve refreshments." Mariah shrugged out of her shawl. "I've heard that when you're at a ball, you get very fancy refreshments."

"You do?" Georgie's eyes sparkled.

"First of all, you eat off plates made of gold. Let me go fetch some." Mariah grabbed a pair of tarnished copper serving plates from the bottom of the hutch. "Is this fancy enough for your ball?"

"Oh, yes!" Georgie danced in place, feathers flying.

A gift. That's what this was. Mariah always prided herself on being an intelligent woman, and despite her thousand flaws, she was smart enough to know when she'd found something precious. Something beyond price. More valuable than all the gold plates in world.

She grabbed a jar of strawberry preserves from the pantry. She had a few minutes before she had to start supper, and the dishes stacked on the worktable could wait. She had plain sugar cookies to fancy up and ordinary apple juice to transform into champagne. A little girl to help to dream again.

She no longer had to be sensible, practical Mariah Scott. She was Mariah Gray. A wife and a mother. A woman who could be loved.

Why did I do that? Nick had asked for the hundredth time since he'd impulsively pulled Mariah into his arms and kissed her. Not a peck on the cheek or a slight brush of the lips kiss. But a full-fledged, baby-you're-mine kiss. The kind a man gives a woman when he wants to take her to his bed and keep her there for the rest of his life.

"Let me clear these plates." Mariah's dulcet voice caressed like silk across his skin and she smiled sweetly as if she knew exactly what her effect was on him. "Betsy found the most delicious chocolate cake at the bakery, and she gave me a portion to bring home to all of you."

"Cake!" Georgie clapped her hands in anticipation. "It's good, too. I already had some, and you didn't, Joey."

"Huh! As if I care about some crummy old chocolate cake." Joey refused to be charmed, even by dessert.

That's my boy, Nick silently cheered. *I'm on your side.* That woman isn't what she seems. No, sir. He'd been dead wrong to think the poor lonely spinster he'd once been sweet on would be the perfect choice for a convenient marriage.

"I have to admit those chicken and dumplings were the best I've ever had." Pop pushed back from the table to rub his stomach. "I'm plumb full, but that ain't gonna stand in my way of dessert."

"Good. Would you like me to put on a pot of coffee? I'll make it twice as strong, just for you."

Pop nodded grudgingly. "That would be fine, Miss Mariah."

Miss Mariah. Nick's fork tumbled out of his grip and clattered to a rest on his plate. *Miss Mariah?*

"Make enough for me, too, while you're at it." Will spoke up sheepishly.

What was going on? The minute Mariah left for the kitchen, Nick turned to his father. "I thought you didn't like her."

"She's a damn fine cook, I'll grant her that. And with a little learnin', she's makin' the coffee the way

I want.'' Pop glanced furtively at the door to the kitchen. ''She's lookin' more pleasant than she used to, don't you think?''

''She sure does,'' Dakota, who preferred silence as a general way of life, chose this moment to speak. ''Marriage becomes her.''

That was a mile short of the truth. Marriage didn't become her, it *made* her. There she was, bustling back in with plates of sliced chocolate cake balanced along one slender arm. She set the plates on the table with the efficiency of a practiced poker dealer.

She was pretty alive, radiant…and so beautiful she made his teeth ache. She'd done something different with her hair. It wasn't pulled back so tight it made her eyebrows taut. Nope, her hair was everywhere. Soft, curling coils of it falling into her eyes and around her face and tumbling over her shoulders. Rich, glimmering locks of gold that begged for a man to dig his fingers in and hold tight while he kissed her.

''And last but not least.'' Mariah shimmered as she slipped a plate onto the table in front of him, her skirts rustling and her hair cascading forward to brush against the side of his face.

Sweet heaven, that felt good. And smelled good, too. The faint scent of lilacs filled his senses. The plate clinked on the table as she released it, and he couldn't help twisting toward her as she moved away. Leaving him hot and aching and breathing so hard, he'd be less winded if he'd run five miles.

She eased into the chair at his side, hardly more than a few inches away, but it felt like a mile. A forbidden mile he wasn't allowed to cross.

Will started up a discussion about the crops and

old man Dayton's predictions for a dry summer. He and Pop went at it, while youngest brother Dakota added a few stray remarks. Normally that was the kind of conversation Nick didn't mind partaking in, but not tonight. No, all his brain could think about was the woman at his side.

"I'm glad you didn't mind that I went to town today," she said in a voice softer than he'd ever heard before, more musical. Happy. "Rayna and Betsy and I have been getting together since we graduated from public school. And afterward, I made my last round of deliveries."

"Good." He took a big bite of cake to keep from looking at her. With the way he was feeling, that would bring nothing but trouble down on his head so fast he wouldn't have time to get out of the way.

"Betsy is going to be taking over my business." Mariah began talking and he tried to concentrate on what she was saying, but he couldn't.

Was it his fault her voice rose and fell in a way that kept him spellbound? He was a man. He couldn't help it. The same way he couldn't stop staring at her mouth. Soft and luscious, with a perfect bow-shaped upper lip and a full, tempting bottom lip. She talked on while he watched.

And remembered. How her mouth had felt when he'd kissed her. Deep and hard and long. She'd tasted like paradise, soft and gentle and pure pleasure. Hers had been the sort of kiss that got into a man's blood, so it was a part of him. The kind of kiss that became all he thought about.

"I'll be helping her for a while, if that's all right with you. I won't shirk my duties here, you have my word on that." Mariah took a small bite of cake, the tines of the fork caressing her luscious bottom lip just as he wanted to do. Slow and easy.

If he kissed her, he figured he could make it last all night long if he had to. Just twist his fingers into that wild tangle of her beautiful hair, cradle her jaw in the palms of his hands and claim her mouth with tender caresses and nips, gentle suction and the stroke of his tongue…

"Is that all right with you?" Her big, gorgeous blue eyes pinned his.

He read expectation in the slight arch of her brows and a happy glow on her cheeks. Whatever she'd said, it was something she wanted. He had no notion what she'd been saying. "Sure."

"I know you've got more than enough work to keep you busy day and night until winter, so this is great of you." Her face softened, becoming so beautiful, she could have been a painting made in brushstrokes of ivory and cream, too lovely to be real.

What in blazes had he agreed to? With any luck she'd say it again. The trick was to listen to her this time, instead of dreaming of her kiss.

"When would be best for you?" A lock of hair tumbled against the curve of her face, caressing the cameo skin he was forbidden to.

The blood in his veins boiled.

"Tomorrow? Sometime next week? If it's all right with Will?"

He blinked, trying to unscramble his brains and cool down. What he needed was to take a plunge in the creek and stay submerged in the cold water for about seven years. "I've got a busted water pipe to repair. If all goes well, next week."

"This means a lot, Nick. Thank you."

"Sure." Whatever he'd just agreed to, he had an overpowering suspicion he wouldn't like it. Not one bit.

That's what you deserve, Gray, for thinking down south, instead of with your brain. No good ever came from that. Just misery and heartache. He ought to know, having made that colossal mistake once in his life. He knew better, damn it.

Then Mariah had to go and say something else with that fantastic, mesmerizing mouth of hers. "Rayna's neighbor's daughter baby-sits her school-aged son when we have our get-togethers. I left Georgie with her, too. You don't mind?"

"Uh…" He searched his mind trying to figure out what to say. He'd concentrated really hard and he heard nothing. Not one word. Just saw the motion of her mouth shaping words and remembered the way her lips had shaped to fit his kiss. Pliable and honey-sweet. "I trust you, Mariah."

She beamed, and her happiness glowed from the inside out, radiating through her like a sunbeam, one that always shone, relentlessly beautiful, so bright it hurt a man's eyes.

A sensible, practical wife, my foot! This woman looked mesmerizing and vibrant and full of needs. Instead of the lonely spinster dressed in widow's black, a woman no man had ever courted much less waltzed with beneath a starry sky, he'd married a siren. A woman so beautiful and alive, she could have her pick of men.

Just as Lida had.

The truth bore through his chest, leaving him empty. Leaving him weak. What was he going to do about that? He'd thought he had Mariah figured out, grateful and quiet and shy. But the woman beside him had needs. Needs he didn't dare try to meet.

He'd made that mistake, too.

The cake tasted like sand on his tongue. The conversation around him was just unrecognizable babble. Georgie wanted down, and Joey was first to hop up to help her. He was eager to leave the table and figured out a way to do it. Smart boy.

Too bad his old man wasn't as quick on the trigger.

"I bet your coffee's done, Jeb." Mariah swept out of the chair in that dress of hers, the new one he was about to be billed for by the dressmaker, the garment that hugged her generous bosom and her waist and draped over her perfectly curved hips.

He watched her walk out of the room, her long hair swinging and sway with each step. Making his pulse kick up a notch in reaction.

You're a fool if you want her. The last thing he needed was to fall in love with his wife.

Look where that got him last time. He poked his fork into the cake. Wasn't hungry. Couldn't stomach it. He pushed away from the table, but didn't bolt out of his chair fast enough.

Mariah marched into the room carrying the enamel pot. The same woman with her no-nonsense gait and her efficient movements and the way she poured coffee like a waitress, the same way she had on the night of the fund-raiser supper.

She was still the same woman he'd married. She'd bought a new dress and changed her hair. Those were superficial changes, and he was not a superficial man. So why was his blood pulsing wild in his veins? Why did he want to rip that coffeepot out of her hands, wind his fingers through her hair and kiss her until she was breathless and begging for more?

Because she'd been his first love. He had been eighteen that May, and the innocence of that attraction had been all-consuming. Of watching her across the aisle of the schoolroom when he was supposed to be working math equations on his slate. Of spying on her as she chatted beneath the shade of the tall oaks with her friends Rayna and Betsy while he played baseball with his buddies. And, when school was out and they'd been graduated, of seeing her across the street in town and wanting her with all the foolish, idealistic love in his heart. Naive, he knew now, to think love could be like that. But he'd been young. What did he know of life? Only what he imagined love to be.

Life had taught him a fateful lesson on the subject of love. He had a heart irrevocably broken to prove it.

"Nick, would you like some coffee?" Mariah's shoulder brushed his as she reached past him to fill the coffee cup. Fiery sensation skidded down his arm, setting him aflame. *This is a bad thing, Gray. A bad path you're looking at.* A smart man would know better than to make that choice again. He closed his eyes for the few seconds it took to get his reaction to her under control.

When he opened his eyes, the cup on the table in front of him was full of dark, steaming coffee. Mariah was moving away to pour coffee for the other men, her arm caressing his shoulder again. It was such a light brush it may have only been her sleeve touching his, yet he felt the impact of it as if it was a sweet kiss on his soul.

Oh, Mariah. This reaction to her had nothing to do with her hair soft as an angel's around her face. Nothing to do with the dress that hugged her like a lover and made her eyes so blue it hurt to look at them. This had everything to do with that tiny seed of love buried in his heart, a seed that had gone dormant for so long he'd thought it to be dead, without life, never to return.

What a fool he'd been.

Pop was talking to Will and Dakota about the horses, and wanted Nick's thoughts on the matter. They could use a new stud—and what did he think about the auction next week in the neighboring county? Nick answered without thinking, acting as if he were a part of the conversation when all he could think about was Mariah.

The clink of her spoon in her cup as she stirred sugar into her coffee. The whisper of her breathing. The faint scent of lilacs that made him remember how he'd reached out and kissed her. Claimed her as his. Hauled her close and kissed her until they were both breathless and he was melting from the inside out.

Time to get out of here. Get some distance between him and Mariah. Get some breathing room. Cool down and try to figure this out.

"I'll be upstairs." He didn't look right or left, up or down. Figured everyone would know he was going to check on his children, even though he could hear the muffled sounds of their voices as he moved closer. They were playing in their rooms, as they often did before bedtime. They were fine.

He wasn't.

Even the hallway reminded him of Mariah. Of how she'd stood in the threshold dressed for bed, looking so soft and vulnerable and desirable. The bedroom door was wide open, the long, webby light before sundown painting the large room in a pink glow. The white curtains shone rose, tinting the white coverlet on the bed. Those things were Mariah's—Lida had preferred dark colors—but the bedstead was the same. The rich, cherry four-poster that his children had been born in. The matching bureau and chest of drawers. Familiar, and yet he hadn't looked at them much in years. This had been his bedroom once, and that his marriage bed.

The soft pad of little feet on the carpet warned him before Georgie slipped her hand around his first finger and held tight. "Pa? Why's Mariah sleepin' in Mama's room?"

"Because she's nice, and I don't want to make her sleep on the couch." He knelt so he could look her in the eye.

"Where's Mama gonna sleep when she gets back from heaven?"

He coughed, struck by surprise at how deep the pain went, like a blade twisting through his guts. "When folks get to heaven, it's not a place they come back from. It's not like going to town."

"Not like shopping?"

"That right. It's a place where you stay forever." He brushed the curls from her eyes.

Her big eyes filled with tears. "An ox and wagon can't get there?"

"That's right." At least she was starting to understand. "Mariah's gonna stay and take care of you from here on out. Is that fine by you?"

"Y-yeah." Georgie dove head-first toward his chest and he opened his arms, pulling her close.

So dear and fragile. He cradled her against his heart, wishing he could right every wrong just for her. For his little girl.

Later that night, as he lay awake in his lonely bed, he stared at the ceiling. The house was silent, everyone tucked safely asleep. Everyone but him. He couldn't relax, couldn't stop remembering that she was in bed wearing her white nightgown with ruffles at the hem. And beneath that cotton garment would be Mariah, and nothing but skin. Creamy and soft everywhere. He quaked from crown to sole, rocked by an emotion too powerful to name. Too overwhelming to feel. Too dangerous to let spark to life in his heart.

Stop thinking about her. He threw back the covers, breathing hard, half aroused and getting harder and hotter. Now that he'd imagined Mariah naked, all soft curves and ivory skin, he couldn't think of anything else.

You've got more willpower than this, Gray. He grabbed his coat at the back door, jammed his feet into his boots and headed outside. Let the cool night rain whip across his heated face. He stood in the shadows until he shivered. Until his desire to be loved and wanted by Mariah slipped away like a leaf in the wind.

He had to be practical. He had to do what was right. He had a family to take care of and a ranch to run. A wife might be a necessity, but loving her wasn't. He figured that with Mariah as his wife, he'd never be in danger of losing his heart. Not again.

But he was wrong. He was as vulnerable to her as he'd been to Lida. He hated that. Hated it to the far side of his soul. Bitterness soured in his mouth like week-old milk, and he couldn't spit out the taste of it. He started walking into the darkness until something powerful stopped him. The sight of headstones at the family graveyard, dark and lonely in the drizzling rain. His stepmother's grave alongside Lida's. And her baby's. The poor sickly newborn boy that hadn't been his.

The betrayal pierced like a barb through his skin and rage exploded in his chest. Rage, because it was a whole lot easier to feel than the hurt that had troubled him day and night through the long years of his marriage. The knowledge that the man he was and the love he felt had never been enough to keep Lida faithful. He'd never been enough to keep her heart.

He'd be damned if he let another woman do that to him.

Mariah. He may have married the wrong woman, but that didn't mean he'd let her have that kind of power over him. That kind of ability to hurt.

"Nick?" Speak of the she-devil. There she was, soft as an angel in that pure white nightgown, with her black shawl draped over her shoulders.

She moved toward him, and it was as if she called not to him but to his heart. He could feel it lurch in his chest, like an infant's first breath, startling him, warming him, flooding him with feeling, and he knew how the world felt the day the sun was made to first rise and give light to the dark.

He tried to speak, but couldn't say her name. He couldn't find the words to say anything, his chest so full and his heart breaking as she walked through the rain. His anguish didn't touch her. Didn't chill her. Didn't diminish her until she was in his arms, warm and damp all at once, small and powerful. When she touched him, she touched the most essential part of his soul. And if he opened up now to her, accepted her comfort and her love and everything she had to offer, then he'd be laid open completely, every part of him. He'd be more vulnerable than Lida had ever made him. This was the power Mariah had over him.

He could hold her close or push her away. Open himself to heartache or stand alone, on his own two feet, with no comfort and no grace on a night without stars or moonlight to guide him. Just the colorless rain in a night so dark it felt without hope.

Knowing the conclusion he had to make, he tore away from Mariah's embrace and chose the dark. Chose the best path for all of them. Rain sluiced down his face, blinding him, but he kept walking. He didn't stop until Mariah was but a brief shadow against the endless night and his heart was as cold as the wind.

Chapter Ten

All night long Mariah held on to the image of Nick striding away from her in the rain, a solitary figure with wide shoulders set, as unconquerable as the darkness. She'd watched him disappear into the night, becoming one with the distance and shadows. She'd waited for him in the rain for more than an hour before she retreated to the kitchen and finally to her bed. She'd lain awake until it was nearly time to rise for the day without hearing his return.

But in the morning when she'd come downstairs to the dark kitchen, a fire crackled merrily in the stove, newly lit, with the oven lid left ajar to let in air. Nick had done that—he'd lit the fire. He'd been here. That meant he was all right. Relief left her dizzy as she added more wood to the cheerful flames, closed the oven door and dug in the pantry for biscuit makings. She'd been worried about him. He'd been in too much pain last night, staring at the silhouetted gravestones cast against the stormy sky.

She hurt for him. She had felt his pain last night the moment she'd touched him. She'd gone to him like water in a riverbed, pulled by some unseen current, only knowing that there was no other way to go. He'd accepted her, allowed her to sink against his chest and wrap her arms around his sides, to hold him and comfort him. The sorrow inside him felt enormous, and he'd pushed away from her. Moved away. Didn't look back.

Why had he turned away from her? Did any act of comfort hurt him? Was it his grief for Lida that made him break away?

Or did it mean he didn't need comfort from her? She didn't have the faintest notion. She grabbed a big wooden spoon and blended the ingredients well.

"Mornin', Miss Mariah." Jeb studied her warily, as if he still wasn't quite willing to trust her. He was a cautious man. "Mighty good coffee I smell. Suppose I'll pour me a cup."

"Is that a compliment you just paid me?"

"Nope. Why would I go and do somethin' like that for? A man appreciates coffee, is all. It's hot. That's all that matters." He grabbed the pot off the stove. "If you're fishing for praise, then I'd say it's passable."

Passable? Mariah almost believed him until he marched to the lean-to, cursed his stiff back when he knelt to tug on his boots, then let the door slam shut behind him. Taking the coffeepot to the barn with him.

Maybe the coffee was more than passable. That made her smile, just a little, as she wiped out the mixing bowl. Would Jeb get all the way to the stable before he figured out he'd forgotten to take any cups?

Boots drummed up the back steps. There he was. She left the bowl on the worktable and scooped four cups from the upper shelf. One for each of the Gray men already hard at work. They were her family now, and she intended to take care of them whether they liked it or not.

"Nick." She skidded to a stop in her tracks, holding the cups in midair. He was nothing more than a shadowed form in the dark lean-to, but she would know the look of him, the shape of him, the feel of him, anywhere. It was as though their hearts were connected and she could feel his sorrow like it was her own. "Were you out all night?"

"Took a long walk. When I came back, I slept in the barn." He stayed in the shadows, away from the light. "How are my kids?"

"Sleeping soundly last time I checked." She set the cups on the edge of the table. With her hands empty, she didn't know if she should go to him or stay where she was. To touch him and try to comfort him or to leave him alone. "I'd offer you some coffee to warm you up, but your father took the coffeepot."

"Yeah, I saw him. I came in to change. My clothes are wet through."

"Oh, sure. Do you want me to heat some wash water?"

"No. I'll take it cold." He prowled in a wide arc around her, like a panther wary of an adversary, sure of its dominance but not looking for a fight.

The lamplight caught him, showing his hair dark with rain and his wet shirt clinging to his chest. He'd been like this all night? She ached for him and the pain he was in. If she knew how to take the grief from him, she would. Only time would dull the pain, but it would never repair the loss.

How deeply he must have loved Lida to be grieving

her so completely. What a good heart he had to love so. It made Mariah love him even more.

''Cold water'll be fine.'' He grabbed the full pail beneath the pump and turned his back on her. Marched away.

He's hurting, Mariah told herself. That's why he's keeping distance between us. It was perfectly natural. Completely reasonable. She'd married him knowing he was newly widowed and he wasn't ready to love again. Not yet.

All things came in good time, and this would be no different. He wasn't trying to avoid her, she realized. He needed her. He needed to count on her. To rely on her. To know his children were cared for and his house was in order.

That's what he needed from her, for now. And he needed a thousand other small things, kind words and gentle touches and understanding. Her love for him was big enough to wait. Strong enough to shelter him. Patient enough to love him without condition. Until he was ready to love her in return.

She'd vowed before God to love and honor Nick. Love and honor him, she would.

Mariah. Everywhere Nick went, there were reminders of her. His freshly laundered clothes in his bureau, folded with preciseness and care, as Mariah did with everything.

He slipped into the clean dry shirt. He could hear the faint clatter of the stove burner; the clump of wood being placed in the fire. The whistle of the teakettle cutting off as she lifted it from the heat. Those telltale signs that a woman was in the room below him…and that woman was his wife. The one woman he never should have married. The woman he never should have kissed.

He regretted that impulsive action more than anything. His groin pulsed from thinking about the warm velvet heat of her mouth beneath his and how a single kiss had made him hungry for more. For the sight of Mariah in her nightgown all spread out on his bed, her golden hair curling across his pillow, her gazing up at him with those fathomless blue eyes. Surrendering to him as he unbuttoned the tiny round buttons that marched from neckline to waist right between her enticing breasts.

He groaned, aroused, hard as wood from thought and not from the deed of undressing her. He hadn't even undressed her in his mind, hadn't gotten past those damn buttons to the breasts beneath. Look at him. Look how he wanted her. He was weak with it and shaking with it, hurting and confused.

He left his shirt untucked and headed down the hall. The doors to both Georgie's and Joey's rooms were shut tight, and all was quiet within, judging by the sound of it. His son, so burdened with responsibility and grief. His daughter still hurting. He'd made the decision to marry Mariah for their sakes.

Was this all one big mistake? He couldn't shake the feeling it was, and it troubled him down deep. He felt as though he was still up the creek without a paddle and being swept right for that waterfall. If he plunged over the edge, it didn't matter much. But his children…

No, he had to keep them safe. Do what was best for them. But what?

He'd thought Mariah was a solution to his troubles, but now she was another person in his boat, heading down the rapids toward disaster. He didn't know which way to steer them in. Which way to lead his family to safety.

It was a damn bad way for a man to feel. Powerless. Lost. Wishing he'd made smarter decisions.

No, he never should have married Mariah. He couldn't fight that thought as he headed downstairs. As he avoided her in the kitchen by going out the front door.

And it would have worked, too, but he'd left his boots and coat at the kitchen door and had to head back through the parlor.

There she was, looking like sunrise in a new calico work dress, one she must have purchased ready-made from the dressmaker's. Nothing fancy. No, not Mariah. Lida would have charged up a bill large enough to choke a horse with fancy gowns and ribbons and gloves and hats to match. But Mariah, she was too sensible. She'd chosen a light yellow calico with tiny blue rosebuds scattered all over. The only trim was a small lace-edged collar.

She's not Lida, remember that. He stopped to gather what wits he still possessed before he strolled into the kitchen.

"Nick." Mariah turned from the stove, even though he'd hardly made a sound. As if she'd been listening for his approach. "Joey's been invited to Rayna's son's birthday party. I thought I'd take him to town early to pick up a gift at the mercantile."

"Fine."

"Is there anything you need me to pick up for you? I didn't think to ask yesterday." She turned strips of bacon efficiently while she talked, and still looked beautiful doing it.

He saw the woman and not the wife. Why did he want her so much? "Don't worry. If I need something, I'll get it."

He sounded too harsh and he knew it. He could hear his voice boom like thunder.

Mariah stared at him with wide eyes. "Fine. I'll remember that."

She wasn't prickly or sharp-tongued or so proud she set his teeth on edge. She was surprised and sounded a little hurt. Not so tough-skinned, after all.

That made him feel more than terrible as he stalked to the door. Didn't bother to put his boots on first, just grabbed them and headed out the door. The porch steps were damp from last night's downpour and his socks were damp before he took two steps. He stood leaning against the rail tugging one boot on and then the other.

Damn it, what was happening to his life? To the life he hadn't liked but had been used to? Lida and he had gotten so good at their separate lives, there had been only minor hitches from time to time.

But with Mariah... She wasn't at all the way she was supposed to be. She was supposed to be a woman who didn't need him. A woman who didn't make him need. But look at her. He could see her through the window standing at the stove, looking desirable and incredible and sincere. He could feel what she wanted. What she needed. Limitless love and attention and promises of forever.

He wasn't the man to give that to her. To any woman.

Disliking himself for it, he stomped through the

mud, turning his thoughts to the work waiting for him. But the image of Mariah remained burned in his mind.

Mariah ladled the poached eggs onto the platter, listening to the clamor of the men shucking off their jackets and boots. Georgie had woken in a teary mood and Joey still hadn't come down from his room, although she'd called him. Maybe now that the men were here, he'd make an appearance. She considered sending Nick up to fetch him, since it had to be hard for the boy, with his grief for his mother so fresh. It was natural he'd have a hard time seeing another woman at the stove where his mother had cooked breakfast.

She'd need to think of some way to reassure Joey. To let him know she understood. She'd put that problem to the back of her mind and work on it. The right solution would come to her. In the meantime...

"Where's Nick?"

Will glanced up from the table and fidgeted. "Well, uh, he's staying with one of the mares."

"Oh." That probably happened on a ranch. Horses fell ill and needed care. "I'll be sure and set aside a plate for him, so he can come eat when one of you goes to spell him."

"Uh..." Will rubbed his head, looking more uncomfortable. "Fact is, he won't be comin' in at all. Lots of work this morning."

"That's a fact." Pop spoke up while the other brother, the quiet and kind of scary Dakota, lifted one dark brow and shook his head.

Nick wasn't avoiding her. That wouldn't make any sense. He needed his breakfast. But her stomach twisted as she reached for a plate and began to fill it from the stove. She grabbed a second plate and filled it, too, working quick since the men were waiting.

He'd been distant last night and more distant this morning. He hadn't looked at her when he'd taken the pail of cold water to wash with, instead of the warm. Instead of the water she'd offered.

He wasn't used to her taking care of him, that was all. It had to remind him of Lida and the love they shared. That was it. Mariah felt a little better as she handed Jeb the platter of sausage and ham. Nick wasn't rejecting her. He was hurting, and it was her job to help him.

She rescued the toast and stack of French toast from the warmer and put on a fresh pot of coffee to brew since Jeb had clunked the empty pot on the table. She grabbed the plate she'd filled for Nick and grabbed her shawl from the peg by the door.

"Hey, where you goin' with that?" Will rose from his chair. "Uh, you're not takin' that to Nick, are you?"

"Thought I might. He's bound to be hungry." Mariah slung the length of wool over her shoulders, wondering why Will was acting so strange. Then again, he usually did act uncomfortable around her. "I'll be right back."

"Mariah—" Jeb called her name, but she was already out the door, moving forward down the porch stairs when maybe she should have gone back.

She wondered what Jeb had to say with every step she took toward the horse stable. That bad feeling in the pit of her stomach cinched up a notch. Maybe she should have let one of the men bring the plate.

She was too proud to turn around now, so she kept going. Stepping around the mud puddles and into the

serene comfort of the stable. The sweet scent of hay
and the comfortable scent of warm horseflesh were a
pleasant greeting. She traipsed down the main aisle,
looking for a sick horse.

She found her husband, instead. Sitting on a grain
barrel gazing out the back double doors, both open to
a view of the rolling plains and the endless horizon.
The way he sat there, elbows on his knees, face in
his hands, there was a sense of defeat. Of something
terribly wrong.

"Nick?" The horse had died. Maybe with Lida's
death, that was too much to lose. She hated that he
was hurting and rushed toward him.

Until he turned his weary gaze on her. And felt his
dread when he looked at her, saw his wariness written
on his handsome, haggard face. He didn't want to see
her. He looked at the plate heaped with food in her
hands and then turned away, staring hard at the distant
horizon. As if that's where he most wanted to be.

"You might not feel like eating, so I'll leave this."
There was a clunk of the plate as she set it on a nearby
molasses barrel. "Will told me about the horse and
I'm…sorry. That's a sad loss."

He shook his head. "Thanks, Mariah, but the horse
is fine."

"Oh, good." She sounded confused.

Why wouldn't she be? She was doing her best to
be a good wife and all that entailed, and he didn't
want her to be. Nick raked his face with his hands,
soul-weary and out of excuses. He didn't know what
to do to right things. But he wasn't about to lie. "I
just said that because I didn't feel like sitting up to
the table this morning."

"I see."

He was hurting her, damn it, and he hated that. Wished there was a better way, but he wasn't going to pretend. He wasn't going to let her keep thinking… Hell, he didn't really know what she was thinking. Whatever he said, it was going to hurt her. That was the last thing he wanted to do. She leaned against the wall, and if he turned his head a scant inch, he brought her into his side vision.

Oh, the sight of her. It made his chest wrench so hard, it was likely to drop him to the ground. She was a vision in that dress, the same color of a newly risen sun, soft and gentle and glowing. This was the woman who'd been hiding beneath the black shapeless dresses and the stern manner. Not a prickly woman who would make a better housekeeper than a wife, but a vibrant woman of wants and needs.

And he wanted her. He needed her. His teeth ached with it. His bones hurt from it. His soul longed for her with a power that scared him.

Wanting and needing her would be the biggest mistake of his life.

But he wouldn't hurt her. He wouldn't say one word to diminish her.

He had no notion what he was going to do. He only knew he had to do something. He had to stop wanting her. Stop craving her. Stop dreaming of having the right to hold her close and naked, intimate and loving.

He wasn't going to open up the shredded pieces of his heart. He was never going to give up his power to a woman, no matter how strong and kind and beautiful.

"I'm having a tough morning," he told her, instead. "I appreciate the plate of food. It was thoughtful of you."

"I'm taking care of you, the way you take care of me. I've never thanked you for building the morning fire. It's good of you, Nick." Her hand brushed his shoulder. A brief connection that he wanted to reach out and cling to.

But what shelter can there be from the storms of life? Women disappointed you. All he had to do was look around. Pop's marriages had been disasters, the last one running off with a book salesman.

As for his marriage to Lida…

He could still see the empty bed and how the moonlight fell through the window, marking the indentation in the feather tick where Lida's weight had been. The hollow chill in the center of his gut that remained while his mind thought up every reason, every disaster, any other excuse why Lida wasn't in her bed. Except the real one.

And that one no one outside the family knew. The shame tore him apart. Lida's words haunted him, her accusations, her belittling, and the angry names she'd hurled at him when it suited her mood. Barbed weapons that cut deep and made wounds that never healed. He'd never satisfied her. Not materially and not in bed when he'd given her his heart… She hadn't minded telling him exactly how clumsy he was when he'd found her in her lover's bed, a married man who kept a room above his store in town. *You could never satisfy me, Nick, so I found someone who could.…*

No, he was never going to let anyone that close. And with the way he felt about Mariah…the devastation would be worse.

"I need to be alone," he told her. "I'd appreciate it."

She withdrew without a word, and his shoulder ached where she'd touched him. Ached for the soft comfort, for that connection that made him feel.

Her step hesitated at the end of the aisle. He winced, realizing she wasn't going to leave just yet. She had to drag this out, and he couldn't take it. He wanted her. And looking at her would only make that want magnify.

"Nick?"

"Yep."

"If you ever need to talk about Lida, will you let me know? I know you loved her." Mariah waited in the silence that followed while her words echoed in the loft and high rafters above.

Nick didn't answer, so she tried again. "You said we needed to have respect for one another. And friendship. I hope you know you can talk to me. As a...friend."

Another beat of silence seemed to sink her confidence right down to her toes. She was probably assuming too much from this man who was full of sorrow, who looked at her and couldn't help but be reminded of the woman he'd lost.

Sad for him, she turned to go. Whatever it took, she'd take care of him. Leave, if that was best for him. Stay, if it wasn't.

She took one step. Another. Kept going.

He didn't call her back.

He didn't need her. Fine. Then she'd go back to the house, make sure his family got enough to eat, his children were cared for and his house kept clean.

She'd do whatever it took. For Nick. Because she loved him more every day.

Joey crossed his arms over his chest—a perfect imitation of his father, and equally as stubborn—as he stood in his room and glared at her. But it wasn't defiance or hatred in his gaze as he watched her put a stack of shirts on his bureau to put away. It was pain.

"Your pa has the horses hitched and waiting." She smoothed the top shirt on the stack. "Georgie and I are almost ready. I'll see you downstairs in a few minutes."

Joey nodded, wordless. The ache in him was so big it felt as tangible as the floor she stood on and the door she pulled closed. Nick's son. Joey was so like him. The shock of dark hair that rose like a cornstalk out of the center of his head fell forward over his brow, just like his father's. Joey had a brow like Nick's, a high and wide forehead, a finely shaped blade of a nose and a dimple in the middle of his chin.

A strange warmth, like the one she felt for Georgie, burned in her chest. This was her stepson. *Hers,* whether he liked it or not. She was going to take care of him, too. She was going to take care of all of them.

If they let her. She stopped at the hall window to gaze out at the lush green prairie below. There was Nick, his shirt stripped off in the sun, bare-chested while he worked, his head bent, his Stetson hiding his face, his muscles straining as he swung a sledgehammer. What a man.

Her blood turned to melted butter, and she grabbed the windowsill for support. She'd never seen a man

without his shirt on before. Never. And the sight…
why, Nick was something to behold. He was bronzed
by the sun from his head to the waistband of his
Levi's. When he lifted the sledgehammer, every muscle in his broad back and in his iron-hewn arms
flexed. Like poetry, he moved with pleasing precision,
a functional beauty that made desire curl hard in her
abdomen.

How would it feel to touch him? Would his skin
be hot as the sun? Slightly rough against her fingertips? She longed to find out. *He's your husband. You
can touch him if you want.*

If only she could. She closed her eyes. Her need
for him pounded hard as waves on the shore, lifting
her up, letting her down. *Please, one day let Nick fall
in love me.*

It took all her willpower to tear away from the sight
of Nick at work. Harder still to turn from the only
window in the house that had such a good view of
him. That husband of hers was mighty fine. Mighty
fine, indeed. It was going to be hard not to think of
him all afternoon long.

Georgie's bedroom door was wide open, giving a
view of the girl seated at her miniature table in a
matching ladder-back chair. There were several items
lined up on the tabletop. A nightgown. A handful of
colorful hair ribbons. A few shiny copper pennies.
Her rag doll. There was a satchel at Georgie's feet,
open. The girl worked carefully and methodically,
putting each item into the bag so it was just right
before reaching for the next.

Mariah knelt in front of Georgie, the satchel between them. "Why are you packing?"

"Cuz we're goin' to town." Georgie bent forward,

her golden curls tumbling like sunshine everywhere. With her hand full of pennies, she carefully considered where to put them.

"Why do you need your satchel in town?"

"Just 'cuz." Georgie moved aside a stuffed bear and lowered the pennies to the bottom of the bag. They clinked together, a strange and tinny sound.

That was how Mariah's heart felt. Georgie still wanted to run off? Mariah tried not to take it personally. Georgie's heart had been broken long before Mariah had come to live here.

The girl grabbed her pile of hair ribbons and dropped them in her lap. "How long is heaven away from town?"

"It's farther than any horse can travel."

"How 'bout your ox?" The satin strips were twisted and knotted, so she took time to pull a red ribbon from the tangle and smoothed it over her knee.

"It's too far for an ox." Mariah rubbed a tear from Georgie's cheek with the pad of her thumb.

The child said nothing after that. She straightened each hair ribbon, until all dozen were in a neat pile on her knee. Satisfied, she laid them gently on the stuffed bear's stomach, where they would ride well on the trip to heaven.

"We don't have much time. We've got to be in town soon." Mariah reached with her fingertips to grab the wool throw from the foot of the girl's bed. "Would it be all right if I helped you pack?"

"You got any cookies?" Tears trailed down her cheeks as she watched Mariah fold the blanket. "I'm gonna need cookies 'cuz I'll get hungry."

"We'll pick up any food you're going to need in town. We can stop by the bakery."

Georgie nodded somberly.

"Let's see what you have." Mariah inspected the contents of the bag. "Let's put your nightgown right here. You've got something to sleep in. You're going to need fresh underthings and another dress."

Mariah tugged open the top drawer of the small bureau and withdrew the small garments. "And a sweater. The nights are still chilly sometimes. You may need your best shoes."

Mariah loaded her arm with every heavy thing she could think of, including a few books. "It's too bad you're going to leave. I'm really going to miss you."

Georgie sniffed.

"Your brother is sure going to be sad you've gone. And your pa. I bet he sits down and cries when he finds out you're gone. We're going to be awful sad without you."

Georgie sniffled harder.

The satchel was small and was quickly filled, and Mariah zipped it shut. "There. You're packed. Are you ready?"

"Y-yeah."

"Is there anything else you want to take? Anything you'll miss?"

Georgie's eyes filled with big silver tears. "No."

"Oh, I know. We forgot your boots. You may need to cross a few creeks on the way. We'll remember to grab those when we're downstairs." Gently, Mariah took Georgie's hand. "C'mon, grab your satchel and let's go."

"Okay." Tears shone in her eyes as she stood. She gulped hard, to keep from crying. Her hand curled around the big strap.

"C'mon." Mariah took a step toward the door, holding tight to the girl's other hand.

"I can't." Those tears fell like anguish. "It's too heavy. It won't come up!" Sobs shook her fragile shoulders. "I miss my mama."

"I know. I'm sure she misses you, too."

Georgie gave another tug on the much too heavy satchel. "She left me. She left. She left."

"Poor baby." Mariah pulled the girl into her arms and held her tight.

Frail arms wrapped around Mariah's neck and clutched tightly. Georgie's little fingers bit into the skin at Mariah's nape, but she didn't care. The pain was nothing compared to the fierce emotion consuming her. The intense need to keep this child safe, to hold her forever, to never let her go.

"What's goin' on in here?" Nick's baritone boomed into the room.

"Pa!" Georgie leaped out of Mariah's arms and ran to her father.

"Guess you packed again. I sure hope you're gonna stay with us, princess." Nick scooped her up against his big bare chest and cradled his daughter tenderly. Protectively. He pressed a fatherly kiss into the crown of her head.

Georgie's sobs began to ease.

"Maybe that worked. Maybe this will be the last time she does this. Thanks, Mariah."

"I didn't do anything. Just filled a satchel."

"A satchel she can't leave with." He cradled Georgie's head in his big hand, holding her as tenderly as a newborn to his chest.

What would it be like to have Nick's child? The single wish surprised her. The longing came to life, filling her with a sharp yearning. She had two step-children she cared about very much. She would be happy taking care of them for as long as they needed her, say another ten or twelve years. But the idea of having another child…

A baby. Her very own baby, hers and Nicks. Maybe more than one, as the years passed. Who knew what the future held? Maybe a large family for the woman who'd never had a real one. The yearning within her expanded, filling her with dreams of children yet to be born, with names yet to be found. The dream of her and Nick happy and in love, and the new life that came from that love.

"I'm glad I married you, pretty lady." Nick reached out with his free hand and hauled her against the side of his bare chest. Bare and hot and brown from the sun…

Mariah closed her eyes, drinking in the wonder of coming against his naked chest. Desire coiled tight deep within her, and she ignored it. Just held him tight. Breathed in the pleasant scent of his salty male skin. "I'm glad I married you, too. So very glad."

His arm came around her, holding her against him. Georgie's sobs silenced and her tears dried.

Hope. It was all around them.

Hope and love.

More grateful than she could find the words to say, Mariah kissed Nick's chest, right over the dependable beat of his heart.

His fingers curled around her nape, holding her. Holding on.

Nick. Mariah thought of nothing else all afternoon. When she chatted with Rayna, shopped and later met with Betsy at the house in town, Nick was in the back of her mind if not in the forefront. The sight of him working bare-chested in the field, with the sunlight caressing his brown skin. Or the image of him standing in Georgie's bedroom, cradling her in his steely arms, protecting her, comforting her, a man made even stronger because of his tenderness.

Nick hadn't come to supper. Will had some other excuse, and this time Mariah didn't rush out to find her husband and force food on him. If he needed time and space, she would give that to him. Remembering how hard he'd hugged her in Georgie's room, remembering the need she felt inside him, made it easier. Nick needed her. That was all that mattered.

Clink. The sound of the plate striking the edge of the basin startled her out of her thoughts. The evening kitchen was pleasantly quiet around her, steeped in shadows, the lamp on the counter casting enough light to work by. The murmur of the children's voices rose and fell in an upstairs room, vibrating through the floorboards, where they played a game of cards with their uncles.

A feeling of contentment filled her. This married life was nothing compared to what she'd thought it would be. Somehow she'd thought it would be easier, not the work, but the people part of it. Like a well run Ladies' Aid meeting.

Fine, she'd been wrong about the depth of marriage life, of being a wife and a mother. She had only her own childhood to judge by. The cold distance of her parents' marriage shocked her now. Never, under any circumstance, would her father have held her when she cried. No, he was more likely to scold her into silence, if not raise a hand to her. Never would he have cradled his wife to his chest, with need in his heart and in his touch.

The only thing her father had ever cradled was a whiskey bottle.

What a gift she'd been given with this new life. The ring on her hand, the vows she'd made and the pattern of her days taking care of these people. Of living with them. And coming to love them a little bit more each day. Her chest ached with the power of it, her poor heart as cracked as an iced-over pond facing the spring thaw. Fissures and fractures and wide broken spaces that let in the sunshine and the darkness, the warmth and the cold.

The love and the pain. Mariah wasn't sure she cared for it, feeling this way wasn't the most comfortable thing, but she was grateful. She could have lived her entire life in her house that rattled with emptiness, dusting knickknacks and tatting dollies and never have known what it was like to want to love a man so much it was in every breath. In every heartbeat. In every thought.

Jeb's hitching gait padded down the hall and into the shadowed corner of the kitchen. Mariah slipped the plate into the rinse water and plunged her hands back into the suds. Jeb's dislike for her was at least less noticeable since she'd made his coffee the way he liked it.

She kept her attention on scrubbing every inch of the plate, getting it nice and clean. She didn't want to look up to see the pained look on Jeb's face. The look that said he thought Nick had made a mistake in choosing her. It hurt, but she'd do her best by Jeb regardless of his opinion of her.

"Would you like me to put on some coffee? The water's hot in the kettle for tea."

"My sweet tooth's troublin' me. Thought I might want some of those baked goods you picked up in town." Jeb regarded her with caution, as if she were a poisonous snake coiled to strike and he wasn't looking to be bit.

"Good idea. I should set the box out." She flicked the soap bubbles off her fingertips and dried her hands on the nearby towel, but Jeb had marched right past her.

"I'll take care of it, ma'am."

Surely dealing with Nick's family would get easier. Right? Her stomach was a tight ball when she turned back to her work. The children's voices rose in glee a few minutes after Jeb ambled upstairs with the baker's box full of iced cookies.

Cookies she'd let Georgie pick out. Any kind. Until the box was full. Mariah had paid for the treat out of her own money. She and Nick hadn't even spoken about the practicalities of money and getting her name on the store accounts in town. Somehow that hurt, and she didn't know why.

She rinsed the last plate and set it on the board to drain. As she reached for the first pan, she felt a sensation prickle at the top of her spine. A tingle of awareness a second before the back door opened.

Nick. She could feel him as if he were a part of her. How could that be? It made no sense. Never, in all of her women's clubs and groups she'd attended over the years, had any one of the members spoken about this connection between a man and a woman. Not only sexual, not merely romantic. Something different. Something more.

The round curve of her left shoulder burned and, sure enough, when Nick crossed the dark room to her, that was the exact place where he placed his hand. A welcome weight that made her shine inside, where she was dark without him.

"Sorry I missed supper." He spoke in her ear and she shivered. "That probably makes more work for you."

"Sure. I had to dish up a plate and put it in the warmer. I'm exhausted from the strain of it."

"I appreciate the sacrifice." His chuckle lashed through her and sank deep like a hook, binding her to him. Her hair caught on his whisker-stubbled jaw as his arms snaked around her waist from behind. "You are sure a sight for weary eyes, ma'am, lookin' mighty fine in that dress."

"Really?"

"Yep. You're the most beautiful woman in the room."

"I'm the only woman in the room."

"Who has ever been in this room," he corrected, and the whisper of sensation across her temple had to be a kiss, just the hint of it. He released her, walking away casually, as if reaching for her had been the most natural thing on earth.

"Sit down, let me get that for you." The pots needed to soak, and she wanted to spend time with her husband. "I've got hot water for tea?"

"Perfect." Nick eased into a chair with a sigh. "Damn, I'm tired. Took all day to get that section of the fence repaired. If you can trust gossip, then the stud I'd give my eyeteeth to have will be comin' up for sale at the next county auction."

"The one your father mentioned?"

"Yup." Nick leaned back in his chair, exhausted to the bone. So sore he wondered if he could get back on his feet again. "The stud's as wild as they come, but he's got breeding. His daddy was one of the best cutters in the territory. I'm busting my back trying to get a corral done in time that'll hold him. Did Joey behave better today?"

Mariah stiffened. "He tried hard. It's going to take him time to accept me."

"You didn't answer my question."

She closed the warmer door and swept toward him through the light and into the shadows, the lamplight clinging to her like mist in the morning air. "Joey is doing fine, considering what's happened. Losing one mother and gaining a stepmother almost immediately can't be easy."

She set the plate in front of him, heaped with thick slices of roast, potatoes seasoned in their skins and gleaming with melted butter, a half dozen of her biscuits that were so damn fluffy it could make a man get down on his knees to thank her. A pile of green beans mixed with onions and bacon, just the way he liked them.

She returned with a cup of gravy and a plate of tomatoes sliced and sugared.

All that she'd done for him, and now she was steeping his tea. As bright as the moonlight, as gentle as the night air. He wasn't used to being treated like this.

"I'll steep a cup of tea for me, if you want company." She gazed at him through her lashes, the question sounding casual, but it was more.

He was no fool. He knew what she was asking. And truth be told, he was tired, he was sore, he was heartsick and she made all of it go away. "Sure. I've gotten used to eating a late supper alone. Don't much like it."

She brought the light with her, the lamp from the worktable, the flame flickering on the wick as she set it on the table. Her hands were small and soft and... *Don't go thinking like that, man.* He stared at his plate, concentrating on cutting the slices of roast beef, instead of the way the light danced across the soft shape of her—her hair, her face, her throat, her breasts...

He stared harder at the potatoes. They possibly might taste better with gravy. Yep, that's what he needed. That rich thick gravy Mariah made....

Her skirts whispered as she took the chair at his side. So close he could feel her body heat on his skin, although they were not touching.

"I helped Betsy today. There's a lot she has to learn about taking over my business."

Mariah started talking with that incredible mouth of hers. No, he wasn't thinking about her mouth. About how incredible those satin-soft lips had tasted. How the brush of her mouth to his made his blood heat and stirred to life a need inside of him he wasn't sure he could control.

"...and the house, I think it would be better for her to live in town. Since she's been widowed, she's been living with her folks..."

He ate, but he didn't taste the delicious roast she'd seasoned and the biscuits that melted on his tongue. Her voice vibrated through him like a string on a fiddle plucked hard and left to resonate. Her mouth was soft and supple and knew just how to fit against his.

He wanted her mouth more than any single thing in this county. He was tired and aching, inside and out, and he'd done nothing but think about her all day. With every swing of the hammer. Every beat of the ax into wood. Mariah. Seeing her in the windows as she moved through the house. Watching her drive off in the surrey with his children. Knowing he could trust her to be where she said and do what she promised. Mariah might be wearing new dresses and wearing her hair down, but she was still the same inside. And he wanted her. The way a man wants to love his wife. Body and soul, complete possession.

No good could come from going down that path. He knew it. But that didn't stop him from wanting. From needing.

Her hand covered his, a touch of understanding. He didn't need to say the words. It was as if she could read his silence. Without a sound, she stood, withdrawing only to circle around behind him. The brush of her fingertips skimmed the back of his neck where tired muscles had kinked into a painful knot.

"You worked hard today." There was a smile in her voice. Her skirts rustled and her mouth brushed where her fingers had been. The heated velvet of her kiss made him forget all about his aching muscles. "Feel better?"

"Yeah," he croaked. His throat had seized up. His lungs stopped working. He closed his eyes, the meal in front of him forgotten, waiting, tingling, quivering, for her next kiss.

There. Soft silk, the outline of her lips on his flesh. Hot and tender, and he fisted his hands to keep from leaping off the chair and hauling Mariah into his arms.

''Did you like that?''

She sounded so uncertain. Completely unaware of her power over him. She wasn't trying to manipulate him. This was Mariah, straightforward and dependable and as steady as the sun. She might not be the wife he'd envisioned, but she was the one he'd always dreamed of. The one who seemed to know what he needed before he did. The woman who could make him feel again after he was certain his heart had died right along with his faith in women.

Her fingertips waltzed between the vertebra in his neck. Twirled slow and sensual in the tight muscles where his shoulders met. Her touch was like magic, replacing pain with pleasure. Her kiss to his neck, the curve of his shoulder, the hollow behind his ear, was like faith newly given.

He wanted her. With everything he was. Every bit of his being. Every inch of his body. He was hard and hungry and had been celibate for over five long years. He bounded out of his seat, blind with need, kicked the chair aside and hauled Mariah hard against him. She fell against him with a gasp of surprise and a smile of delight. He kissed that smile. Kissed her hot mouth that molded to his as if she were made for him. Maybe she was.

She melted against him, and he cupped a hand at her hip, holding her to the part of him that was hard and growing harder. He wanted her. He knew it wasn't wise, wasn't smart. He was probably making another huge mistake he was going to regret, but Mariah's kiss was like a poison in his body, taking over, making him crazy and weak and shaking with a desire so strong, there was no logic.

There was only the sweet taste of her tongue as he

sucked the tip of it into his mouth. He needed the soft comfort of her love and her body the way the earth needed the sun. He ran his hand over her throat, along her collarbone, down her arm and up her side, his thumb curving over the rise and the peak of her breast. Her nipple pebbled beneath the pad of his thumb. He groaned, shaken to the soul by this proof that she wanted him. The same way he wanted her.

He kissed her deep, cupping both hands at her hips, rocking her against his arousal, hard and throbbing. The soft curve of her stomach made him crazy, but he kissed her slow and deep, fighting for control. He had to stay in control. Mariah was a maiden, and this was new to her. He gritted his teeth, holding on, overcome at the pleasure as they rocked together. He needed her. Only her.

Those buttons marching from her collar to her waist were troubling him. If he just released a few of them, then he could kiss his way down her throat to the swell of her breasts. When he kissed the sensitive curve beneath her chin, she moaned in pleasure. Her fingers curled in his shirt.

"Like that, huh?" he murmured against her throat.

"Nope. I hate it. I'm just submitting like a good wife."

"Teasing me, are you?" He blew gently against the dip at the column of her throat and she shivered. He laved the spot with his tongue then blew again.

He felt the pleasure shiver through her and into him.

"Fine. If you don't want me to kiss you, I'll stop."

"No! Don't you dare." She grabbed his head and held him there, offering him her throat and her breasts. And more. So much more.

Tenderness left him dizzy as he popped the top buttons of her dress with one hand. The fabric fell away to reveal a lace-edged corset cupping full creamy breasts that were so beautiful they couldn't be real. Just a dream. Just as she was.

"Mariah," he rasped her name, and he didn't care if his voice was raw with his feelings. He felt like a man who'd been lost in a distant and vast desert for an entire decade and here was his first sight of home. This woman was what his scarred heart had been craving, and she was the only one who could make the pieces whole.

She tugged down the fabric, loosening stays so he could free her from the garment. Lush, rose-tipped breasts filled his hands and he feasted on them, taking one nipple into his mouth and then the other. He loved the way she arched up, making little sounds of pleasure deep in her throat. Her fingers wound through his hair, holding him to her breasts.

What are you doing, Gray? He tore away, breathing hard, blind with need.

It took all his willpower to fold the scraps of lace over her breasts, and every drop of control he had to fasten the buttons and step away.

Embarrassed by his weakness, he didn't know what to say. Was thankful for the shadows that hid his face from hers.

"Good night." He didn't know what else to say. How to explain his desire for her.

And why he'd married her.

Mariah was a good woman, and he wasn't going to hurt her. He wasn't going to let her see the man he truly was.

"You sleep well, all right?" He kissed her nose,

tenderness welling up like water in a well, rising higher and higher, pure and deep. "I'll see you in the morning."

"Sure."

"I'll take the plate with me." He grabbed the flatware and his food and strode away, steady and strong as he always did.

Except this time he took her heart with him.

Mariah stood in the shadows a long while, waiting. Hoping that he'd come back for her.

He didn't.

Chapter Eleven

Mariah stared at the ceiling. She couldn't sleep. Her mind kept replaying what happened in the kitchen over and over again. It wasn't where he touched or how he touched her.

It was the way he made her feel, as if by the caress of his fingertips and the brush of his lips he could call forth some magic spell that made her feel how he loved her. And made her heart open like the wild roses that cover the prairie come summer, from hibernating root to the first tender bud.

She wanted to know that kind of love. The kind that felt ready to blossom in her heart. It hurt, the thought of waiting. And what about Nick? He was hurting. He was still hurting. She knew it. She could feel it as steady as the night all around her, in every beat of her pulse through her veins.

He wasn't all right. He'd reached out to her tonight. He'd needed her. She wanted to help him take away the pain like a soothing balm that heals a wound. Not that she was presumptuous enough to think she could heal the grief from a ten year marriage, but she could offer him all he needed to find comfort. To find the path back to being able to love again, with a whole heart.

She listened to the eaves creak in the wind. The sounds of the night deepened. Nick had reached out to her with his need tonight. Should she take the risk of reaching out to him? Would he pull her close, or send her away? Love her, or reject her?

Fear of his rejection kept her in bed, clutching her blanket in the dark.

He'd never felt so alone and it hurt like a thousand blades in his flesh, imbedded deep. Nick didn't know how to fix it besides heading downstairs to the liquor cabinet and drowning his pain with whiskey. A temporary solution, but anything was better than this unrelenting pain.

And it was stupid, too. The real solution was two doors down the hall from him—Mariah, lying asleep and peaceful in the dark. Probably wearing the white nightgown that flowed around her like a dream. It *was* a dream to think he could be with her, have the right to unfasten the tiny buttons at the collar and help himself to heaven.

He closed his eyes. He was rock-hard. Blood thrummed through his groin, making his shaft so engorged there was no way to ignore it. Mariah had aroused him completely. Unlike he'd ever been before.

Why did he want her so much? The sensation of her kiss remained a whisper on his lips. The heat of her skin, the warm weight of her breasts, the little sounds of pleasure she made…

Remembering made desire explode through him, leveling his willpower like a dynamite blast, leaving him shaken and shattering any chance he had of falling asleep.

He tossed the sheet off his restless, aroused body and marched in his drawers to the window. A quick shove against the stubborn frame and humid air breezed over him. Storm clouds nudged at the sickle moon, casting a half darkness over the land. Over his life.

It's a sign, man. A storm was brewing if he went against every shred of common sense he had, headed down the hall, flung open Mariah's door and claimed her as his wife, his woman, his love. His. Forever and ever, until the end of time, until not even death could part them.

That's how he wanted her, with his entire body, his broken heart, his wounded soul. Every part of him ached for the haven only she could give him.

And what good would come of that? His carnal hunger for Mariah was proof enough that he'd lost control of his cool detachment, the distant and convenient marriage he'd planned on. He'd blown that plan to bits, and now it was dust. Dead and gone and buried. And why? Because he didn't know he'd want her like this. With a wanting that could make him weak and strong, incomplete and whole.

He was tired of being alone. Of being broken and always in charge and always strong. Life was a tough place, and it wore on a man. Even a brave man. He did his best, heaven knew, but he felt like a man alone in the storm with lightning flashing and thunder clapping and rain on its way. With no one to care. No one to hold close and lose himself in and love the night through until he was strong enough to meet the new day. A man changed for the better.

The wind swept his face and he watched the storm gather to the west. If the wind held, the storm would bypass them, hitting a good distance north. A distant thread of lightning stabbed into the black sky. He felt as dark as the night. Without hope, as if the light was being slowly snuffed out of him, the way the clouds blotted out the stars, leaving only a fathomless void in their place.

Mariah. He turned toward the door before it opened. Moved toward her before he saw her standing in the threshold, her hair down. She was angelic temptation in her pure white nightgown, the buttons undone to show the upper swell of her breasts. She was a vision of beauty, a dream and too good for the likes of him. He reached for her anyway, pushed the door shut and pulled her into the room and into his arms where she belonged.

He wasn't alone anymore. He hugged her to his chest, loving how she felt against him, soft and female. Everything about her, her soft hair catching on his unshaven jaw, her hands splayed against the planes of his back, her breasts a pillowed heat against his chest, the slight curve of her stomach against his hard shaft. She had to feel it, and didn't back away. She tilted her face toward his, and he needed no more invitation.

His mouth covered hers. She was velvet heat and untried passion and sweet woman, and she moaned. Her fingers dug into his back as she held on, surrendering to his kiss. His possession. She was so incredible, so tender. He needed her so much. Overwhelmed, hungry for her and only her, he cupped her face with his hands. Kissed her hard, taking the comfort she offered. The sweet comfort that burned like a lone candle in a dark night.

"I'm so glad you came." He crushed her to him, burying his face in her hair.

"I wasn't sure if you would want me."

"Of course I want you, Mariah. There's never been a question about that." The choice was out of his hands.

It was as if this moment had been written in stone long ago. As if fate knew at this moment in time he'd need her more than air. He couldn't take the pain, the sadness or the loneliness one moment longer. He'd been alone for years, unwanted.

And here Mariah was, come to him, wanting him.

And he was going to have her. It wasn't because she was a woman and available and naked beneath her nightgown that fueled his need. It was Mariah. Her touch. Her beauty. Her comfort. He needed her now, before he thought about it, before common sense showed up and intervened. And if he didn't, he feared the loneliness tearing him apart would never end.

The scant starlight painted her in shades of silver as he took her hand in his and led her to his bed. Right where he'd always wanted her. From the first moment he'd cast his gaze on her in the schoolroom when he'd been sixteen and new to town, he'd thought she was an angel. And the natural progression of that attraction could not be stopped. Not by her father then and not by his discipline now.

He shouldn't do this. It was wrong and he knew it, to want her like this. To need her with everything in him. The bed ropes groaned as she sat on the edge of the feather tick, angel and woman, seductress and healer. She knew what he wanted. It was plain to see the hard buds of her nipples against the thin cotton nightgown. And the knowledge in her eyes, dark with desire, as she pulled her nightgown over her head. The disappearing starlight saw a woman naked and perfect and impossible to resist.

He went to her like a cougar on a hunt and kissed her hard. So she knew she was his. His wife, his love—and no other man's. Ever. He crushed her hair in his fist, holding her mouth to his as he laid her down on the bed. She stretched out willingly, all soft, inviting woman. Vulnerable and naked and shivering with need.

"I want you to love me," she said into his kiss.

"I already do," he whispered against her lips. Then he hauled off his drawers and tossed them into the dark.

Unable to turn back, knowing she didn't want him to, he fit his knee between hers and opened her gently. Her soft thighs parted and he stretched out over her, never breaking their kiss. He settled onto her and knew he'd come home. Lying with her this way was exquisite. Like finding heaven and hell all in the same moment. The woman he needed to heal his soul would be the one thing that could destroy him.

"Oh, yes," she moaned as his hand curved down the length of her throat, rising into his touch like a cat being stroked. The starlight on her face showed a woman lost in sensation, needing his love.

Did she hurt this way, too?

"Mariah." Her name was a broken sound.

Like whiskey to flame, he ignited and burned. Touched her and kissed her and loved how her breathing changed. How her body softened, grew fuller, more welcoming. How she arched into his touch, moaned for it, became consumed by it. She cradled his head as he suckled her breasts and kissed them. She lifted up to his kisses on her stomach and along each rib. Sighed when his fingers skidded along the sensitive skin of her inner thighs. He could feel her leg muscles tighten, unsure.

"Just trust me," he whispered against her belly, glancing up the length of her stomach and over the beautiful peaks of her breasts to her lovely face.

"I've never…"

"I know, but I have." He knew that would make her smile, and it did. He had to reassure her. He had to make this count. He wouldn't hurt her for the world.

"Typical of you, Nick. I should have known you'd be twice as arrogant when you had me naked in your bed."

"Not arrogant. Lucky. I'm one fortunate man to have you for my wife."

It was as if he'd torn through her rib cage, plunged inside and grabbed hold of her heart. Tears burned in Mariah's eyes. "I'm lucky, too. You're a good man."

"If I were a good man, I wouldn't be doing this. Taking advantage of you."

He looked tortured, his brow furrowed, his eyes darkened. His heart ached. She could feel it. She reached out to place her hand there, in the center of his chest, over the pain.

"You're not taking, Nick. I'm giving."

He closed his eyes. His throat worked. She could feel the struggle inside him. See it in the sharp way he breathed. In the tendons cording in his neck. Then, decision made, he grabbed her jaw, and kissed her with a tender passion that melted every bone in her body. His hands parted her thighs, leaving her open and exposed and more vulnerable than she'd ever been. She fell back on the bed, closed her eyes and gasped.

His thumb traced the crease between her extreme upper thigh and eased upward. White-hot pleasure spilled into her where he was touching her. He wasn't only caressing her body, but also the center of her, the core of her, and she opened to him like a spring flower to the morning sun. Eager. Defenseless. Hungry. *This* is what the women in her clubs had talked about. This liquid pleasure. This heartbreaking thrill.

She never wanted it to end. Her eyes drifted shut, her hips arched, lifting her into the palm of his hand. His touch warmed her like the midsummer sun. Stirred to life feelings so dormant she'd thought them dead. Her chest ached with it, her soul hurt with it. She clung to Nick's steely arms as he came to her, easing his weight onto his elbows, his big, hard, male body on hers. She opened to him, accepting his open-mouthed kisses, welcoming the first hard nudge of him into her body.

She gasped at the intrusion. A push of hot steel that did not yield. She was going to break apart, not just her body, but her heart. It was too much, this first thrust, the amazing presence of him within her. It hurt, but not the way she thought it would. It hurt in her heart. She felt as if she were unraveling. It was too much. Her body twined around his, open and clinging and craving him like winter dreams of the sun, and she was afraid. Afraid to let him into her heart. She was afraid to love him wholly and truly. What if she wasn't enough?

''Trust me, sweetheart.'' He pressed his forehead

to hers, a tender comfort. Kissed the tip of her nose, a gentle touch. "I'll take good care of you."

"You always do."

His kiss was a promise, caring and true. He wouldn't hurt her. She trusted him. Whatever came from this, whether she disappointed him or not, she wanted to know this man's love. To feel him deep inside her, to hold him in the greatest intimacy. He was a steady pressure against her tightness, and she let go, opening to him, releasing the last shred of her fear.

"That's right," he murmured against her mouth. "Are you okay?"

"Great." She choked on the tears in her throat. Opening more. Letting the hard iron of him sink deep until he was wedged so completely inside her neither of them could move.

"Still doin' okay?" His gaze searched hers.

"Y-yes." She leaned her forehead into the hollow of his throat so she wouldn't have to look at him.

This was too much, this joining, being stretched around him. It was too much pleasure, too much sensation, too much emotion in her heart that felt as if it was breaking. How could being in love with him shatter her heart?

He pulsed inside her, that hardness thrumming against her, stretching her more. Amazingly, she pulsed around him, too, a pleasure so sweet and painful it brought tears to her eyes.

"Let me see you, pretty lady."

She could no longer hide. He would look upon her face and see all that she felt for him. Every scrap of love. Every bit of devotion. He would see her heart.

How could she let him? He didn't love her, not yet. He wasn't free of his past.

"C'mon, beautiful." His thumb grazed her cheek, a tender request.

She could see the dark pool of his eyes in the shadowed darkness. She could feel the intense pull as he studied her. Exposed and wide open, she trembled deep, from the outside in.

He moved, stroking away and thrusting home. A purely physical act that wasn't physical at all. It was so much more as she held him inside her. They trembled together. A curve of a smile touched his mouth as their gazes met and locked. He didn't look away as he stroked again, harder this time, withdrawing only to return.

Incredible. She thrummed with it, felt wild and calm at once. His forehead met hers and he stayed, holding inside her. She was so full of him, overwhelmed by him. He filled her senses. His hardness, his strength, his heat, his breathing, his weight, his kiss. She couldn't seem to breathe, so she clung to him, feeling as if she were ready to shatter apart and lose herself.

All she felt was him. The man he was, good and true. He thrust again, driving unbearable pleasure straight through her. She clung to him, helpless, and everything within her stilled. She buried her face in the hollow of his throat, overwhelmed, feeling the cracks in her heart widen. She was breaking, falling, afraid. She held on, feeling his kiss to her brow, his touch at her nape. He cradled her tenderly as he rocked them beyond pleasure and into something else.

I love you, Nick. She loved him more than anything. More than her life. She could feel his face in her hair, kissing her as they came together again and again, slow and tender and incredible. He tipped her face to his and kissed her deeply. Tender as his lips played with hers. So incredibly tender. She could feel his affection for her, hidden quietly in his heart. Could he feel hers?

They made love as if they had all the time in the world. Wanting nothing else but each other. There was only the two of them, bound together, close…so very close. Mariah cried out as he set a faster rhythm, thrusting hard and deep. Surprised how the intense rush of pleasure moved through her into him and back to her. Tears filled her eyes as she broke apart inside, shattering into a thousand pieces, in a huge wave of sharp pleasure that decimated the wall of ice around her heart. That left her open completely to him as he moved inside her, driving so deep their hearts touched.

"Mariah." He said her name with a shiver, sighing hard as his back stiffened and he lost control.

She held him tight and accepted the hot rush of his seed. Tenderness raged through her, and kissing him wasn't enough. Holding him like this didn't bring her close enough. She felt broken and whole. Lost and found.

He collapsed, his face buried in her hair, so vulnerable. Mariah kissed his temple, so tender. She ran her fingertips over his neck to the crown of his head, gently. Her body thrummed around his thickness still inside her. She was full of him, her heart aching from loving so deeply. She hugged him while he rested. Kissed the shell of his ear and loved how he shivered in response. He was hers now. Her man. Her love.

"We're joined forever, beauty, just forever," he mumbled as he climbed back onto his elbows.

He thrust hard, driving deep, so good. His hand settled on her hip, showing her how to rock with him. How to increase their pleasure. So incredible. How she loved this man. She felt wild with it, calm with it, accepting his kisses, giving more of her heart. Nick was amazing, such a man. And she tried to keep her heart open, to accept all he wanted to give her. It was more than sex now, a different kind of togetherness, and Mariah held him inside her body and inside her heart, letting him in where she was most vulnerable. She loved him. That much.

He was touching her face, talking to her, gazing into her eyes to her soul. There was love for him there, too, that deep down. It hurt too much and felt too much, and she hid her face in his shoulder and held on tight. She was overwhelmed by her love for him. There were his strong arms around her and his kiss in her hair as he rocked them both, hard and gentle. They came together and he emptied into her, more than his body, all he was. She felt the depth of his love for her. As deep as hers was for him.

His arms came around her, cuddling her close, holding her to his heart. She held him in hers, grateful in the contented silence that settled between them.

So, this is what love is. She pressed kisses along the outer curve of Nick's neck and along the crest of his shoulder. His skin was damp with sweat and tasted salty and wonderful. Her heart ached, strangely full.

She didn't know love could make you new.

"Are you all right, sweetheart?" he mumbled into her hair.

She nodded, too happy to speak.

He kissed her forehead, infinitely tender. It was a kiss he meant. She could feel it.

He loved her.

She held him tight. *I love you, too.*

"Is it all right if I stay here inside you?" His palm stroked over the side of her head, tender and possessive.

Nice. She nodded again, snuggling against him. He was hers. Hers to love. Hers to touch. Hers to kiss if she wanted to. Just to prove it, she stroked a kiss across the underside of his chin.

"Hmm, you don't want this to end, do you?" He smiled down at her lazily.

"Does it have to?" Was he going to love her again? Desire curled strong and hot within her, and she felt him swell inside her. Tenderly, she kissed him again.

"Mariah, you don't know what you're doing." He tensed, his hand freezing on her hip.

"I do now." She was sheer seduction, in the way real love was, as she caressed the curve of his jaw with her lips.

Desire ripped through him with the fury of a cyclone's leading wind, and Nick fought for control. Fought to hold on. He didn't want to. It was wrong, but he was already hard, already thrusting. Mariah's head rolled back and he caught it in his hands. He cradled her while she moaned in the pleasure they made together. Moving as one heart, one soul, with only their love to guide them on this bleak night as the starlight faded and wind tapped against the siding.

He held on to her and let the darkness take him.

The bed shifted and Mariah drifted awake. For a second she was disoriented and then she realized she was in Nick's bed. Alone. The rustling she heard was him as he pulled on his trousers. "Are you all right?"

"The storm's kickin' up." He sounded grim as his buckle jingled. "Got to keep an eye out. Looks like lightning's heading this way."

"Will that be a problem for the livestock?"

"The cattle can get spooked and stampede. You stay here warm and snug." He leaned toward her in the pitch dark, his presence a warmth she could feel before his lips brushed hers. "Get some sleep for me, okay?"

"I'll even have a good dream for you, too."

"Hmm…as long as it involves a sunny afternoon in my hammock, that'll satisfy me." The rough pads of his fingers traced the curve of her chin.

She loved how he touched her so tenderly. "You be safe out there."

"I'll dodge any lightning bolts. Promise."

He left her smiling. Nick could feel it even though she didn't say a word. What had happened tonight? He'd give just about anything to have stayed in that bed, where experience and common sense couldn't touch him, and love Mariah one more time.

He'd never be able to go back to her again.

Logic and common sense had been waiting for him right outside the door, or so it felt like. And with every step down the hall, the trouble he was in only got clearer. *You messed up, Gray. Wanted to get yourself in more trouble, didn't you?* Life wasn't challenging enough with the problems he had. No, he had to go and make love to Mariah. Take a step on a path there was no coming back from.

Dakota's door opened. "Heading out?"

"Trying to stay ahead of the storm. Doesn't feel like twister weather."

"I disagree, big brother." Dakota followed soundlessly on the stairs, a wraith in the dark.

"You think we'll have trouble?" he asked once they were outside in the high wind.

Dakota took a minute, standing with his hands on his hips, scenting the air, feeling the storm. "Yep. Might not be too bad, though."

Nick had learned long ago his baby brother was always right. "Let's get moving. We've got work to do."

"Will is not lying around in a warm bed if I've got to be out in this." Dakota grabbed a rock and sent it sailing against the upstairs window with a sharp tap. "That'll wake up our lazy brother. We'll make him ride point and take the brunt of the wind."

"He deserves it."

The wind changed direction halfway to the stable. Coming straight from the northwest in a cold, mean line. The dark twist of clouds in the distance, glowing with spears of lightning, was heading their way. A possible twister storm, and the first of the summer.

There were horses to bring in, cattle to herd, and haystacks to cover before the brunt of the storm hit. But the work wasn't enough to drive thoughts of Mariah from Nick's mind. Battered by hail and wind strong enough to knock him on his butt, he couldn't stop thinking about her. About the way she'd reached out and touched his heart.

No doubt about it. He'd married the wrong woman, and it was too late to undo it. Too late to go back, to reverse the night and erase the love they'd shared.

There was nothing to do but to step forward on this path that had no happy ending for any of them.

Mariah listened to the wind turn cruel against the side of the house, rattling a loose board, and climbed out of Nick's bed. She shrugged into her nightgown and padded down the hall. Only the children's bedroom doors were closed tight. She imagined the others had wakened with the worsening of the storm and headed outside. It might be a long night.

A flash of distant lightning lit the window in the hallway. Thunder rolled like a stampede through the dark. A distant sound, but not strong enough to rattle through the house. *Yet.* Mariah wondered how Georgie fared through lightning storms. She opened the girl's door, but Georgie was sound asleep, her breathing a near silent rise and fall.

Good. Mariah vowed to come check on Georgie again, just to be sure.

In the kitchen, she lit a lamp and blew the banked embers to life in the stove. While the kindling caught with loud popping crackles, she measured coffee beans into the hand mill and ground them. As the lightning flashed through the kitchen, Georgie's scream filled the air. "Mama!"

Mariah turned down the damper so the kitchen wouldn't catch fire and raced up the stairs with all her might. Georgie's scream had faded, but the sound of her sobs led Mariah straight to the child's bed.

"I want my mama," Georgie wept, huddled among her pillows, hugging her rag doll tight to her chest. "Mama, Mama, Mama," she chanted, crying harder with each word.

"Poor baby." Mariah sat on the bed and pulled the

child into her arms. Georgie put up a struggle, then just as suddenly stopped, slumping against Mariah's shoulder. She smelled of cookies and soap and little-girl sweetness that tugged at Mariah's heart. She cradled this child, her stepdaughter, and pressed a kiss to her brow. "You're safe. I promise you. The storm can't hurt you here."

"I want my mama." Georgie's muffled plea rang with pure heartache. "She's gone. Long gone and far away."

"That's right, sweetie." How could anyone have left you? Mariah hugged her daughter tight, rocking her gently. "You're safe here with me. And Joey, he's across the hall. And your papa and your uncles and your grandpop. You're not alone at all, see?"

Georgie nodded, sobs shaking her little body. So frightened and fragile. We all are, Mariah realized. Maybe it was simply part of being human. Part of walking through this journey of life. The blessing of it was that no one had to walk that path alone. She'd never known what family was before, what it was like to love a man and his children, to have a house where she was more than safe. Where she was accepted and wanted and loved for who she was.

She felt the ghosts of her childhood slip away, the experiences that became memories and for nearly three decades shaped who she was. No, who she'd *thought* she was. She'd been prickly, sharp-tongued Spinster Scott, behaving as she did to keep everyone away. To prove her father was right.

But he was wrong, and tonight had been proof of that. She was lovable.

She was no longer the little girl too afraid to speak at night when her father returned from the coal yard in a bad mood. She was no longer the girl watching her mother work long hours cleaning other people's homes, only to work long into the night washing their laundry and cleaning their house. She was no longer the names her father had called her, worthless, a burden and cold-hearted. Useful only when it came to doing housework. That part of her slipped away like a ghost in the night, quietly and irrevocably.

She felt stronger. Brighter. The Mariah she was meant to be. Mariah Gray, wife and mother.

She smoothed the sleep-tangled locks out of Georgie's eyes, damp from the tears still brimming her eyes. "Don't you worry. I'm going to stay and take care of you."

"Until my mama comes back?"

Mariah knew Georgie had heard all about heaven and how no one returned from there, but she didn't understand. How could she? "I will stay and take care of you for as long as you need, okay?"

Georgie nodded, tears still falling, not satisfied, but better. She snuggled against Mariah's shoulder, sweet and precious. "You ain't goin' to heaven, too, are you, Mariah?"

"No. I'd rather stay here with you."

"Okay." With a shaky sigh, Georgie rubbed away the last of her tears.

"Why don't you come downstairs with me, and I'll make you some cocoa."

"Yes, please." Georgie wiped her face on Mariah's shoulder, apparently exhausted.

She cradled Georgie carefully, holding her close and safe and tight. Now, if she could manage to keep hold of the child and somehow get them both off the bed…

"Let me." Nick's near whisper rumbled with the same booming note as the thunder rolling in the sky overhead.

Her love. Mariah's heart swelled simply from watching him cross the dark room. She couldn't see him, but she could hear the brush of his boots against the carpet and the rustle of his clothes as he bent close. The heat of his kiss brushed her lips.

"Had to make sure Georgie was doing all right." His hand brushed Mariah's as he lifted Georgie out of her arms and into his. "Come here, princess."

"Papa. The house is rattlin'."

"I know. The thunder is mighty fierce, but I don't want you to worry—" Nick's voice faded as he carried his daughter down the hall.

Mariah climbed to her feet, weary. Lightning flared nearby, bright enough to throw light into the room, and a few seconds later thunder drum-rolled across the top of the house, shaking the windows in their panes. Downstairs, she heard the rattle of the stove door.

The fire! It was probably out by now. Mariah hurried through the dark, following the faint glow of light at the bottom of the stairs and into the kitchen where the lamp cast a warm puddle over the table where Georgie sat, her hair tangled and tears drying on her reddened face. She looked up with watery eyes. "I wanna cookie, too."

"Just one." Mariah ruffled the girl's hair on her way past the table.

Nick squatted in front of the stove, balanced on the balls of his feet, stacking kindling on the fledgling fire. "Thought I'd help you out before I head back outside."

"I appreciate it, but you have work to do." She knelt beside him, her hand falling to the hard curve of his knee. "I can do this."

"I know. You're a capable woman, Mariah." He hefted a few sticks of wood in a cross pattern so the fire could breathe. "You can build a fire, too, but I want to do this for my wife."

"What a thoughtful husband I have." She brushed a kiss to his cheek, a brief caress of heaven against his face.

"Thanks, beautiful." He rose, leaving the door ajar to give the fire more air. It was hard to sort out all he was feeling, and there wasn't much time for that now. Lightning illuminated the kitchen, followed by a slap of thunder that shook the house. "I've got to go."

"Don't go, Papa!" Georgie's cry rose above the first wave of rain against the side of the house.

He kissed her brow, recalling the image of her safe in Mariah's arms. That was one worry gone, one problem solved. "Mariah will take care of you. Be good for her."

It wasn't easy walking out, but responsibility was riding on his shoulders. Lose this ranch or a portion of his livestock, and he was in deep trouble. He had a family to provide for and brothers to keep gainfully employed. He hesitated on the walkway, with the straight-out wind beating at him and the hail bruising his head, to turn toward the kitchen window, glowing golden and bright, like a lone beacon in the infinite dark.

Through the glass panes he could plainly see Mariah, her hair tangled from their lovemaking, sweeping across the room toward the window and Georgie.

The love on her face was unmistakable as she knelt in front of the girl and brushed the tears from those cherub's cheeks.

You can't mess this up, Gray. He felt as if he were dying inside as he turned his back on the woman he loved and the bold glowing light that shone so bravely in the night.

Mariah set the coffeepot on a trivet to keep warm. She'd done her work quickly, and there was nothing more to do. Leftover biscuits from supper were in the warmer, along with a plate of sausages and scrambled eggs she'd fried up just in case the men were hungry when they came in from their work.

Hail rammed into the west side of the house, echoing like a thousand hammer strikes through the still rooms as she turned the lamp down a notch. It was enough for the men to see there was food for them. Satisfied she'd done all she could, she lifted a drowsy Georgie out of the chair. The girl's head nodded to a rest against Mariah's throat. Lightning flashed and thunder boomed, jerking Georgie awake. Seeing she was safe, Georgie gave a vulnerable, rattling sigh and struggled not to doze.

The scent of sweet chocolate clung to Georgie's face and fingers, a pleasant scent that accompanied them all the way upstairs.

"Don't wanna go to bed," Georgie whined, rubbing her face in Mariah's shoulder.

"Would you like to sleep in my bed?"

Golden curls bobbed against Mariah's chin as Georgie nodded.

"We'll be snug and safe together," Mariah assured her.

Lightning led the way through the room as she stepped into it. Thunder cracked a second later, so loud it made the silence that followed ring.

"Don't like thunder."

"Neither do I. We'll be safe from it under my comforter. Go ahead, climb under it." Mariah lowered the girl to the pillows, trying to lift the coverlet at the same time.

Georgie crawled under it like a cave dweller, tented by the fabric.

"Like normal, Georgie," Mariah instructed, lifting the top sheet.

A half second of eye-burning lightning caught Georgie in the act of crawling beneath the sheet, then the darkness came so quick, it hurt Mariah's eyes. Thunder crashed like a runaway train through the house. Even the floorboards quaked.

"Scary." Georgie reached out.

It was. The wind sounded mean, but not dangerous. Mariah knew that if there looked to be a chance of a twister, Nick would come fetch them.

They were safe, and Mariah slipped into the bed. She burrowed beneath the covers, pulling Georgie close. They cuddled together in the soft pillows as the next flash of lightning seared through the dark, showing a dark-haired boy standing in the open doorway, and then the thunder pealed.

"Joey, come in."

"I'm not scared of the lightning or anything." He sounded defiant.

"That's good." Mariah wasn't fooled. The storm was practically overhead, and it was scaring her. Lightning was dangerous, and she couldn't think about Nick outside on his horse, a perfect target for lightning to strike. "C'mon in and join us. Georgie would probably feel better if you were here."

"Yeah. Because of Georgie." As if it pained him beyond all possible words, Joey crawled into bed on the other side of Georgie.

Mariah lit the bedside lamp and stole a book from Georgie's room. Once back in bed, she read out loud, while Georgie yawned and Joey pretended not to be interested in the story. Lightning crackled and hail hit the roof, sounding like rocks falling from the sky. They snuggled together, safe and warm, and listened to the storm rage.

Cold and dog-tired, Nick kicked off his boots. He was the last man back in the house, and he'd wanted it that way. He'd needed the space as he rode one last sweep, assured the livestock had made it through the storm without trouble. The hail was melting in a steady sluice off the porch roof, a pleasant sound as he headed into the kitchen to find his brothers and father at the table, forks clinking against their plates, silent as they ate. Coffee, he expected since he'd re-built the fire for Mariah, but all this…

"That wife of yours ain't half bad," Pop commented around a bite of a flaky biscuit. "In fact, I've never seen a woman work so hard. And to think she did this out of her own thoughtfulness."

"Must have figured we'd be cold and hungry," Will agreed. "She fried up a lot of food for us."

"Don't look at me, I've always liked her." Dakota pushed away from the table, plate in hand. "I'm headin' up. Will, you've got first rounds in the morning."

"Me?" Will eased off the chair, stiff with fatigue,

and followed Dakota to the worktable, where they left their empty plates. Their low, rumbling argument went with them through the house and upstairs.

So, the tide was turning. He was surprised it had taken this long for his family's opinion of Mariah to change. Nick grabbed the platter with the leftover sausages and eggs and dug in. "Couldn't leave a biscuit for me, could you?"

"Nope." Pop didn't look sorry. "Figured I'd best do my duty and eat every last one of them."

"I surely do appreciate that." He loved Mariah's biscuits. "Are you likin' her a little more?"

"I figure you showed some wisdom in marrying her."

That was the closest Pop had come yet to admitting he'd been wrong. Just Nick's rotten luck, or a bad sense of timing, or something. Whatever it was, it wasn't right that the moment his father began liking Mariah, Nick wanted to send her away. Troubled, he finished the rest of the food, sucked down a cup of coffee hot enough to scald his guts, and headed up.

What was he going to do about Mariah? Every step up those stairs took him closer to her. What if she was waiting for him in his bed? With her hair tangled, naked between the sheets, the way he'd left her when the storm had interrupted them. What if she was naked, all smooth warm skin and soft curves, on this dark night when he needed her most?

He groaned, unable to take the image. He wanted Mariah as he needed air and sustenance and sleep. He'd give anything for the right to climb into bed with her after the long workday was done, to find comfort and pleasure in her arms, and fulfillment in her love.

A thin line of lamplight beckoned him down the hall. It came from Mariah's room. She wasn't in his bed? He was both disappointed and relieved. He wanted her. He didn't have the right to love her.

His steps stilled. He raised one hand to lean against the threshold and soak in the sight. Beautiful Mariah had fallen asleep propped up in the pillows with a book open on her lap and an equally asleep Georgie snuggled close, using Mariah's stomach for a pillow. Joey lay on his side, asleep. The lamp's gentle glow framed them like a picture.

Life had never been this way. Lida hadn't climbed out of bed and made sure a hot meal was ready for them at three in the morning. She hadn't read Georgie to sleep. She hadn't brought this sense of peace to their home. His life was transformed without the resentment and the sadness.

He'd never been happy, not like this. Not this in-the-guts, to-the-bone, down-deep sense of contentment.

But his children's lives…that was the real change. Joey wasn't pale and worried anymore. He was cool and reserved around Mariah, but a new stepmother was a lot to get used to. Nick had faith in his son. The boy would come to love her, when he was ready. Look at him now. Asleep in bed with his sister, without one worry line on his face. And Georgie, her small hands fisted into the skirt of Mariah's nightdress, holding on for dear life, even in her dreams.

Mariah *was* the right woman. The best mother for his children. The finest housekeeper and cook. The perfect match for his soul. Marrying her was the best thing he'd ever done.

Making love to her was the worst.

Torn, he padded to the bedside table and turned down the light. Tenderness ached in his chest for his wife. As the flame died on the wick and darkness stole Mariah's face from his sight, he grieved for it and for what he had to do. The night felt as endless as his loss. He closed the bedroom door the same way he closed his heart. Final. Certain. His soul was as dark as the night, as cold as the wind, as spent as the storm.

He locked his bedroom door, stripped to the skin and fell into the bed where he'd made love to Mariah. His pillow smelled like lilacs.

He could not sleep.

Chapter Twelve

The morning star twinkled like a promise in the clear predawn sky as Mariah hesitated at the kitchen window, a stack of plates tucked against the curve of her arm. It was going to be a beautiful sunrise. Remembering the love she and Nick had made together, it was sure to be a magnificent day.

She played the night over in her mind as she set the breakfast table. Savored in memory each tender kiss and the loving way he'd caressed her. Held close the pleasure of having him inside her, and the harmony of his soul touching hers.

She felt like the dawn, as if the sun were newly rising within her. A new woman, she flipped the pancakes on the griddle and listened to them sizzle. As they cooked, she fetched syrup, jam and butter for the table. It hardly seemed like work to finish up the pancakes, start the ham sizzling and begin sorting the clothes for tomorrow's weekly washing. Instead of doing laundry for hire, this was for her own family. How her life had changed—and for the better.

Jeb ambled in, unshaven and tousled. Dark circles bruised his eyes from the interrupted night's sleep.

"A cup of your coffee would be heaven right about now."

"It's brewed and ready." Mariah was all too happy to carry the coffeepot to the table.

"Thank you kindly, Mariah." Jeb folded his powerful frame into the chair. "Sure is something what you did for us last night. Want you to know I appreciate it. You're a good woman, and trust me, there ain't many of those in this world."

Mariah glowed more brightly inside. "Thank you, Jeb. That means a lot coming from you."

"That's right. I'm a tough old bird and don't you forget it." He winked, his grisly face wrinkling into a rare grin.

Feeling like the first beams of sunshine that were lifting above the far edge of the eastern prairie, Mariah returned to the stove. She flipped the ham slices on the griddle, squished them closer together to make room for the bacon strips, and decided she'd fry the morning's eggs sunny side up. Nick's favorite.

Nick. Joy surged inside her. He'd be here soon, striding through the threshold with his wind-swept hair and the confident swagger she loved so much. She couldn't wait to see him, her husband. Her love.

As dawn chased away the long shadows from the night, Mariah felt it all the way to her soul. It was going to be an incredible day.

All it took was one look, and Nick knew he couldn't do it. He'd planned to fill his plate and head out to the fields. He had the excuse of needing the corral finished by the end of the workday all ready to use.

One look at her, and he couldn't move.

"Nick." Mariah, spatula in hand, shone like a new diamond. So bright, it was a pleasure to his eyes. "Good morning, handsome."

"Morning." He wasn't used to that kind of greeting or that shine of affection on a woman's face. Lida had never treated him like this. But Mariah… She was an entirely different problem.

"You're just in time. I'm ready to put the eggs on the table."

His favorite kind. He didn't miss that piece of information. Or the smirk from Will already at the table drinking coffee that said it all. *You're in trouble now, big brother.*

Yep, he surely was. Last night was proof enough. He couldn't get it out of his mind. The magic of making love with her, of thrusting gentle and deep. It had been real love, not sex, but bigger, deeper, more tender and intimate. Looking at her this morning, changed into someone new, he saw himself in her eyes. He felt changed, too. Her love was a blanket surrounding him and on the inside, too, warming his heart and soul.

She reached out to him. Her hands settled on his shoulders. Her kiss played against his mouth. Incredible tenderness swelled inside him like a soap bubble expanding in the air, lifting above the ground, higher and higher…

He squeezed his eyes shut and stepped away from the woman he loved. It took all his strength, but he did it.

"The food smells good."

"Thanks." She beamed at his compliment, and it was easy to see her heart. The love he'd felt when they were together last night shone in her now, as bright and steadfast as the sun. She was lovelier today than he'd ever seen her.

Love threatened to overtake his good senses and he walked away. The wise thing to do. The smart thing. But he ached, suddenly lonely. He wanted her in his arms where he could hold on to her forever.

This had gone too far, and he didn't know how to stop it. He sat in misery at the table, passing platters of meat, fried potatoes, eggs and pancakes as he did every morning. He wanted to make love to Mariah again. He wanted to reach out and simply hold her hand. To bask in this rare gift of love and make the most of it.

But he couldn't. This was never going to work out. Love never did. And he didn't have enough heart left for another woman to shatter. He feared that, when Mariah fell out of love with him, she'd destroy him irrevocably. Not only his heart, but rip him clean down to the soul. He loved her that much.

He had that much to lose.

"I wanna 'nother apple." Georgie clasped her hands together, standing in the waist-high bunch grass, the wind stirring her blond curls and snapping the hem of her pink calico dress. The sun worshiped her like an angel. "Please?"

"You can have the last one." Mariah tugged the remaining apple from her apron pocket and handed it to her little girl. "Careful with your fingers."

"Bad Boy tickles." Georgie giggled as the big ox nosed the sunbonnet brim, trying to decide if the hat was good to eat. Georgie jabbed the apple at him. "Stop it! Here."

Mariah patted the gentle steer's neck as he deftly

lifted the treat from those small fingers and crunched
into the fruit. He was much happier with the other
oxen. Nick had a matched set for breaking sod and
hauling that was too heavy for the horses. Bad Boy
rubbed his poll on Mariah's hand, begging for affection.

"We may have to start calling him Good Boy."

Georgie laughed. "That's not a real name."

After apologizing for running out of apples, and to
escape the other oxen coming to see if they could get
apples, too, Mariah grabbed her basket, took Georgie's hand and led her toward the split-rail fence. The
oxen followed like puppies waiting for a treat.

"Tomorrow," Mariah promised. Nick would be
out of town at the livestock auction, and he'd be gone
for a few days. She'd have plenty of time to fill.
"Georgie, go ahead and climb through."

"'Bye, Bad Boy! O-oh, he kissed me." Georgie
wiped her cheek thoroughly before crawling between
the ground and the lowest fence rail.

"More roses!" Georgie scampered through the tall
grass, nearly head-high on her. She was only a bobbing crown of blond curls topped by a pink calico
sunbonnet. She disappeared, kneeling into the grasses.

Mariah went on tiptoe, watching as the little girl
found a fistful of wild roses from the low spreading
bushes sprinkled across the prairie.

"There's more, Mariah! Come pick 'em! They're
stickery."

Mariah was already cutting through the thick
grasses. Grasshoppers sprang out of her way. Mead-
owlarks scolded. A hawk circled lazily overhead, as
if keeping an eye on them. Mariah knelt beside Geor-

gie, took out the clippers weighing down her apron pocket and carefully snipped the stems.

"They'll make our supper table smell nice, won't they?" Mariah asked as she held the blossoms up for Georgie.

She buried her face in the soft fragrant blooms. "Pretty. Like my dress."

The colors were the same. Mariah slipped the roses, the first of summer, into her basket. The hawk overhead glided away. The birds had quieted. Remembering the incident with the coyotes, Mariah scanned the tall, rustling grasses. She couldn't see any danger, and they were close enough to the house.

Still, she took Georgie's hand. "Let's go find your papa, okay?"

They skipped together through the flowering pasture, the prairie daisies, bluebells, asters and sunflowers waved in the warm breezes. The vibrant white and purple and yellow blooms scattered color across the grassy plains for as far as she could see. She felt like those wildflowers, newly open to the warm sun, dancing for the first time in the wind.

She'd never been so happy.

"Papa!" Georgie ran, arms outstretched, toward the shirtless man hard at work in the afternoon sun, face shaded by the dark brim of his Stetson.

As he turned toward them, pivoting from his boots, turning his lean hips, setting his broad shoulders, the sight of him hit her deep in the chest. Like a blow from a boxer's glove, she reeled. This man was hers. Hers to love with her entire heart. Forever and ever.

It was as if he felt it, too. As Georgie raced across the last ten yards separating them, an invisible connection looped from Nick to Mariah. A connection that lifted her up in a way nothing ever had.

"Papa!" Georgie flew into her father's arms.

"Howdy, princess." His drawl was gentle with affection. "Did you come all this way to see your old pa?"

"Yep. Know what me and Mariah did?"

Mariah noticed Joey in the background, lowering his hammer into the tool bucket. He sauntered over to his father, so like Nick in the cut of his profile and the stance of his young body. It was easy to see the good in the boy as he checked to make sure his sister was cared for.

Her family. She took a step toward them, and then back, unsure.

Nick held out his hand. "Come over here, pretty lady. Whoever your husband is, he's daft for letting you wander all by yourself. Someone might get the notion to steal you away."

"Oh, and who would want me?"

"Any man would call himself lucky to have you, but I, for one, would be the first to fight for you."

"That would make me the lucky one." She slid her hand on his, palm to palm. The gold of her wedding band flashed in the sun, as if the angels above were granting their approval.

"With Joey's help, I've got the corral ready. We did a good job, too. It'll hold that stallion I intend to bring home." Nick released her, stepping away.

It was a small thing, but she felt distance, instead of intimacy. Her palm felt cool where he'd touched her, even in the steady sunshine.

Maybe it was nothing. He was tired. He'd worked

hard since before sunup, and had little sleep last night. What the storm hadn't interrupted, she had.

Remembering made her blush. Made her want to feel the power of being joined with him. *Tonight.*

"Do you two lovely young ladies want to come to the creek with Joey and me?" Nick's invitation was spoken to Georgie, who chanted, "Yes! Yes! Yes!" But over the top of Georgie's sunbonnet, Nick's gaze lassoed hers. Need shone in the tired depths of his eyes.

Need and fear. Mariah could feel both emotions. She needed him, too. She feared this love that sizzled between them, a connection more binding than marriage vows and shared goals and one night of physical intimacy. So much more.

When the four of them headed toward the stable, Nick casually kept the children between them.

She was killing him, and more completely than Lida ever could. Nick splashed through the ankle-deep water, the shallow end, where minnows and water bugs skidded out of his way. Mariah had her skirts tied above her knees, wading barefoot alongside Georgie. Heads bowed, woman and child gazed into the sparkling water.

"There's one!" Georgie's call startled waterfowl from the trees and small trout from their shady resting places beneath rocks and the jagged bank. Water splashed as she plunged one fist into the water. She came up empty-handed.

"Let me try." Mariah reached down into the sparkling creek and pulled up the desired pebble. She held it, dripping, on her palm.

"Oh, pretty!" Georgie added it to her skirt pocket,

which made the left side of her dress scoop downward, dangerously close to the water. "Oh, get that one."

"This one?" Mariah moved into the deeper current, reached down without concern for her new dress. She had a streak of mud on her cheek, and her sunbonnet was slightly askew. Her dress bore wet patches in several places.

"That one." Georgie confirmed, studying Mariah carefully, then changing her stance so she stood exactly as straight, with exactly the tilt of her head as Mariah did.

Nick stopped in midstride, letting the creek's current caress the tops of his feet and his ankles, cool against the hot Montana sun. *Look at what you stand to lose.* It was right here in front of him. He'd been playing newlywed last night, not thinking with his brain, instead of sticking to his guns.

Look at Georgie, beginning to recover from Lida's loss. There was Joey, sitting on a fallen tree over the creek, fishing in the shade. There was no burden weighing down his shoulders. No worry stark on his face. He was a boy again. He'd spent all morning riding his pony. Half the afternoon helping to finish the corral. Playing and riding and hanging out with his pa. Just like he used to do. Seeing his son like this, was everything.

His children were going to be all right, and he knew who to thank. It was Mariah's doing. Selflessly, and without condition or complaint, she'd walked into their lives and their house and healed everyone she touched. She was a hundred times the woman Lida was.

"Look! I gotta trout!" Joey stood on the tree trunk,

holding the struggling fish up for all to see. "He's pretty big, too!"

"Good job, son." Nick hopped onto the bank. "Let me help you clean that."

"It's big enough for me to fry up for your supper," Mariah offered in that soft voice of hers.

"If I catch more, will you fry 'em up, too?" Joey asked, fidgeting with excitement.

"Of course."

"I could feed our whole family!"

"I got it! Look." Georgie held a pebble on her palm, water dripping off her chin.

"Good job," Mariah praised, the honest, hard-working, sincere woman Nick had always loved, beautiful because of all the ways he loved her.

From the sixteen-year-old schoolgirl he'd first been enamored with, to the spinster whose loneliness matched his own, to the beautiful wife and lover who'd eased the lonesomeness from his heart.

His chest ached, and he couldn't stop the pain of it. The scent of her lilac water was still on his shirt. Faint, but noticeable, calling back the sensation of holding her in his arms. Soft and sweet and sensual. Of loving her last night as if there could be no yesterday and no tomorrow, just that one moment frozen in time.

His trousers were tight again, because seeing her was wanting her, craving the absolute bliss he'd found in her arms. Mariah was all woman, no simpering girl, no petulant child, but a woman grown and all the more beautiful for it, and she made him feel…

She made him *feel*. There was no blissful indifference around Mariah. No simple, heart-frozen, indifferent, one-foot-in-front-of-the-other life that he'd been living. Last night she'd opened him up, like an ax splitting a stubborn piece of wood. He felt the resulting fissure from outside in. His heart suffering from it. That's what love did to a man, what a woman did to a man, and he would not allow it.

"Pa, I'm gonna catch more of these." Joey hopped to the bank, proud of his catch. "Are you gonna come fish with me?"

"You bet, cowboy."

Love was many things, and the kind that came with responsibility came first. Over the sparkling creek and the afternoon so beautiful it hurt to look at, Nick turned his back to Mariah and made his choice.

She'd felt Nick's distance all afternoon, growing stronger as the hours passed. Because he and his brother were leaving for the auction tomorrow, Nick spent time with the children. After he tucked them into bed, he disappeared into his room to pack.

Mariah dried the last of the pots and pans, putting them away on the shelves of the shadowed kitchen. She could hear the tap of Nick's gait on the boards overhead as he moved from the closet to the bed and back.

She'd finish up here and go to him. Offer any help he might need. Maybe even offer herself naked on his bed. She burned inside, remembering how he'd behaved when she'd come to his room last night. The way he'd led her to his bed, steady and silent, as if he were perfectly calm. But the shiver of his breathing and the tight grip he held on her hand said everything. This was no casual meeting. No convenient marriage. No, it was a union based on love. She shivered, wanting him so much. Nick, her love.

She tossed out the wash water and tipped the basins up to dry, all the while buzzing with excitement. Nick was still in his room. She was definitely going to go up to him. Only Jeb was in the parlor to say good-night to as she whipped by and flew up the stairs. Breathless and eager, she headed down the hall toward the splash of light from Nick's room.

It was amazing to think he was her husband. That she had the right to walk through his house to his bedroom. To reach out and pull him close. All the years she'd longed for him, and now he was hers. Hers to love and cherish for all time.

His back was to her as he gazed out the window. His shoulders were straight and his arms were lifted, braced on either side of the frame. He was a big, powerful man that made desire curl through every inch of her. Love filled her in a quick swoop, like a hawk racing straight up into the sky.

She closed the door behind her. "All packed?"

He glanced over his shoulder at her. He didn't smile as he turned. "Yep. I'm all ready to go. Dakota and I will be gone before first light."

"I packed breakfast and lunch for you both. It's down cellar keeping cool."

"That was mighty fine of you, Mariah." Nick winced, looked troubled, a man resolute and rigid at the window. He didn't take a step toward her.

So she went to him. "Just taking care of you, like I promised." And she wasn't finished yet. Nope. She wanted to honor and cherish him for the rest of the night. She splayed her hands on his wonderful chest, so iron-hard and perfect.

The muscles beneath her fingertips went rigid. Nick stiffened. His jaw clamped shut. Ridges furrowed his brow. He didn't want her? She didn't understand as his fingers clamped over her wrists, stopping her. Seconds beat between them, stretching out as if each were an eternity. In those few precious moments she saw the depth of him, the dark broken places in his soul, the wounds he covered up like a door closing and locking. His heart shuttered, as if he'd shut a window and pulled the shade.

He broke the connection between them.

Mariah stood in front of him, separated, isolated, her heart beating alone. His grip on her wrists became impersonal and distant, like a stranger's touch. What was happening? "You're tired. I understand. Come to bed and I'll give you a back rub. Your shoulders look tense."

"No." He released his hold on her, pivoting hard. "I've got to get some sleep while I can. I've got to be up at three. It's a five-hour ride, and I want to be there before the auction starts."

How should she interpret that? His words were harsh and sharp. What was troubling him? She laid her hand on his shoulder. "What can I do to help?"

"You can sleep in your own bed tonight." Hard words.

She could hear the pain beneath. He'd needed her last night and reached for her in the dark, where it was easier to hide vulnerabilities. How hard was it for a man as strong as Nick to take down the steel walls around his heart? Lamplight filled the room, showing the shadows beneath his eyes and the pain on his face.

He was still grieving. She had to remember that. He needed her; she'd felt it in his soul last night. He'd clung to her, needing her love. She would give him no less now, in the light that worshiped him like the great man he was. She closed the curtains and turned down the wick until darkness swept through the room, hiding him from her sight. But not her senses. He smelled like sunshine and prairie wind and horses and leather. The faint scent of his evening cigar clung to his shirt as she swept her hands over the back of his shoulders, feeling his muscles turn to iron.

"I can't do this, Mariah." He sounded choked, torn, ashamed as he twisted away, storming through the darkness and out the door. His steps rang loud and then faded away, leaving her alone in the silence.

He didn't want her? Did he regret their lovemaking? His rejection struck like a sledgehammer to her unprotected heart, the one she'd opened wide to love him. Tears pooled in her eyes, and she breathed slowly. Cold, stinging pain filled her chest.

Surely he wanted her. He was exhausted and managing his grief. It had to be hard for him, losing the mother of his children and the wife he loved. Harder still to recover from that catastrophic loss and love another woman, as if the heart and the love that blossomed there could be turned on and off like a water pump on demand.

She ought to know. Nick could walk away from her, reject her, and the love in her heart kept going. Like the tough prairie roses, not even the brutal Montana winters could stop them from blooming each summer.

She waited for him to return, and when he didn't, she retreated to her own room. Lying beneath the sheets, with the warm night air fluttering the curtains, she listened for his footstep in the hall.

He never came.

At ten minutes to three, she couldn't take it any longer. She went downstairs to kiss him goodbye.

He was already gone.

With every rocking step of the gelding down the road in the dark, Nick thought of the woman he'd left behind. He'd rejected her. She had to be hurt. Maybe even crying. It took every ounce of discipline he possessed to keep his horse facing east and his bottom planted firmly in the saddle.

It killed him a little with each passing minute. He'd treated her badly. Acted as if her touch was the one thing he didn't want. When her love was the one thing he craved more than his life.

He rode on, with his brother at his side, as the world awakened. Birds gathered to herald the sacred coming of the new day, the chirping became a din that hurt the ears and silenced the moment the sun began to rise, a reverent light that brought color and warmth to the earth.

Like Mariah to his life.

He grimaced as the pain set deep. He had to stop thinking about her. Had to cut the woman from his soul and keep her where she belonged, as his housekeeper and cook and the woman that shared his name. Nothing more.

His children needed stability. They needed a stepmother they could count on. One who would love them and care for them. They couldn't have her falling out of love with their father and thereby thinking she could love them less. As Lida had done.

Georgie was too young to understand, but Joey was old enough to have felt some of it. A mother more interested in daydreaming about her latest lover, and more in love with the lover's child she carried than with the two beautiful children she had. Nick was a grown man, he could handle her rejection. It hurt, no lie about that, but he was tough. He could survive. But children were vulnerable and needed care. He would not walk down that path again with another woman, always wondering if she was holding up her obligations, hating that she did the bare minimum with the kids and the house, just doing enough. Never more.

Love wasn't dosed out like helpings at a supper table. One scoop of compassion, a half scoop of concern, a spoonful of sympathy. His kids deserved more than that. A mother who stood by them. One who was sensible and practical...

"Missing your wife?" Dakota broke the hour-long silence.

"Not overly much."

"Liar. If I were you, I'd never have left her bed. She's a fine wife. Takes care of those she loves. Unlike some people."

Lida. That was true enough. Mariah was steadfast and loyal and committed, just as he knew she'd be.

She was also angelic and sensual and wanted a part of him that he could not afford to give.

Every mile that passed took him farther away from her. That was torment.

And a blessing.

Chapter Thirteen

"**M**ariah!" Ellie McKey called from the busy boardwalk. "We missed you at the last book club meeting. I heard you married and quite well, too!"

Mariah held the bakery boxes stacked in her arms upright as she closed the bakery's heavy glass door. "Hello, Ellie. How are you?"

"The real question is, how are you?" The woman swept up in her tailored dress and matching bonnet, with a parasol raised to protect her complexion from the hot sun. "A practical marriage like yours must be a hardship."

Digging for gossip, are you? Mariah's pride went up along with her chin. "Nick and I are quite happy, thank you. That's a lovely dress you're wearing. I'm running late and can't stop to visit."

"Fine. I hope to see you at the next Ladies' Aid meeting. Hope you're not too busy to come."

Ellie seemed pleasant enough, but she and Ellie had never been friends. It seemed even less likely now that she could feel the sharp prongs of Ellie's stare boring into her back. Ellie was one of those women who rarely spoke of her husband with whispered joy.

For the first time in her life, Mariah understood why. There was a difference between a happy marriage and an unhappy one.

That made her think of her own marriage. What if her love wasn't enough? What if, when Nick came home today, he turned his back again and rejected her?

She had felt his heart that night when they were intimate and as close as a man and woman could be. His love for her was true and as wide as the horizon. Why did he turn away?

It troubled her all the way home. She realized she was running late when she spied Rayna's buggy parked in the shaded yard. She checked her pocket watch—she was only a few minutes late. Rayna came outside as Mariah was tethering the gelding.

"Sorry I got here a bit early. Jeb said to make myself at home, so I did."

"I'm glad. I'm the one who's sorry. I got held up at the shoemaker's. I had Nick's work boots patched for him." Mariah grabbed the baker's boxes, turning to look over her shoulder at the squeak of Betsy's buggy wheel. "Why, look who's driving up late. It's the most notorious member of our group."

"That's right. I'm wanted in five counties." Teasing, looking happy, Betsy pulled her mare to a stop. "I've put my life of crime behind me to take over your laundry business and to embroider in my spare time."

"Did you start a new project?" Mariah waited for Betsy to climb down from the seat.

"Pillowcases. The pattern is violets and nosegays, and I think it's going to go perfect with my quilt."

The three of them retreated from the hot sun into

the cool, shaded kitchen. Rayna had already set the pitcher of cool tea and glasses on the table.

Mariah lowered her packages onto the edge of the table. "I got us some treats."

"So did I." Betsy pulled a small box of confections from her sewing basket. "And truffles to have with our tea. I thought we ought to have something extra, since this is our first get together at Mariah's new home."

Home. Mariah stilled, considering the word, as she tucked away her reticule and untied her bonnet. It made her think of security, like a welcome hug, like a crackling fire to settle down by. Home was the steadiness of a man's love that did not fade.

That's what she wanted with a desperation that scared her. *In time.* Nick was coming home today with his new stallion, if all went well. Perhaps time away was what he needed. Time alone to think, without the demands of the ranch and the family. Time to sort out his grief.

Maybe he missed me. She hoped so, because she missed him. Nick Gray was wonderful and strong and kind, and the tenderness he showed her was unlike anything she'd ever known. Longing filled her. She wanted to be in his arms. Love brimmed her heart, full and patient, just for him.

"Have you given any more thought to running for president of the Ladies' Aid?" Rayna asked with a knowing wink as she poured the tea. "Or will you be too busy with your new *obligations* to your husband?"

"It's true I have a lot of work between the house and the children, but I have time for the meetings." Mariah was glad that unlike some husbands, Nick didn't mind if she took a few hours to herself a week to visit with friends or serve on the Ladies' Aid. "I might not stay with the book club—"

"I wasn't talking about those *obligations.*" Rayna waggled her brows.

"Marital obligations," Betsy hinted.

Mariah's face burned. "Why, I don't know what you mean."

"He's that wonderful, huh?" Rayna's grin broadened. "I'm glad to know you and Nick are getting along just dandy."

"Yes, that's *always* a good sign of a happy marriage," Betsy added as she circled around the table and chose a chair to slip into. "When the husband and wife are committed enough to meet one another's *needs.*"

Mariah felt even hotter, but pleased. She fetched the sugar bowl from the pantry. Luckily, Betsy and Rayna turned to discussing the latest town news and saved her from further embarrassment.

As Mariah was returning to the table, she caught sight of a bay horse through the kitchen window. A horse she didn't recognize. Nick's new stallion? Was Nick home?

Excitement exploded through her like a lightning bolt. Before she could take a single step, Nick strode into view. His gaze fastened on hers through the open window. Time froze like eternity when their eyes locked. Was he glad to see her? Did he need her? She couldn't tell.

He broke away, turned his back and went to help hold another lead on the unhappy stallion.

"Goodness, is that the wild horse everyone's been

talking about?'' Rayna spoke with alarm. ''He *does* look wild. I hope no one gets hurt handling him.''

''Nick's a fine horseman,'' Mariah commented, feeling rooted to the floorboards. She couldn't pick up her feet and her pulse was booming in her ears.

Nick had turned away from her. He hadn't smiled. He didn't wave. He didn't lift a brow in acknowledgment. He'd turned his back, coldly and efficiently, as if he had better things to do than say hello to his wife. To the woman who was no longer a necessary wife, but the woman he'd made real love to.

He's busy. She tried to excuse him. He'd had a long journey, and he was probably worried about getting the new animal settled. He would probably come in shortly and show her just how much he missed her. Right?

A part of her wasn't sure as she settled down at the table to chat with her friends.

He couldn't avoid her forever. Nick knew she'd be coming out with a plate of food about now. If he leaned to the left, he could just see the house and the corner window, and it looked as if everyone had just sat down to supper. There was Joey talking away to Pop, and Mariah in the background, setting platters of food on the table.

Mariah. Her name could rock the earth from beneath his feet. That's how vulnerable he was to her. That's how much power she had. Making love to her had laid him open entirely. Every part of him.

She could use that against him—and, as a woman, probably would one day. To manipulate him. To get every little thing she wanted. Even to break him. Like Lida.

His chest ached in the place where his heart used to be. Hurt for all the times he'd tried to love Lida and she'd pushed him away. And not just physically. It wasn't only his heart that had died, but a piece of his soul. He'd paid a high price for trying to love a woman. He'd never do it again. *Ever.*

The trouble was, he already loved Mariah. With all he was. With every bit of him. How was he going to keep his pride and his heart intact? She was so far inside him, it terrified him. To be so exposed. Vulnerable. Open and aching.

If he was like this now, how much worse would it be when the blush of love wore away? When love wore down to the quick, because life had a way of testing a person. He didn't want to live like that again. Miserable, always keeping his guard up, keeping control, keeping her where she belonged—away from his heart.

Mariah was headstrong. She was a woman with her own strength and force. Would their future be a constant battle? Or would it, in time, end up as it had between him and Lida, separate beds, separate lives, separate hearts?

No, he couldn't stand that again. He didn't want an unhappy wife looking for love in another man's arms.

And what about his children? What about their happiness? Their stability? What happened if Mariah stopped loving them, too?

It was too late to go back, but if he could, he would undo their night of passion. He would have turned his back on her instead, and turned her away. He would have said anything to send her scurrying back to her bed, so every one of them would stay safe.

"Nick?"

He loved the sound of her voice. The whisper softness of her step. The way the marrow in his bones shivered when she came near.

He couldn't look at her. He watched the stallion scent her approach, head up, ears back, nostrils flaring.

"He's a beauty." Her admiration shone like a gem—no, she did, rare and flawless and true.

How his heart ached for her. He wanted to reach out and pull her close, seek comfort in her arms, breathe her in like the evening air and cherish her as if their love would never end.

"I brought you some supper. Your favorite."

He could smell it. He didn't have to look at the plate she thrust at him, heaped with delicious food. Everything there was what he especially liked, from her buttermilk biscuits to the baked potatoes in butter and green beans with onions and bacon. "Chicken potpie. This was a lot of work."

"I picked up dessert in town, since I was running errands. I'll make you come into the kitchen later for that, so I can ply you with chocolate and then tempt you upstairs to your bed."

He choked. He couldn't look at her as he balanced the plate on the thick fence rail. How was he ever going to get that suggestion out of his head? Suddenly all he could think about was pushing the chocolate cake aside, lying her on the table and helping himself.

Good job, Gray. Now that's all you're going to think about for the rest of the night.

It took discipline to clutch the fork, instead of to reach for Mariah and bury his face in her silken hair. It took a mountain of fortitude to pierce the tines of the steel fork into the soft center of the buttery potato when what he wanted to taste was the passion he and Mariah could make together.

"Dakota said your trip went well." She leaned her slim arms on the rail beside him and let the wind play with her hair.

The way he wanted to. To feel the silk between his fingers, the soft scent of lilacs and woman as he held her close. The softness like paradise against his jaw and cheek. He recalled holding her like that in his bed after they'd made love, her naked warmth against him. They'd rested together, intimate and still joined.

Nothing in his life had felt as good as holding her at that moment, not even the love they made, and why that was, he couldn't say. Maybe it was because he'd felt complete. As if no matter what happened from that moment on, he would have the sheltering comfort of Mariah's love and the sweetness of being in her arms. His heart no longer ached where it was broken. His soul no longer hurt where it was scarred.

"He said the stallion was a handful to bring home." Mariah kept talking as if the silence between them was companionable, as if he hadn't been avoiding her.

That made it worse. He felt guilty enough leaving the way he did without saying goodbye. Guilty again for returning home without kissing her hello. She didn't know how fiercely he'd missed her at night when he lay awake on the lumpy mattress in the hotel longing for her. She didn't know how many times he wished to see her—just see her. Through the window at work in the house or walking in the sunny fields with Georgie. Splashing in the creek with her skirt hiked to her knees.

Love twisted his chest like a belt drawn too tight.

His eyes blurred with the intensity of it. The broken places inside him felt endlessly dark.

What was he going to do? He wanted Mariah. He couldn't let himself want her.

"The stallion kept me and Dakota on our toes, I'll admit it," he said around a mouthful of biscuit. "But his bad temper benefited me. I got him at a mighty fine price, and that's something right there. Look at the wide barrel. He's strong. He's got good composition and he's going to sire some mighty fine foals, once I break him."

"You sound determined. About as determined as he looks to break you."

"He can try, but I'm pretty damn tough."

"I've noticed."

How warm her voice, like the first soft fall of moonlight coming over the eastern prairie, and how it lured him.

He cleared his throat, popped a bite of succulent chicken into his mouth and chewed. If he concentrated on the food and not on her, he might make it through the evening without hauling her down into that grass and letting her love him, his flaws and all, and damn the consequences.

She touched him, soft as starlight on a lonely night, and the connection was more than flesh and bone; it went beyond the physical. It was as if she'd touched the deepest part of him. He gritted his teeth, torn. He wanted her solace. He wanted her love. He felt her in his soul, and he didn't understand it, only knew that he stopped hurting when he was with her, when she touched him, when she came to him with this love as amazing as starlight and as steady as eternity and as familiar as his own soul.

How could he let her any closer? He shook with the fear of it. The uncertainty. If he gave in and loved her, then how long would it last? If how things had gone with Lida were any indication of how marriages went, then in a couple of years the bitterness and disappointment would accumulate like snow on a roof. One day it would be too heavy and the wood holding it up would break and the roof would collapse.

No, he'd walked down that path and had the broken pieces to prove it. His love for Lida had been nothing like this remarkable, infinite love for Mariah. What would it do to him when she turned away? When she realized he was simply a man, nothing more. He tried to be strong but he was human. Tarnished and with broken places, no different from anyone else walking this earth.

Behind her in the falling twilight shone the windows of his house. His home. Pop would be in the parlor about now, enjoying an evening smoke, reading the paper and probably keeping an eye on the kids.

His children. He had to remember what was important. He'd married Mariah for their sakes. Not for his.

Mariah's hand slid up his arm and swept over the curve of his shoulder. She was sweet heaven, and what good was heaven to a man like him?

He closed his eyes. He wanted to run. He wanted to stay.

Her fingertips were sheer bliss on his poor, tired muscles. "I hate that you've been avoiding me."

He squeezed his eyes shut, no longer hungry, no longer anything. "I'm truly sorry about that."

"It's all right. I want you to know I understand."

Gentle, her words. Soothing, her touch. "You loved Lida with your whole heart. I know what that's like now, and to think of losing someone you love so much... I can't imagine the pain."

She thought he loved Lida? He shook his head, truly lost.

She kept on going, in that dulcet voice of hers that swept through him like a hymn. "I don't want you to hurt any more than you already do. If you're not ready to make love with me again, I can wait. I'll give you anything you need, Nick. Please, just don't think you have to avoid me. That's not good for you or me."

"What would you have me do?" He didn't know if she was sincere or if she was playing him the way Lida always had. Then again, how could she be so forgiving? He'd hauled her into his bed, taken her virginity and every bit of comfort and pleasure he could because he needed it. Because he could no longer stand being alone and hurting. Because the aching void in his soul filled whenever she touched him.

As she was doing now. Touching him, soothing him.

"I want you to take your time," she said, and pressed a kiss to the corner of his jaw. "Be good to yourself. I want you to ask me for what you need, and I'll do my very best to give it to you."

"What do you mean by that?" Surely this was going to be leading in the direction that women took things—what did Mariah really want?

He rubbed his brow, overcome, disappointed; he couldn't stop feeling as if here it came, what he was afraid of. He'd made love to her, loved her with his whole being, and she was going to start using it against him. Trying to herd him like a runaway into a corral of her choice.

And, like the stallion in front of him, he'd fight. And if he gave in, he'd be miserable.

"I mean, if you need a friend to talk to, I'll listen. If you need someone to hold you, I'm here with open arms." Her fingers stilled, and so did the reverent twilight. "If you need to be loved, then I will do that, too. Without condition. Without end. Just like I vowed to do. To honor and cherish you."

She was too good to be true. It was as simple as that. "I didn't love Lida. Not the way you think."

"Of course you did. You married her and were raising a family with her." She felt as sincere as nightfall, gentle but certain. "She was the mother of your children."

"I married her because she was pregnant and I was responsible. Not because I loved her."

"But you did." She sounded as if she had endless faith in him.

Not for long. She might as well know the truth. "You think I'm pining away for the woman I loved. Sure, I loved her, but the passion we shared was dead long ago. The truth is, we could barely speak civilly to one another the last couple of years she was alive. I'm sorry for her passing, and, sure, I loved her in a way. But that isn't the reason I'm out here with the horse, instead of inside the house with you."

"It isn't?"

He heard the vulnerability in her words but kept right on going. It was the only way he could right the boat and keep them on the correct course, safe and out of danger. "I married you out of necessity, Mariah. I needed someone to keep the house and care for my kids and cook the meals. That was our bargain.''

''It sounds so harsh when you say it like that. A bargain. But marriage is more than that. We vowed to love, honor and cherish each other. I know you're torn apart inside, I can feel it. Somehow I can feel what's inside you, and I will do anything to heal your pain.'' Her hand splayed across his chest, over his beating heart. ''I'm your wife, Nick. When we made love—''

''You're my housekeeper.'' He tore away from her, unable to take it, breaking apart from the inside out because she wanted the impossible from him. The one thing he couldn't afford to give, because she was as dangerous as a tornado roaring across those plains, coming straight at him, destroying everything in her path.

She wasn't like Lida. Not in the least. Mariah meant every word she said. He could feel it. The truth of it. In his heart, and in hers.

She wanted his love, that was all.

It was too much.

''Just your housekeeper? You can't mean that.'' She sounded so sure.

He squeezed his eyes shut, fought with everything in him, and kept walking.

''Nick?''

His hands fisted as the last vestiges of twilight faded and night fell and he melted into the shadows. Mariah could not distinguish him from the darkness of the vast plains.

Yet she could feel him like the wind on her face— nothing that could be touched or seen or measured, but it was there just the same, a force that was endless and had a power of its own. A force that came quietly or fiercely, and she could feel his heart in hers and feel his hopelessness.

He's not ready to love me. Mariah took solace in that. He was still grieving, that was all.

He's hurting, he's confused, he needs time. She wrapped her arms around her waist. There was a tight knot of pain in the center of her chest. What had he said? He'd admitted he didn't love Lida. That he was not grieving her. That wasn't the reason he walked away into the night. His hurtful words echoed inside her.

He wasn't grieving Lida. The truth of it sunk in, hitting her hard, and the tight ball of pain inside her began to unwind. *I needed someone to keep the house and care for my kids and cook the meals.*

Sure, he needed help. She understood that. She'd married him knowing he'd married her for practical reasons, but he'd chosen her. Out of all the women at the dance who were younger and prettier. Out of all the women in town who were softer and sweeter and more accommodating.

You're my housekeeper, he'd said. But there was no way that was true. Never. She'd felt the way he loved her. With every touch, every kiss, she'd felt his love. And it was like a slow, steady lightening of a predawn sky, glowing with the promise of the day to come.

Then why had he said that? She hugged herself more tightly, alone. She had never realized how dark a night could be.

She stood a long while, waiting. But Nick did not return to her. *In time.* She wished it with her entire being. She could not let go of the hope he would come to her.

But the doubts began to feel as wide as the horizon as she trudged through the grass. The house was lit up like a beacon, the windows glowing warm and bright, as if unafraid of the night.

You're my housekeeper, kept echoing in her mind.

As Papa had always told her, *What man would want you, Mariah? You're as cold-hearted as your mother, and there's only one thing a woman like you's any good for and that's hard work.*

She died a little, but kept on walking.

It was late, past time to put the children to bed. And, as always, there was more work to be done before she could sleep.

The wind rushed through the open window to snap the curtains hard enough to wake her. Mariah rolled over in her bed, alone, wearing nothing but her night rail. She'd kicked the sheet off her in her sleep. The wind billowing into the room was humid.

The distant roll of thunder told her another storm could be on its way. Had Nick come in while she was asleep? Or was he out there somewhere in the endless dark? She yanked the window closed and the curtains fell silent. Lightning snaked across the sky to the northwest. The sky was glowing strangely with an eerie light.

She pulled on her housecoat and padded down the hall. Nick's door was open, his room empty. His bed unmade. The bed where they'd made love, where they'd come together as one, and the impact of it still ached inside her. Wasn't that what marriage was supposed to be? That special bond, physical and emotional? Why had Nick pulled away?

The wind was blowing harder by the time she stepped outside. Whipping up dust and snapping through trees. There was a sense of expectation in the air as Mariah picked her way down the path, the landscape made translucent by the glowing sky. A strange color twisted in the clouds to the north.

She found Nick on the rise, sitting in the waving sea of grass, arms around his knees, watching the storm. The wind was too loud for him to hear her, but his shoulders stiffened. His spine straightened. He cocked his head, listening for the sound of her gait on the crackling, dry grass.

Would he send her away? Or ask her to stay? There was only one way to find out. She gathered her courage and slipped to the ground beside him. "I figured you'd be out here watching the storm."

"Twister weather, but tonight's storm ought to miss us."

"As long as the wind doesn't change direction."

"That's why I'm sitting up here, to be sure."

He sounded so distant. How did she reach across and pull him close? She didn't know.

He seemed to lean away from her. When he spoke, he could have been a stranger. "Thanks for tucking in the kids tonight. I didn't get in to tell them goodnight."

"Joey read himself to sleep. I took the book out of his hands and turned off the lamp." Mariah remembered how the boy had awakened when she'd lifted the Mark Twain novel out of his grip. Joey had pretended to go back to sleep, but she knew he hadn't. What was it about the men in this family? Why were they so obstinate? So hard to win over? "I read to Georgie and she went right to sleep."

"My children are doing better. You care about them."

He sounded like her employer, not her husband, not her true love. "Yes, I care about them. They're my children now, too."

"You always surprise me, Mariah."

"Is that good or bad?"

"I sure as shootin' don't know." He raked his fingers through his hair. Did she always have to be this difficult? Why wasn't she the convenient, practical wife he'd bargained on? "You'd best get back in the house."

"I'd rather be with you."

Don't hurt me like this, Mariah. Nick rubbed his face, wishing he could wipe the scars from his soul as easily. "No, go in. It'll be hailing in a few minutes."

"I don't mind a little hail."

It would be wrong to use her again. Wrong to make her think he loved her—when he couldn't. It took a big part of him to turn away. "No, I'll keep an eye on things. If it looks like trouble, I'll come wake you."

"You're eager to get rid of me."

"Nope. Just to be alone."

Mariah grimaced, feeling the pain down deep. So, he'd answered her question. He didn't want her.

She couldn't go. Not until she knew for certain. "You didn't mean what you said, did you? You married me because..." *You wanted to love me.*

He covered his face with his hands. He was shadow and darkness, silhouetted by the oncoming storm, his dark hair lashed by the wind. Defeat gusted over her like the cruel storm. "I told you, Mariah. I knew you'd do your best with my children. And I was right. Look how well they're doing."

She couldn't speak. Her hands trembled. Then her arms. Then her shoulders. A cold, bone-rattling kind of shaking spread through her.

"My children are all that matters to me," he continued, honest and as resolute as the prairie surrounding them. "I meant what I said when I married you. I'll treat you with respect. I'll take care of you. In return, you care for my house and my children. That was our bargain."

"But we made love."

"No." He choked, rubbing his face again. "That was a mistake, and it isn't going to happen again. I don't need a wife."

I need a housekeeper. She could hear his thoughts like her own.

Thoughts he meant.

At least you're useful, girl. You work hard. There's no other reason to keep you around. Papa's voice flashed through her head as a bolt of lightning forked across the clouds where a dark funnel began to descend from the sky to a far corner of the sleeping prairie.

The twister wasn't a threat to her, but Nick was. Heart breaking, Mariah climbed to her feet, brushed the grass from her housecoat and ran to the house. A piece of their conversation played in her head. *We made love,* she'd told him.

That was a mistake, he'd said.

A *mistake?* He couldn't have hurt her more if he'd

taken a whip to her and lashed her until he broke through the flesh and muscle to the bone beneath.

He didn't want her? All this time she'd thought…

It didn't matter what she thought. It was over. Nick was never going to want her. He'd tried to love her and it was impossible. A mistake, he'd called it. Trying to love her was a mistake.

She refused to let that hurt. Refused to feel the pain. She wiped the wetness from her eyes, because she *was not* crying, and pushed through the back door. The kitchen echoed with the pad of her feet and the rustling of her clothes.

Empty. Alone. That's how she felt. When she climbed into her bed, that's what she was. Not Nick's wife, but the woman he did not want.

Her heart shattered, like a glass window struck by hammer, cracking into a thousand tiny shards. Destroyed. Never to be made whole again.

She listened to the sounds of the storm swell and fade until there was only silence. Then Nick's step rang in the hall. He didn't hesitate by her door as he ambled past.

He continued on as if she wasn't there.

Chapter Fourteen

The fire was lit and crackling cheerfully in the cookstove as it had every morning since she'd become Nick's wife. Mariah knew it was out of courtesy that he lit that fire and nothing more, the same way he took his work boots off at the back door or brought wood in from the shed or mucked out the barn. He considered it his duty.

As she looked around the lonely kitchen, she realized she had her duties, too. Not as Nick's true love and not as the woman he'd always wished he'd married over the years, but as someone to take care of his house and his children.

You're not good for anything else, girl. Papa's voice still crept into her thoughts, the low rumble of it and the drunken slur. *Why are you starin' out the window like that? Think someone is gonna wanna marry the likes of you?*

It didn't matter what Papa had said years ago. She didn't need to think of him ever again. He was dead and buried and gone from her life. Then why did it feel as if he were here, making all the old wounds in her heart fresh and new?

Because he'd been right. She'd thought that Nick loved her because of their night together, but now she wasn't sure. *She* loved Nick. There *had* been so much love, an incredible tenderness, but maybe it had all been hers. Not his.

Maybe Nick had needed comfort from his loneliness, that was all, and she'd been there, coming to him in her nightgown, naked underneath. He'd needed comfort. She'd wanted true love.

A mistake. No wonder he felt it necessary to let her know how he felt. *You're my housekeeper, Mariah.*

Nothing more.

She closed her eyes against the pain.

"Mariah?" Jeb's gruff baritone boomed sharply, like a general barking orders in the heat of battle, and it echoed around the kitchen like a gunshot.

She could only stare at him, the present and past oddly blending together, seeing the image of her father in the kitchen doorway over the top of Jeb Gray striding toward her, his brow furrowed, his mouth a grim, uncompromising line.

"I'm sorry, Jeb. I don't have your coffee ready. I'll make it right now." Her fingers didn't work right. She was upset, was all, but she dropped the measuring spoon and cringed when it clinked against the counter. Clumsy, her pa would have said.

She grabbed the coffee mill and, in her hurry, the drawer slid out and fell in a perfect arch from shelf to floor, clattering to a stop in front of Jeb's left toe. Her heart stopped as he knelt to retrieve it.

Tears of shame burned behind her eyes. She grabbed the coffee bag, determined not to spill that, when Jeb's big gnarled hand closed over hers.

"You look mighty exhausted, girl." Kind words, gently spoken. "I can make the morning's coffee."

"But it's my job."

"I thought my son had gone plumb loco marrying you, and I'm not too proud to admit when I'm wrong. But you are a fine woman, Mariah, and I don't come to admire too many women. Give me the coffee beans."

Foolish tears blurred her vision as she handed over the coffee bag. "I'll do better tomorrow."

"You're doin' fine today." His hand lighted on hers, just for a moment, but the connection was unmistakable, like a father to a child, not a bond that hurt but one that healed.

Blinking hard, she set about her work. Putting the ham and sausage on to fry. Whipping up biscuits. The kitchen didn't feel lonely and neither did she, sharing her workspace with Jeb.

"What kind of eggs would you like for breakfast?" she asked.

"I love how you scramble 'em," Jeb replied.

There was a harmony she'd never known, working side by side as she flipped the sausages and he ground the coffee. She dolloped spoonfuls of biscuit batter onto a baking sheet as Jeb set the grounds to boiling.

"I'll be back for that," he said, gruff as always, but with a sparkle in his eye. "When I do, will you let me steal one of them biscuits hot off the rack?"

"Chances are good." She felt warm inside, as if she belonged.

Was it a sign? If Jeb could learn to accept her, even maybe like her, then could Nick? A small hope flickered to life inside her chest. While she worked, she nurtured that hope for a true love, a real marriage and—maybe—a baby one day.

It was such a tiny hope, but she held on to it with a fragile need. A mistake, Nick had said. Exactly how much did he mean that? And was she wrong, maybe too desperate, to hope the love of her life might one day love her back?

As she scooped the last of the scrambled eggs from the pan, she heard the fall of Nick's step on the porch. Felt his sure, steady presence like the heat from the stove on her skin a moment before he opened the screen door.

The Stetson's dark brim shaded his face, hiding the deep-set eyes she loved so well, the strong line of his nose and the hard curve of his mouth. The stony cut of his jaw looked rigid, as if he was tensed for battle as he stalked into the sunny kitchen like a hungry predator. The power in his lean, well-honed limbs, the strength in his trim body and the magnetism of him, of his character, filled her with longing.

Such a man. She wanted him with the depths of her being, and she felt alive as he strode straight toward her, cutting through the lemony rays of the new sun streaming into the kitchen.

"Can I have a plate?" he said. Not "Good morning, Mariah." Not "I'm sorry for what I said last night. I didn't mean it." Not "I love you."

He held out his hand, palm up, waiting.

The tiny seed of hope died within her. Since she was just the housekeeper, she fetched a clean plate for him and dished his food right from the stove.

"Thank you." As if she were a stranger, he tipped his hat and strode right out of her kitchen and into the new day. The sunlight didn't touch him as he disappeared from her sight.

One brief look, a few spoken words to her, and she was all Nick could think about with every step he took toward the corral. Mariah. He ached with a longing for her he couldn't explain. Maybe it defied all logical explanation. It just was, and that made it dangerous.

"Hey, son. Wait up. Thought I might join you."

Nick took one look at the old man carrying his heaped plate of food in one hand and a steaming cup in the other. What was Pop up to? "You never eat outside."

"That ain't entirely true. I've been known to take my meals in the field a time or two."

"When you had a wife you wanted to avoid. I remember, long ago when I was a boy. Just never thought I'd be doing it."

"Life will surprise you, that's for sure." Pop caught up. "Are you heading to the new corral?"

"Yep. I want to spend some time with my new stallion. Get him used to me hanging around."

"Good. Get him used to your scent and your voice. Let him see you're not gonna hurt him." Pop nodded his agreement. "Say, that's a fine woman you've got in your kitchen. Thought you should know."

"I thought you were the one who said I shouldn't have married Mariah."

"I spoke out of turn, and I apologize." The older man settled his plate on the flat joint of the split rail fence. "But I'm not the one doin' her wrong now."

"So that's why you came out here." Nick balanced

his plate on the rail, staring hard at the delicious food piled high. He wasn't hungry. Again.

What was happening to his life? He wanted peace, not chaos. He wanted a predictable, orderly life that wasn't going to rip his soul to shreds. He didn't want his days filled with angry silences and glares, or his evenings torn apart by accusations and lingering unhappiness. He didn't want nights spent alone in his bed, knowing his wife wasn't in hers.

He wasn't going to let any woman make him feel that worthless. He wasn't going to let any woman climb her way past the steel walls protecting his heart.

Especially Mariah.

Pop finished his first sip of coffee, taking his time, as if considering his words. "Keep in mind, you're not nine years old anymore, but you'll listen to what I have to say. You hear?"

"Don't think you can lecture me. I don't need advice on how to handle my wife."

"I think you need more than advice, son. Keep in mind this woman can cook. She can bake. She can take care of those children with a mother's kindness."

"You're makin' my head hurt." Nick rubbed his forehead, irritable. He should have grabbed a cup of coffee while he was in the kitchen. It's just that Mariah unsettled him, stirred him up so that he was inside out, upside down and longing for her kiss, craving her touch, wanting to love her so hard and so much, he couldn't tell where he ended and she began.

"Son, I know Lida wasn't a good wife to you, and I sure am sorry about that." Pop stopped slurping his coffee and set down the cup. "It breaks my heart to see you like this. She made you unhappy, and now you think misery is all a woman is gonna bring you.

But your mother, before she died in childbed, God rest her soul, was a fine woman. Sweet, soft, gentle. Loving. You remember her.''

''I was three.'' All Nick recalled was the scent of vanilla as he'd clung to his mother's skirts and a soft voice that was like singing. A woman's memory grown indistinct with time. ''You just recall the good, because my mother's gone and you loved her. You of all men should know how hard a marriage is.''

Pop hung his head. ''There's no denying my second marriage wasn't so good.''

''You were miserable.''

''I was no different from you, with a ranch to run and a child needing a mother's care. I married out of desperation.''

''Maybe misery is the state of marriage.''

''No, son, I'm sorry if that's what you think. If you grew up watching me unhappy with my wife, and then you went and found unhappiness with yours, but you're wrong. If your mother had lived, you would have seen what love can be.''

''Love doesn't last.''

''Love is the only thing that lasts. Nothing, not even death, can stop it.''

''That's a funny philosophy coming from you, Pop. The man who told me to marry someone who can cook because that's what mattered.''

''I didn't know you would be given a rare chance.'' He raked his fingers through his salt-and-pepper hair, looking troubled, looking weary. ''I had that chance once, and it was taken from me. But the love I had for your mother never died. It lives to this day in my heart and, somewhere, in hers.''

"What are you, a poet?" Nick thought his father was tougher than that. Tougher than anything.

He pushed away from the fence, startling the stallion, who was approaching with nostrils flared, and cursed. His temper felt on the edge. His senses full-loaded and his control ready to crumble into a thousand pieces. He felt as if he was back in the boat again, caught in a river without a way to haul them in to shore and the rapids were approaching. "I don't need any help, Pop."

"I think you need more than that. A swift kick in the britches, so you'd best listen to your old man, and listen good."

"I can manage my own wife."

"She's more than a wife. She's a damn fine woman who works without complaint and does everything she can for everyone in this family. She keeps the house clean and the children cared for, and have you noticed how she looks at you?"

"Yeah, Pop, I've noticed. That's why I'm out here with my food getting cold, instead of eating inside at the kitchen table." How could he say it? Whenever he looked at Mariah he felt as if he were breaking inside. The hard walls and defenses and shields he'd built to cover up the truth that Lida figured out and Mariah would in time—he was just a man, with flaws, with broken places. He made mistakes, said things he regretted, and fell short of the man he wished he could be.

Now was one of those occasions. What he wanted to do was to open his heart to Mariah and love her, as if he'd never been hurt, as if he knew beyond doubt that love never ended and that he'd never fail her. They'd never fail one another. They'd grow old together, happy and complete, as husband and wife, friends and lovers.

But if he let her in, he let in the rest of it. "The truth is, Pop, love ends. People disappoint one another, and those disappointments build into resentment and bitterness and even hatred."

"Sometimes that's true. We both know it. I'm not gonna deny it." Pop sounded so wise, looked so sure. "But sometimes, love is even stronger."

"Than bitterness? Than a wife who's tired of hard work and being trapped by her children?" It tore at him, the uncertainties that lingered down inside.

With Mariah, he'd chosen a woman who didn't mind hard work. Who had a few social clubs to keep her happy and friends to visit. But she was also practical and didn't look to fancy things to keep her happy. He'd chosen Mariah because she was so lonely, she would be happy to care for children not her own.

And that made him remember something. What was it that Mariah had said? It troubled him now, and with the rising sun in his eyes, burning away the darkness, stinging so that his vision blurred, he struggled to remember. He'd been over there on the rise. He'd been watching the storm for twisters, and they'd been talking about his kids. *They're my children now, too.*

"Trust me, son. Mariah's a rare woman with an unbreakable heart."

"That's not possible. Hearts break. You know that. I know that. And then you figure out it's better not to get close to anyone and go on with your life. Or marriage." Nick had heard enough. He turned his back on his father and walked away. He'd do anything to escape the pain crackling to life inside him.

"I don't mean her heart can't break." Pop's wise words lifted on the wind, inescapable. "I mean no matter what, Mariah will keep on loving with the broken pieces of her heart, and in the broken places, and that kind of love will never end. If you can find a woman like that, then the least you can do is love her the same way in return."

How can anyone love with the broken pieces? Nick had the image of Humpty-Dumpty, the children's nursery rhyme, and all the king's men couldn't put him back together again. That's what life did to a man. Testing him day by day, leaving scars here and bruises there, in his soul. Every flaw felt as huge as a mountain. Those flaws were what drove Lida away. And they'd drive Mariah away, too. He felt her in his soul every time she smiled at him, every time their gazes met. It was too much. Too damn much to hand over. He didn't need his soul shredded and torn at his feet, too.

He kept walking, his conscience biting, his anguish large enough to choke on. This was killing him, tearing at him deep inside, and as much as he was hurting, he longed for Mariah with his heart and his body and his soul.

He couldn't live like this. That was all he knew as he kept on walking through the shimmering prairie grasses with the hot sunshine all around him.

He felt dark and cold.

"I bet you win the most votes," Betsy predicted as she poured a cup of coffee in the church basement where the Ladies' Aid gathered. "I voted for you and so did Rayna."

"That's right." Rayna appeared through the small

crowd at the refreshment table, balancing three plates of sliced chocolate cake. "You put in so much extra effort, I'm sure most of the members respect that. You'll make a great president."

"Thanks, but either way, my friends are more important to me." And my family, she added. Fine, she'd love to be president, but she'd be fine if she wasn't. For the first time in her life, she could say that. For the first time in her life, she wasn't alone.

But she *was* lonely. And it was odd, because she was with her closest friends at her favorite social club, basking in the glow of success from their last fund-raising event and already making plans for the next one. She had a wedding ring on her hand and step-children waiting for her at home. Her life had been transformed. *She* had transformed.

Where her life had been empty, it was now full. But inside her soul, that's where she was lonely. In a place she hadn't known existed until Nick had taken her to his bed and awakened it.

She ached for him the way the earth craved the dawn, the way winter wanted for spring. Nick didn't love her. He didn't want her. He'd driven his rejection to the point inside her where it would hurt the most. She was furious with him. She wanted to hate him. She ought to throw things at his head and cry and shout and give him a piece of her mind.

It would be so much easier if she could. If she could rage at him for hurting her. But the truth was harder. The feelings more deep and complicated. She loved him truly, down deep in those places he'd breathed to life inside her heart and her soul. In the places where love could not die.

Even when she wanted it to.

"Gather around." The elections chairwoman, Ellie McKey, clapped her hands, silencing the din of nearly three dozen women talking in a small, enclosed room. "I have the results."

"O-oh, I hope we both win." Betsy fidgeted with excitement.

"For treasurer…" Ellie's voice rang out.

So, what did she do about her marriage? Mariah's thoughts took her away from the applause to earlier this morning when Nick wanted a clean plate and not her. All he did was walk away. From her questions, her uncertainty and her pain. When she was hurting and when she needed him to hold her, to come to her, instead of turning away, where was he? Turning his back to her. Every time she needed him.

But he certainly had no problem reaching for her when he was in need. He was the one who'd taken her to his bed. He wasn't distant and uninterested then, oh, no, he was—

"Betsy Hunter, vice president," Ellie announced, jerking Mariah from her anger, but the argument still continued in her head.

Nick wanted what he wanted. To be left alone, to be loved, to be served his breakfast, to have his house clean and his children cared for so he didn't have a single worry, and all *his* needs seemed to be met—

"Mariah Gray."

Applause roared, bringing her back to the room. Betsy had grabbed Mariah's hand and was jumping up and down. Looks of approval were beaming her way from her friends in the group. She was president?

"And those are our new officers for this coming year," Ellie continued. "About the upcoming Fourth of July church breakfast. We're going to need…"

Mariah took plenty of congratulations as the meeting finally adjourned and she, Rayna and Betsy made their way outside. Mariah couldn't believe it. She'd finally been elected president. She'd worked long and hard putting in extra hours over the past year, with her eye on that lofty position. She was happy, yes. She'd do her best for the club, as she did with everything, but being president of the Ladies' Aid wasn't her greatest wish.

Being loved by Nick was.

After saying goodbye to her friends, Mariah ran a few quick errands to the mercantile and the grocery. She mulled over her situation all the while. Standing in line at the mercantile, the clerk finished tallying her purchases.

"Shall I put this on Nick Gray's account?"

"Yes." That was the final blow. Nick still hadn't added her name to his store account. And why should he? She was merely his *convenient* wife.

Rage blinded her. She felt cold with it, hot with it, and so powerful she felt as if she could take on a charging bull and win. Gathering up her parcels, she marched to the door with such speed, everyone darted out of her way.

Good. Because this was the beginning of her anger. How dare Nick treat her like this? He knew how she'd been raised. He knew how lonely she was. He knew how she felt about him. And he'd had the nerve to call their beautiful lovemaking a mistake.

Well, then, she was a mistake, too. And that hurt enough to level her. Her heart was broken into sharp and jagged pieces, and broke even more. He'd done that to her. Knowing she loved him, he'd given her a taste of paradise—of what their marriage could be—

and then yanked it away from her as if he were in charge.

Well, he wasn't. She had some say, too. She shook with fury. The road ahead of her was a brown strip between fields of green. Good thing the road was easy to make out because her vision was blurry. Her eyes burned. Tears pooled there, collecting but not falling.

Mariah pulled the surrey to a halt in Rayna's neighbor's driveway. Before she could set the brake proper, the *bang!* of a screen door slamming open resounded in the pleasant afternoon air. Feet pounded on the hard-packed earth.

"Mariah!" Georgie came running, arms outstretched. "You came!"

"I'll always come for you, princess." Mariah knelt, holding out her arms as Georgie rammed into her. Reed-thin arms cinched around Mariah's neck and held on tight.

So tight. "We gotta make mud pies."

"Is that why you have mud all over you?"

"Yep. We had fun, but we have to wait for the pies to bake."

"Can you leave them? I bet Molly will make sure the pies bake up properly." Mariah smiled at the thirteen-year-old girl who was ambling down the dirt pathway. She slipped the gold eagle into the girl's palm, thanked her for taking such great care of Georgie, and lifted her stepdaughter into the surrey.

"Do you know how to make mud pies?" Georgie asked, once they were under way. "I could show you."

"I'd like that. I bet you're pretty good at it."

"Yep." Georgie started chattering on about her stay with Molly and how she and Rayna's son had climbed trees and pretended to be birds and played in the mud by the well.

Mariah listened, as always, filling up with more love for this child, so dear and precious. Then it hit her like a rock to the forehead, and she nearly tumbled from the seat.

She'd never have Nick's baby. There would be no more children, with him sleeping down the hall from her in his separate bed. There would be no baby to hold. No baby of her own.

"...an' then I tole Molly..." Georgie scooted over on the seat, right up against Mariah's side.

Mariah slipped her arm around the little girl, tugging her close and keeping her there. How she loved Georgie. How she loved Joey. They were wonderful children.

But there would be no more. The rage in her chest broke apart, because she couldn't stay angry with Nick forever. He'd tried to love her. Maybe he'd given it everything he had. He'd tried hard and still, when the lovemaking was over, he'd gazed upon her face and couldn't feel love.

He couldn't love her because she was unlovable. *What man is gonna want you, Mariah?* Pa's hard words mocked her. He was right, and she hated it, and she hated Nicholas Adam Gray for proving it to her. She hated him with a passion for choosing her out of all the women to marry. He chose her, and, instead of living alone insulated in her lonely life where being a spinster was her choice, he had to go and make her a wife and a stepmother and show her what she couldn't have. What she wasn't good enough for. He had to take her to his bed and love her as if she were priceless, the piece of his soul lost and now found, and his one true love for all eternity. When she wasn't.

He made her feel this way, damn him. It was all his fault—

It wasn't his fault at all. The horses turned onto the long driveway toward home, as if sensing she was too preoccupied to drive. At the first rise of the prairie, the ranch house came into view, a neat, tidy, two-story house with friendly dormers marching across the roof and a wide front porch inviting visitors to come on up and stay a spell. An ideal home. She'd thought she'd find an ideal life in it, in time. She'd been arrogant to think that one day Nick might fall in love with her.

The truth was, no one could. Her father was right. Every cruel word he'd said to her bit like the edge of a razor into her soul. No, it would have been better—safer—to have stayed a spinster. To never have known this pain.

She was unlovable. She was only good for hard work.

"Mariah." Georgie held out her arms expectantly.

Mariah blinked. Somehow they were home. The horses had stopped and were waiting politely, their tails twitching in the heat. The brisk wind ruffled their coats.

"Let's get you inside. It's past your nap time, young lady." Mariah's feet touched the ground.

Georgie was already climbing into her arms. Mariah accepted the sweet weight, settled Georgie on her hip and carried her toward the back steps. The maple leaves rustled hard, as if in protest, at her approach. The sun faded in intensity. When she looked up, she saw a thin web of clouds over the sun and the giant white cliffs of thunderheads building along the horizon.

There would be another storm. Would Nick use that as an excuse to stay out of the house? He probably was saying his thanks right now to those thunderheads, because they were his allies. He'd spend his night watching them, not lying in bed worrying if she was going to come open his door and impose herself on him.

Shame ached in her, in those broken places of her heart. Nick had been pretty dang kind, considering. Turning away from her, instead of using cruel words, as her father had.

Fine, she understood it now.

After lying Georgie down on her bed and tucking her rag doll beneath the blanket, too, Mariah hesitated in the hallway where the window gazed down over the fields. A rise of smoke pinpointed his location— he was bent over, wrestling a calf to the ground while Jeb lifted an iron brand from the hot flames of the fire.

She squeezed her eyes shut, refusing to look a second longer. Love beat in her heart and stirred in her soul. Love for this man she hated, this man who couldn't love her even when he'd tried. True, unbreakable love that she wanted to turn off like the kitchen pump and couldn't.

She wiped at the tears in her eyes. Marrying Nick had been a hard lesson. She didn't need to make it worse by wasting time on foolish wishes. What she had was a convenient marriage to a man who didn't love her. Just as Nick had told her from the moment he'd proposed.

She had no one to blame but herself.

"Joey?" She rapped her knuckles on his door. His room was empty. He was without a doubt outside helping his father and uncles brand the cattle. So she tugged the book from her skirt pocket—the latest by Mark Twain—and set it on the foot of his bed, where he was sure to find it.

That's when she saw it, when she was coming out of Joey's room. Nick's door was open, directly across the hall, giving her a plain view of his room. His empty room.

He'd taken out every stick of furniture. Every bit of clothing. Emptiness echoed around her the moment she stepped into the room.

He'd moved out.

Nick had found a way to tell her that he wanted nothing to do with her. This was no longer a convenient marriage.

She *was* just the housekeeper.

Chapter Fifteen

"Hey, big brother." Will skidded his horse to a fast stop, swinging down with the grace of a born rider, looking about as mean as a thunderstorm. "You'd best get up to the house. There's trouble."

"Trouble?" Whatever it was, he didn't want to deal with it. He was tired and hot and dirty. Grit stuck to his face as he wrestled the calf to the ground, poked his knee in the animal's ribs. He used his body weight and every bit of his muscle power to keep the thrashing animal still.

Pop came in with the red-hot iron. Nick prepared for the animal's reaction to pain, holding the powerful steer steady as the brand hissed and burned.

"Okay." Pop stepped back, swinging the iron safely away.

Nick released the animal, bounding out of the way of striking hooves and sharp horns. The steer sprang onto his feet and shot out into the field, bawling. Were they done yet? Nick took one look over his shoulder and started cursing. He'd been doing this since sunrise and the pen was still half full. His battered body was protesting up a storm.

"Mariah can handle it," he told Will. Whatever it was—fire, flood or a collapse of the roof. He'd married the most capable woman in three counties.

"The problem is Mariah."

"Now don't go lecturing me on how I shouldn't have married her. I'm gettin' tired of—"

"She's packing up her wagon," Will interrupted.

"Does she need help?" She probably had something to do in town, something to do with one of those clubs she belonged to. "Why don't you carry anything she needs carried? I'm busy here."

"Nick, Mariah's leaving you."

The lasso slipped from his hands, hissing to the ground, coiling like a snake in the grass in front of him. "She's not leaving me. Mariah wouldn't leave."

"Then I don't know what you'd call putting her things in her trunks and dragging them through the house and into the yard, but right now she's trying to get those trunks into her old wagon. She even hitched up her ox."

"No." He didn't believe it. "You go down and help her with what she's really doing. Maybe she's giving her trunks away. She won't be needing them."

Because she was staying right here with him. End of story. Forever. Until death parted them. That was their bargain. For better or worse, a convenient marriage.

"Go look for yourself." Will swung into the saddle.

Mariah wasn't the kind of woman to leave. Nick refused to believe it. His feet started moving, despite his belief in her, taking him to his mare. He rode over the rise and down the draw and up to the knoll where an ox stood in the shade of the maple, hitched to

Mariah's old wagon. Mariah wiped sweat from her brow with her sleeve, then bent over and began shoving one of her trunks onto its side.

One trunk was already in the wagon bed.

His blood iced. "Hey, you takin' those into town?"

"Yes." She didn't sound happy. She didn't look happy. She hefted the trunk, got it off the ground, but it was too awkward. She dropped it, cursing.

"Here, let me help." Those were empty, he knew it. Until the moment he knelt and heaved the trunk off the dirt and realized it was packed full.

She was leaving? Mariah? The one woman he'd thought would stand by him no matter what? That couldn't be right....

Fury blinded him. Like a lightning strike, it seared from the top of his head to the bottom of his soles, making his purpose clear. He balanced the trunk on his shoulder. He wasn't going to make this easy for her. They had a bargain, sealed by vows and a wedding ring. She wasn't getting out of this. He was stuck, and so was she.

"Hey! Where are you going?" Her gait pounded behind him all the way to the house, angry, too. "I want that in the wagon, not in the house."

"Too bad, because you aren't going anywhere, lady."

"Oh, and who are you to tell me what to do?"

"I'm your husband."

"No, you're not. You're not living in this house anymore." She leaped up the steps, circling him to block the back door. "I saw your room."

"I figured things would be better between us if I moved into the barn." He hated this. She might look as mad as hell, but tears stood in her eyes, unshed and genuine. He knew it had to hurt. He was responsible for that. "Look, I can't be what you want. You keep looking at me with those moon eyes of yours, so bright and shining and hopeful, and that's not what we have here, Mariah. We had a deal, and we blew it."

Every time I look at you, he wanted to say, *I remember being in your arms.* More vulnerable and more exposed than he'd ever been. Every time he looked at her, he wanted her with a fiery yearning that started in the bottom of his soul and pulled upward through every part of him.

And look how right he'd been to hold back. Mariah already wanted to leave. She was packed. She was out the door. She stood in the threshold, blocking his way.

"Nick, I don't understand." Her touch was like melted gold, precious and rare and so lustrous, he was spellbound. "You don't want me. You made that clear. Not as your lover, because you keep pushing me away. Not as your wife, because you don't need me. Not even as your friend. I don't know why you married me, but I..."

She had no idea? He didn't understand it, and it terrified him. He wanted her so much. If only she could see who he really was. Tarnished by life, just as anyone was, with a list of flaws a mile long. He'd let her down, disappoint her, and how would she feel about him then?

Her love would die, that's what. He didn't trust her. He didn't care what his father said. No woman's heart could be that strong. He didn't believe it. Not even of Mariah.

"I love you, Nick." Her words trembled, raw and

thin. One tear slid down her cheek, just one. "I regret marrying you because all you wanted was a woman to do the work around here. You know how I was raised, darn you, and you did this to me? I can't stay here in this house full of a family that isn't mine."

"You're going to leave, no matter what I do, aren't you?" His eyes darkened until they were nothing but shadow. "Even if I haul every trunk back into the house and guard the door with a shotgun, you'll find a way to leave."

"I'll keep my promise to you. I will cook and clean. I'll watch your children. But after I tuck them in at night, I'm going to my own house. Betsy will let me have my old room back, and we'll live there together. I'll be all right. I'll survive."

Barely, but she didn't want Nick to know that. "I'll be the housekeeper you need, I'll raise your children and I'll care for them as my own. But I can't pretend to be your wife. I can't live a lie. I won't. I won't sit at the breakfast table every morning and hurt like this. I can't. It's already killing me. Will you let me go?"

"Yes." The hardest words he'd ever said, but Nick managed. He turned around, carried her trunk to the wagon and heaved it into the bed. "Guess you've got this all figured out."

"I do." She didn't look happy. She was white as a ghost and moved like one, too, as if the life had drained out of her.

It drained out of him, too. He could feel her pain, in his own. She could move out of his house and drive down that road, but she was still a part of him. Why that was, he couldn't say. He didn't understand it. He only knew that he'd been right to withhold his heart. Look at her, leaving him. Just as he knew she would.

"Would you mind lifting the other trunks for me?" she asked in a thin, raw voice trembling with emotion. With hurt.

He wanted to haul her into his arms, drag her to the ground and love her with every bit of his soul. He wanted to be a part of her, joined with her. Every broken place in his heart yearned for it with an unbearable pain.

"Sure. I'll get the trunks for you."

"Thank you."

That's all she had to say? Thank you? Now would be the perfect time to start in with the demands. The list she'd already made up while she'd packed of how she wanted life to be, and how he was supposed to act and the things he was supposed to do to keep her from leaving.

He was braced for it, his heart protected, his feelings buried deep. She could do her worst, and he wouldn't let her hurt him. Give him any tongue lashing she wanted. Any berating. Any torrent of anger. He could take it, because wasn't that the way a marriage went?

Mariah stepped close, bringing his heart with her. Her hand lighted on his shoulder and the touch to his skin reached all the way down to his soul. One touch. That's all it took, and he was laid bare to her, open and exposed, the most vulnerable parts of him.

"I don't know what this is between us," she said quietly, simply, "but it's the reason I can't pretend. I love you, Nick. With my entire being. I think you feel that way, too."

She laid her hand over his heart and, like a boom of thunder, her touch rolled through him.

I love you, he wanted to say. The words were right

there, but he couldn't say them. What game was Mariah playing?

"I'll be back to serve supper." She brushed a kiss to his cheek.

So incredibly tender. She wasn't playing games. She wasn't trying to hurt him. She wasn't that kind of person.

"Take good care, all right? I've asked Will to find someone to keep an eye on Georgie while I'm gone."

"Pop will do it. Be careful to keep an eye on the storm. Those thunderheads are building fast. With this heat, it could be twister weather."

"I know." She climbed into the wagon and gathered the reins.

For one brief moment their gazes met and locked. Love burned through the broken pieces of his heart. Love that could heal him. Make him whole. Make him surrender.

He took a step toward her, unsure. No, he couldn't do it. He couldn't trust her that much. He didn't think he could trust any woman, so he let her go.

Although the house was in the distance and out of her sight, Mariah could still feel Nick in her heart. In that little piece only he possessed.

And always would.

The wind battered her sunbonnet brim and swept the tears pooling in her eyes onto her cheeks. She wiped at the wetness, hating this weakness. She didn't cry. She *wouldn't* cry.

If Nick couldn't love her, no one could.

She had to accept that. Had to find a way to go on, to walk into Nick's house every morning and make breakfast, to take care of his children, to clean his house and do his laundry, and all the thousand things needing tended to in a day. She had to do all those things and keep her heart from shattering into even smaller pieces.

She was of half a mind to request a divorce. Shocking, she knew, but that would be the solution to the overwhelming anguish. She could go back to being Mariah Scott, the fearsome and sharp-tongued spinster who didn't need anyone. Ever.

She had her friends and her social clubs. She was the president of the Ladies' Aid, the most prestigious group in town. She didn't need Nicholas Adam Gray, not one bit.

Liar. She wiped more wetness from her eyes, darn that wind, and squinted in the hazy sunshine. The clouds overhead were gathering in the heat of the day. Like an enormous mesa, the gray clouds rose high up into the sky, ominous and breathtaking. In the distance a gray curtain fell from sky to earth—rain. Lightning forked across the pewter clouds.

It was a good thing she would reach town soon. She didn't like the look of the weather. Nick would be keeping an eye out, even though he was probably hard at work and not missing her in the least. If the clouds turned green, then she knew he would make sure Georgie and Joey were safe in the cellar.

Stop worrying about them. She was the housekeeper, not the wife. She was more like a hired woman. The cruelty of it slapped her in the face like the leaf on the wind, sailing right into her cheekbone.

The cottonwoods shook with a hard gust and the ox snorted in protest.

"Just keep going," she told him. "I'm in no mood to deal with your stubbornness."

He must have believed her, because he picked up speed, pulling her into the shelter of her stable in town as the storm hit.

"Georgie! You answer me right now," Nick boomed, at the breaking point. He felt as if every bone, every muscle, every organ in his body had been ripped in two by a dull blade. No, he wasn't feeling terribly patient as he marched through the house, banging open doors. Where had that girl gone? "Pop, you were supposed to be watching her."

"I turned my back for a minute. That's all. She must've been waiting for her chance, because I was watching her like a hawk." Pop hauled the lantern out of the lean-to. "I'll get Joey down to the cellar and be out to help look for her."

"Joey won't stay down there by himself. When he finds out Georgie's missing, he'll go looking for her." Nick grabbed his jacket and headed for the door. The sight of a young sapling sailing horizontally across the length of the backyard didn't comfort him any. It was twister weather, for sure. With any luck, the worst of it would hold off until after he'd found his daughter. "Whatever you do, Pop, stay down cellar with Joey. Make sure he's safe. I couldn't stand to lose both of them in one day."

Pop bowed his head, choked up.

Damn Mariah. She did this. Fury propelled him down the steps and into the storm where the force of the wind stung. Or maybe it was the bits of dust driving into his skin.

"I've got some tracks." Dakota rode up on his paint and with a second horse at his side. He tossed Nick the extra reins. "Hard to say, but there's not much time." He gazed up at the storm as lightning flickered far overhead. "We gotta find her."

"Let's go." Nick was in the saddle, pushing to ride point, but Dakota was the better tracker. Thank heavens for his little brother, who set off on his mare, into the lethal wind. A fence board, ripped loose from somewhere, sailed past Dakota's head, heading right for Nick's jaw. He ducked and the board, with nails attached, flew by.

Georgie. Terror filled him, leaving no room for rational thought. She was out here in this, run off for heaven again and, damn it, she couldn't have chosen a more dangerous time. Between the lightning, the wind-driven debris and those changing clouds, he'd be lucky to find her at all. Ever.

Dakota dismounted and crouched on the ground. He studied the grass carefully, then shook his head.

The wind had disturbed the grass. They'd lost Georgie's tracks.

The prairie stretched as far as Nick could see, from horizon to horizon in every direction. Lightning streaked from the sky, a giant arrow of light that scorched a tree on a far rise. The sky opened up and hail pounded to the ground, drumming like bullets into the earth, so loud they couldn't hear Georgie if she were to cry out. So dense, they couldn't see her. The ice covered the ground, erasing the last of Georgie's tracks in the broken grass.

"Maybe I should keep watch," Betsy said from the kitchen table where she was ironing old man Dayton's work shirts. "Pour yourself a cup of tea and relax, Mariah. It's just a storm. If a twister comes, the cellar door is two feet away."

"It's not that." She couldn't explain it. Ever since she stepped foot inside this house, she'd felt anxious. As if something were terribly wrong.

Things *were* wrong. She'd just left her husband and walked away from the first real home she'd ever had. She'd left her stepchildren...*that* bothered her. Greatly. She hadn't explained, she'd been so upset, hurting as if everything inside her was dying. She'd left, thinking that a housekeeper to them would be the same as a stepmother.

And that wasn't true. She couldn't in good conscience stand here safe in her kitchen. What about Georgie? She'd be up from her nap now. She'd want to play dress-up or tea party or cuddle her rag doll. She liked cookies and warm milk after her nap.

"Here, I poured you a cup of tea. Sit down and relax. I know you're upset, but this can't be good for you." Betsy's caring was nice.

But nothing could stop the strange panic. It shivered through her, taking over, leaving the pit of her stomach hollow and afraid. Something was wrong. She *knew* it. She'd never felt this before, and as she called out a goodbye to Betsy at the door, she wondered if she was a little touched in the head.

Probably, but she couldn't sit in her kitchen. It was as if an unseen hand was pulling her out of the house and into the stable. She borrowed Betsy's older mare, a gentle creature, snapped the lead rope around on the halter ring in place of reins and climbed onto the animal's broad back.

The mare obeyed, heading out into the storm. Hail drove like nails into them. It was only then that Mariah realized she'd forgotten her coat. She wasn't wearing a hat or gloves. She shivered and urged the mare into a gallop. The clouds overhead were twisted into an angry curl of pewter and green.

Lightning crashed and thunder boomed. Mariah kept riding.

"Twister." Nick spotted it the second it left the clouds. A lethal column of wind, louder than a freight train speeding by on a downhill slope. He was looking death in the face and had to keep walking toward it.

"She's following the road." Dakota hopped onto his paint, shouting to be heard above the deafening storm. "I think she's heading to town. A guess, because there are no tracks."

Where was she? They ought to have found her by now, and it was killing him. Mariah ought to have stayed with Georgie and kept her safe.

He should have kept her safe. He should have done what it took to keep Mariah in their house. He should have handed over his heart, his soul and his life to her, if that's what she wanted.

He thought of her in his bed, how he'd melted into her. She'd left him, and had taken his heart and soul with her. And he still loved her. That made him mad. It made him sad. It made him ashamed.

She'd driven away, but he'd been the one to let her go. All he'd had to say were three words and she would have stayed.

But for how long?

"Watch out!" Dakota's warning yanked Nick out of his thoughts.

He dove in time to miss a tree branch, big enough to kill him.

Georgie. Fear iced the blood in his veins. They rode as fast as they dared as the twister rolled toward them, maybe a half mile away and coming fast. Shingles sailed past like a flock of birds, nails bared.

Nick took several blows, one to his head, another to his shoulder, another to his thigh. He didn't feel the pain. Just fear for Georgie.

He'd ride into that twister, if he had to.

He wasn't stopping until he found her.

Mariah felt her nape tingle. There was something different in the wind. Something high and afraid and human…*Georgie.*

With a mother's instinct, she leaped off the mare and started running through the air dark as night. Every breath sucked in dirt, but she didn't stop. Bits of broken boards and trees and fencing rained down on her with the hail. She tasted blood, aware that she was bleeding, but she didn't stop. She couldn't stop.

There! She heard it again, the tortured sound of a terrified child. Mariah only had to follow her heart through the darkness to find the little girl huddled against a rock. It was too dark to see anything but her trembling form.

She heard her name being called over and over again, and suddenly Georgie was in her arms, sobbing, wet and muddy and bleeding. Shaking from cold and fear.

"My poor little girl," Mariah soothed, holding her so tight. Thankful, so incredibly thankful this precious child was safe. "Why aren't you at home with your grandpop?"

"'Cuz I didn't want you to go to heaven, too." Georgie's sobs shook her entire body.

"I love you, Georgie. I told you I would never leave you like that. I was coming back for supper."

She wanted to cradle this child, hold her safe forever, but a bucket landed an inch from Mariah's elbow. The wind howled, chugging like a train, and an entire side of an intact roof sailed a foot over her head.

Time to find shelter. The horse had probably run back home to her safe stall, but that didn't matter. They couldn't outride the storm. The wind tore her hair from its pins and the collar from her dress. She couldn't see the twister, but she could feel the suck of it.

It was too darn close. The world had turned pitch-black and she couldn't see a foot in front of her. Where could they go?

The creek bed. It wasn't the safest place, but it was all they had. Something hard struck her shoulder, something harder crashed into her back. She ran in the dark, stumbling, with Georgie cradled in her arms, protected from the wind.

Something hit her again, driving deep into her upper back. Pain left her dizzy. Where was the creek?

She turned her ankle on uneven ground. This had to be it. She lowered Georgie to the ground and they crawled through the clay and into the wetness. She nestled Georgie into the shelter of the dry bank, where the earth could protect her. Water lapped at her knees as she laid over Georgie, covering the child with her body.

If the twister came this way, they'd be dead. But if it kept away, then they'd be safe from some of the debris.

"Scared." Georgie sobbed against Mariah's throat.

"I know, but you stay right here, whatever happens, all right?" She stroked the child's hair in the dark, wincing as an entire tree branch scraped along the ridge of her back, cracked into her head and kept on going.

Pain made her dizzy, even in the darkness. The force of the wind felt as if it was sucking the skin off her limbs and the hair from her scalp. The roaring was worse. Lightning flashed across the prairie for one brief moment, and in that second Mariah realized the tree on the bank above them was struck. Fire snapped down the trunk to the ground where they were. Her and Georgie.

She covered the child the best she could as the tree exploded and thunder shook the earth. Pain shot like a lightning bolt through her head. The roaring faded. The darkness claimed her. Then there was nothing, nothing at all.

A riderless horse dashed close, shied from a falling shovel and disappeared in the dark. Nick *knew* who'd been riding that horse.

"Mariah!" Nick swung off his horse, even though Dakota was telling him they had to find shelter. The twister was closing in and the winds were too strong. He hit the ground and the wind knocked him over. Good thing, too, because an uprooted cottonwood flew by, right where he would have been standing.

Lightning seared overhead, so close, the hair on his head stood up. His nape prickled. The light burned his eyes and for one moment he could see the prairie spread out in front of him, the lethal funnel heading in a northeast path toward them and a splash of yellow against the shadowed grasses.

"That's Mariah." Dakota saw her first, bolting into action.

Side by side they went, into the hail of debris. Nick

didn't feel the strikes against his face, his chest and his torso. Not even the twister could stop him. Nothing could.

Mariah. It was all he could think about, lying face-down in the creek. Face down…alive or dead? Determination steeled him, and he found her, trapped by a fallen branch. Motionless in the dark storm.

For one brief second he thought she was dead, and he died, too. For a moment everything inside him stilled. And then he touched her warm hand and felt the flutter of her pulse at her wrist.

"Papa," came a tiny whisper.

"Why, howdy, princess."

Her fingers curled around his and held on tight. Mariah was hurt and was unconscious, and there was nowhere to go. The twister was coming too close for comfort.

"The debris still falling." Dakota's hand pressed on Nick's shoulder, easing him down over his wife. Side by side they covered woman and child, protecting them as the onslaught continued.

He felt Mariah move beneath him. Just a little bit, she turned toward him, seeking his comfort. This woman who had protected his child with her life.

As he was protecting hers.

If he needed any more proof of her love, and of his, this was it.

"I shouldn't have left you," she choked.

He could hear the regret and pain in her words. What had Pop said? That Mariah had an unbreakable heart. That if her heart broke, she would still love him with the pieces of it and with the places in between.

Nick finally understood it, because that's how he loved her. He couldn't hold it back anymore. The steel walls melted and the defenses tumbled down, leaving his heart exposed. He wasn't perfect, he was as wounded as anyone was in this life, because life left its marks on a person. But it was the broken places that made him strong. And his love stronger. Like a fractured bone when mended, it was harder to break.

He curled his hand around Mariah's nape, leaning to protect her with his body, with his heart, with his soul. He said the words that made him whole, that brought him into the light. "I should never have let you go, my love, because that's what you are, my one true love."

Epilogue

Mariah gazed around at the Harvest Day festivities. This might be their most successful fund-raiser yet. Old man Dayton's fiddle began the first sweet strain of a waltz.

"Ma'am, may I have this dance?"

She shivered at the brush of Nick's lips against her neck. She leaned back into the steely arms that banded her. His iron chest was unyielding. His hold on her was both gentle and strong.

"I suppose I might permit you to dance with me," she teased, laughing when he blew a raspberry against the curve of her neck. "Since you've done a bit more than merely waltz with me."

His hands curved over the curve of her belly where their baby grew, nestled safe beneath her heart. Her fingers laced through his and held on. Love renewed in her heart, born again as it was every time they touched.

Nick turned her gently in his arms and tugged her tenderly against his chest. They came together like the earth and the sky. She placed her hand on his shoulder, as strong as steel. He kissed her brow as he led them in a slow, sweet waltz.

"Mariah! Papa!" Georgie giggled as Jeb swept close, teaching his granddaughter to dance. "Look at me."

"Are you sure you want another one of those?" Nick teased, his words a kiss along the hollow of her throat.

"Absolutely." Joey was somewhere, playing baseball with his friends, no doubt. Georgie sparkled as Jeb swept her up onto his shoulders.

I'm happy. Finally. She was loved with a family of her own and a husband who cherished her. *What a man.* Mariah buried her face in Nick's shoulder, holding him tight, letting him whirl her to the rise and fall of the music. Together they moved like poetry, like the night. Two lovers and one heart. Their love would burn forever bright.

* * * * *

Savor the
breathtaking romances
and thrilling adventures
of Harlequin Historicals®

On sale November 2003

MY LADY'S PRISONER by Ann Elizabeth Cree

To uncover the truth behind her husband's death,
a daring noblewoman kidnaps a handsome viscount!

THE VIRTUOUS KNIGHT by Margo Maguire

While fleeing a nunnery, a feisty noblewoman
becomes embroiled with a handsome knight in a
wild, romantic chase to protect an ancient relic!

On sale December 2003

THE IMPOSTOR'S KISS by Tanya Anne Crosby

On a quest to discover his past, a prince masquerades
as his twin brother and finds the life and the love
he'd always dreamed of....

THE EARL'S PRIZE by Nicola Cornick

An impoverished woman believes an earl is
an unredeemable rake—but when she wins
the lottery will she become the rake's prize?

Visit us at www.eHarlequin.com

HARLEQUIN HISTORICALS®

HHMED33

Sometimes, there *are* second chances.

SUSAN WIGGS

ENCHANTED AFTERNOON

Beautiful, charming and respected as the wife of an ambitious senator, Helena Cabot Barnes is the leading lady of Saratoga Springs. But beneath the facade lies a terrible deception. Helena has discovered—too late—that her husband is a dangerous man.

Unable to outrun her past, Helena turns to Michael Rowan, a man she once loved, a man who broke her heart. For Helena, the road to trusting Michael again is long and hard. But Michael has just discovered a shattering truth… and a reason to stay and fight for the woman he once lost.

With a deft hand and a unique voice, acclaimed author Susan Wiggs creates an enchanting story that will take your breath away as it reaffirms the power of love and the magic of forgiveness.

On sale September 2002 wherever paperbacks are sold!

MIRA®

Visit us at www.mirabooks.com

MSWBWIBC02

PICK UP THESE HARLEQUIN HISTORICALS®
AND IMMERSE YOURSELF IN RUGGED
LANDSCAPE AND INTOXICATING ROMANCE
ON THE AMERICAN FRONTIER

On sale November 2003

THE TENDERFOOT BRIDE by Cheryl St.John
(Colorado, 1875)

Expecting a middle-aged widow, a hard-edged
rancher doesn't know what to do when his new cook
is not only young and beautiful, but pregnant!

THE SCOUT by Lynna Banning
(Nebraska and Wyoming, 1860)

On a wagon train headed to Oregon, an independent
spinster becomes smitten with her escort,
a troubled army major.

On sale December 2003

THE SURGEON by Kate Bridges
(Canada, 1889)

When his troop plays a prank on him, a mounted
police surgeon finds himself stuck with an unwanted
mail-order bride. Can she help him find his heart?

OKLAHOMA BRIDE by Carol Finch
(Oklahoma Territory, 1889)

A by-the-book army officer clashes with a beautiful
woman breaking the law he has sworn to uphold!

Visit us at www.eHarlequin.com

HARLEQUIN HISTORICALS®

ITCHIN' FOR SOME ROLLICKING ROMANCES SET ON THE AMERICAN FRONTIER? THEN TAKE A GANDER AT THESE TANTALIZING TALES FROM HARLEQUIN HISTORICALS

On sale September 2003

WINTER WOMAN by Jenna Kernan
(Colorado, 1835)

After braving the winter alone in the Rockies, a defiant woman is entrusted to the care of a gruff trapper!

THE MATCHMAKER by Lisa Plumley
(Arizona territory, 1882)

Will a confirmed bachelor be bitten by the love bug when he woos a young woman in order to flush out the mysterious Morrow Creek matchmaker?

On sale October 2003

WYOMING WILDCAT by Elizabeth Lane
(Wyoming, 1866)

A blizzard ignites hot-blooded passions between a white medicine woman and an amnesiac man, but an ominous secret looms on the horizon....

THE OTHER GROOM by Lisa Bingham
(Boston and New York, 1870)

When a penniless woman masquerades as the daughter of a powerful marquis, her intended groom risks it all to protect her from harm!

Visit us at www.eHarlequin.com

HARLEQUIN HISTORICALS®